"*What Isn't Remembered* is an extraordinary work of fiction: Kristina Gorcheva-Newberry has given us stories that are immersive and so richly imagined, alternately elegiac and slyly comic, always arresting and lyrical. I wanted to live in the worlds Gorcheva-Newberry has so skillfully created in one story after another. I loved this book."

—Christine Sneed, author of *Little Known Facts*

"You can read Kristina Gorcheva-Newberry's *What Isn't Remembered* for a revealing look into the lives of Russian immigrants in the U.S., or for the fearless depiction of relationships between women; but most of all you should read her for the startlingly gorgeous language she employs to powerful effect in story after story, from the title piece, 'What Isn't Remembered,' with its lavish allusions to classical music and the convincing correlations between life and love and art, to the heartbreaking 'Boys on the Moskva River,' with its portrait of a family struggling to survive during the slow collapse of the Soviet Union. *What Isn't Remembered* may be a literary debut, but Kristina Gorcheva-Newberry is a writer who comes to us in full blossom. She has clearly traveled a long road to bring us this brilliant first collection of stories."

—Edward Falco, author of *Sabbath Night in the Church of the Piranha: New and Selected Stories*

"Short stories beg for brevity but can accommodate plenitude, demand velocity but can in one shaken snow globe reveal a whole winter. Skilled authors can startle us with stories of consequence, gravity, and comedy in modes both elegant and earthy. Kristina Gorcheva-Newberry is such a writer. Her passionate stories about desire, loss, longing, guilt, and displacement are stunning. Her characters have wrested their survival from all manner of entanglements with lyricism and force, empathy and recognition. Gorcheva-Newberry empowers them with her own impressive trove of knowledge—the language of medicine, food, music, anatomy, apple gathering. She reveals life in the raw. Yet these are love stories, too, and can crack the heart. *What Isn't Remembered* is an enthralling, beautifully conceived collection by a gifted writer."

—R. T. Smith, author of *Doves in Flight*

The Raz/Shumaker Prairie Schooner Book Prize in Fiction

EDITOR
Kwame Dawes

WHAT ISN'T REMEMBERED

STORIES

Kristina Gorcheva-Newberry

University of Nebraska Press
LINCOLN

Acknowledgments for the use of copyrighted
material appear on page 252, which constitutes
an extension of the copyright page.

Library of Congress
Cataloging-in-Publication Data
Names: Gorcheva-Newberry, Kristina, author.
Title: What isn't remembered: stories /
Kristina Gorcheva-Newberry.
Description: Lincoln: University of Nebraska
Press, [2021] | Series: The Raz/Shumaker
Prairie Schooner Book Prize in Fiction
Identifiers: LCCN 2021007059
ISBN 9781496229137 (paperback)
ISBN 9781496229229 (epub)
ISBN 9781496229236 (pdf)
Subjects: LCGFT: Short stories.
Classification: LCC PS3607.O5928
W47 2021 | DDC 813/.6—dc23
LC record available at
https://lccn.loc.gov/2021007059

Set in Adobe Garamond by
Mikala R. Kolander.
Designed by N. Putens.

For
Randy, Albina, and Albert

She looked at the steps; they were empty;
she looked at the canvas; it was blurred.
With a sudden intensity, as if she saw it
clear for a second, she drew a line there,
in the center. It was done; it was finished.
Yes, she thought, laying down her brush
in extreme fatigue, I have had my vision.

—VIRGINIA WOOLF, *To the Lighthouse*

You think that would have changed
things? The answer is of course,
and for a while, and never.

—ALICE MUNRO, *Too Much Happiness*

CONTENTS

WHAT ISN'T REMEMBERED

Boys on the Moskva River

When my brother died in the winter of 1998, the snow fell all night and all day and all the following week, so they didn't find him right away, the contour of his body barely delineated but otherwise indistinguishable from the shrouded, ice-etched forms. Out the window of my brother's luxurious apartment, the Moskva River appeared frozen, layered in white as though bandaged with strips of gauze. But if you stared at it long enough, if you let your eyes adjust to the ossifying whiteness all around, you could see the river tremble and shift underneath the snow, wet and sunken and hollow in the middle, like a puncture wound.

"We need to find your father," my mother said, filling her cup with more coffee. "He can help carry the casket."

"You need to eat something, Mom," I said, turning away from the window that still held the misty imprint of my hand. "Really. You don't sleep, you don't eat. You'll get sick."

She peered into her coffee, her forehead strained with wrinkles, eyes squinting hard as though she were trying to read her fortune in the impervious blackness of the cup.

Our father left us two months before my birth. He didn't find another woman, and he didn't hate our mother or his two-year-old son, who was always sick and crying and not sleeping. But our father wanted to be free, free like birds. If he had wings, he'd told my mother, he would fly away. But he had legs, and so he walked and didn't come back, his fate a mystery.

"Somewhere, in the old phone book, there should be his parents' number and address. Perhaps he's there," my mother said.

"What will I say to him? Your older son is dead, and even though you haven't seen him for twenty-six years, asshole, we need you to be a pallbearer? And what about me, Mom? Technically, he's my father too."

She didn't respond, her face buried in her hands. She wasn't old, although right there and then she could've been a grandmother, dressed in a stretched dark-brown sweater, with her gray hair swept behind her ears, frail, sunless skin, shoulders weighed low from the years of servitude—to her parents, to us, to my brother.

"It isn't about you, Leova," she breathed out the words.

"It's never about me. But always about him. Tell you what, Mom, he didn't care about us. He preferred the city, the streets, to his family. He was just like our father."

Again she didn't respond, her eyes tracing after a covey of flurries spinning webs behind the window glass. Somewhere in the yard there was my brother's shoe, buried under a heap of snow.

* * *

THE YEAR IS 1980; I'm eight and my brother Konstantin is ten. It's one of the hottest summers we've had. There's no rain, and there's no wind. The sun is a pyre in the sky, a blazing vessel of ceaseless heat. The air is dry and brittle, it tingles on your lips. Every living thing, every bug, every leaf pines for rain. The grass sighs and turns to dust, the flowers shrivel by midmorning; the trees offer little shade and no reprieve. They don't move or sway their branches or rustle their leaves but stand still as though painted on a piece of paper, the colors waver and melt away.

We're swimming in the Moskva River, my brother and I, and he teaches me how to float on my back. Dragonflies dapple the surface, pinpricks of golden light, and for a moment Konstantin disappears and I'm left alone, drifting softly, limbs akimbo. I feel his arms wrap around my chest and yank me underwater so quickly the sun shrinks to the size of a fist, and then all is dark and murky, a pillar of silt rising from the bottom. I hold my breath for as long as I can, until Konstantin lets go and I push through the water, climbing higher and higher, guided by the trembling rings of light.

"Fight for your life, little brother," he says as soon as I shoot out. "Because no one else will."

I flounder and suck air and paddle ashore with all my strength.

Our mother is home, doing laundry or frying fish; she doesn't know we've gone to the river or that I've almost drowned. She worries about Konstantin being too thin, squirming like a worm out of her loving arms. I'm too heavy for my age, thick and sturdy, a stump of a boy.

* * *

ON THE DAY of the funeral the cemetery was a giant cocoon of snow, with monuments poking out here and there and tall three-barred crosses. From afar, they resembled crippled frozen birds caught midflight. The gaunt trees stood crystalized-white, the limbs gave an impression of being broken and soldered to the trunks at odd angles.

It was impossible to detect where snow ended and clouds began, all fused together, the sky and the earth and the thin whitish air like a muslin cloth suspended on trees and threaded through our fingers. The four of us agreed to be pallbearers—me, our neighbor, and two of Konstantin's friends. The casket felt heavy, heavier than I'd expected, as though the snow, too, had added to the weight of Konstantin's body. My father didn't wish to attend the funeral or speak to my mother, and he didn't call me by name during our short conversation. Just before hanging up, he said, "Your brother, was he mean to you? You two must've gotten into a lot of fights."

"Some," I had replied. "Some fights."

The grave wasn't long enough, and we waited, shivering but otherwise not moving, as the gravediggers hacked and chopped away. The sounds of their shovels and pickaxes shook the dumb earth and my mother's shoulders. Every now and then I would glance at her stooping in that bulky sheepskin coat Konstantin had bought for her last year. The coat seemed two sizes too big, or she two sizes too small, wilted inside its dyed-black fur so that only the tips of her ungloved fingers were left visible and her face, like a frostbitten apple, dark and lonely. Once, she'd seemed tall and proud to us, indomitable, with a broad, sturdy back eager to support our weight and carry us into the future. But with years, as we thrived, she withered, as though she'd given us not only her energy and her labor but her skin, her hair, her blood, all her vital powers. We were like vampires who couldn't control their urges, seduced by the sight and smell of such tender, familiar flesh, and who kept gorging on her life to sustain their own.

My mother had decided not to cremate the body and not to open the casket, even though Konstantin's face wasn't mangled; the first bullet had entered his heart and the second the back of his head, becoming trapped, permanently lodged inside his brain. For years afterward I would dream about it—him sauntering down the street, whistling a Beatles' song, "All the Lonely People" or "Yellow Submarine," shooting spit between his teeth and raising the collar of his leather coat like an American-movie gangster, like someone for whom death meant no more than a change of scenery or a new costume. I imagined the hit man too, screwing a silencer onto his gun, loitering behind a building, aiming the gun first at the distant sprawl of trees, then at my brother's back, then at his head, his broom-bristle hair always cropped so short. Occasionally in my dreams it would be me trudging toward Konstantin's apartment complex, awaiting the bullet to enter my skull and tear into the cerebral cortex, and I would feel it tunnel through the lobes—occipital, parietal, frontal, temporal—nestling into my thalamus or even not sinking that deep, segueing into the furrow between the two hemispheres. I would wake up drenched in cold sweat, cradling the back of my head, expecting to find the bullet hole, the raw ugly edges of the wound.

* * *

THE YEAR IS 1984, the last winter before perestroika. We're twelve and fourteen, and we're shopping for groceries—milk, eggs, beef cutlets rolled in bread crumbs that crunch between our teeth after our mother has fried them in butter, or rather sunflower oil, but we don't know it then because everything tastes like butter, rich, delicious. The grocery store is invaded by people, who scour the half-empty aisles, foraging for food, plucking off the shelves anything they can spot, be it a pack of soup bones, gamy meat, or sprouted purple-eyed potatoes. We've been warned that the country's supply of flour will peter out in less than a month. But as boys we don't really know how long a month is, how short. Konstantin strays off in hopes to procure beef cutlets while I'm ordered to guard two bottles of milk, a bag of millet, a can of herring, and half a loaf of black bread.

It's been awhile since Konstantin has left, and my arms begin to tingle from heat. I untie my earflaps and take my rabbit hat off; my hair is wet, sticking to my scalp. Herds of people jostle by, but Konstantin isn't among them, and I begin to panic, a lump of fear swells in my stomach. I abandon the tote on the floor, just for a minute, I think, and scuttle toward the meat department; my brother isn't there but a few older women haggling over pig feet to boil for *kholodets*. It suddenly occurs to me that perhaps Konstantin has already gone home, and I weave through the crowd, pushing between the heavy doors, swallowing snow.

I'm almost back to our dingy graffiti-scarred apartment building when I hear him whistle behind my back.

"Hey," he says. "Dickhead, where're you going? And where are all the groceries? Where's the bag?"

I halt, my heart nudged tight between my ribs, and I think about my mother reaching into the chicken's cavity that morning and yanking out the slimy pebble-shaped organ, then rinsing it in cold water and frying it in oil.

"Quit being such a baby," Konstantin says. "Stop the fuck crying and wipe that snot. Disgusting." He's tall and wiry, with a mean cleft in his chin he's already begun to shave and not because he has hair but because he wants it to grow faster.

"You disappeared," I say, sniffling, shielding my face with my sleeve. "You left me for an hour."

"I said I was coming back. And I did, didn't I?" He pulls a *chekushka* of vodka out of his pocket and unscrews the lid, takes a long hard swig; it's the first time I see him doing something forbidden, something adult.

* * *

IN A CROWD of friends and family, I noticed a young woman with a little boy, three or four at most, bundled up in a down coat and with a red scarf noosing his neck and mouth. He fidgeted with the scarf, pushing it down, but the mother pulled it back up, making sure the boy's face stayed swaddled at all times. The young woman kept her eyes on the casket while the red-scarfed boy rolled a snowball between his tiny gloved hands; both the mother and the child stood closer to the trees than to the grave and appeared separate from the rest of the mourners. After the burial, she didn't follow the crowd toward the gates, but moved behind the thickest of trees until all I could discern was a small patch of red flashing in the distance like a bullfinch or some other scarlet-breasted bird.

Weeks would pass before I would see them again, weeks filled with silence, more snow, and mounds of tedious paperwork concerning the inheritance. My father had contacted us a few times insisting on his share, but we ignored his impertinent demands. Soon Konstantin's bank account became privy to us and also his ritzy apartment, where my mother and I relocated. She wanted to be as close to her son in death as she couldn't be in life. She moved about the five richly furnished rooms of his home silently, like a ghost, fading into the forms and shapes of his life, the pearl-inlayed tables and curvy velour couches and solid-oak bookcases, with shelves upon shelves of American movies: *The Godfather, Goodfellas, Prizzi's Honor, Once Upon a Time in America, The Terminator, Die Hard.*

My mother sat in her son's soft, cherry-suede chairs and lay in his field-wide bed, refusing to strip off his sheets. She fingered his clothes—jeans and cashmere sweaters and expensive leather jackets—and lingered by the tall velvet-draped windows, her quiet presence often unnoticed yet somehow palpable, like a sudden breath of warm air on the nape of your neck. I bought groceries and cooked most mornings before work, but she would forget to eat it, forget there was life after life, hers after Konstantin's. She became so thin, threadbare, you could see through her, could see her heart pulsing slower and slower, enmeshed in silence and grief. I had her all to myself now, and yet she was slipping away, dissipating into the darkness.

As for me, I enjoyed living in my brother's apartment. I put on his flamboyant, if a bit arrogant, lifestyle like an ill-fitted glove of oiled, supple leather—it stretched with wear and gave a nice shape to your hand. I could now continue my education, as opposed to managing a small food-and-liquor kiosk for the rest of my life, and enjoy the view of the city and the Moskva River while eating my meals, gazing dreamily out the snow-brushed window. There was darkness out there, and there was light, the city quilt patched with shadows. The outside world was like the river itself—treacherous and invisible, protected by snow that would soon melt, exposing deep cracks in the ice, through which the water would try to escape, gain a semblance of freedom.

When the doorbell rang, I was loading the dishwater, and my mother had dozed off in Konstantin's desk chair, a picture album hugged against her belly. I recognized the woman and the boy from the cemetery and felt obliged to ask them in, nodding and stooping, awkwardly, as though I were the one who had appeared on their doorstep with a stern, urgent gaze and a clump of snow underfoot. The young woman had a smooth face, small inconspicuous features, except maybe for the mouth—too broad, too pulpy, intimidating. She said nothing while she undressed the boy, hanging his red scarf and coat on the hall tree. Squatting, she pulled off his boots one by one before producing a pair of fuzzy slippers from the backpack. She fitted them on his feet, set the boots next to mine by the door, then got up and squeezed the boy in her arms, his sweet scared face nuzzled into her fur coat.

"He's your nephew," she said and pushed the little guy toward me with such a force, he bumped against my hip.

"What do you mean he's my nephew? Who are you?"

"Unimportant. But you must take care of him because I can't, not at the moment."

"No way. You fucking kidding me?"

With her sad, dark eyes she studied my sweater or rather Konstantin's—gray with purple stripes. It was a little too snug yet long in the sleeves, but I loved how soft it felt against my chaffed, wintered skin. "I bought it for him," she finally said.

"That doesn't prove squat."

"No?"

"Konstantin hated children. Compared them to asshole hairs, dirty and annoying."

"I really must go. But I'll be back. I promise."

"When?"

She shrugged. "Soon. Be good to him. He'll eat anything, and he's stranger-friendly." She opened the door and walked out, scurried down the steps with dull thuds. I stared at the puddle of water on the floor and then at the boy. He didn't move, half leaning against me, his kitten-gray eyes brimming with tears.

"Shit," I said.

"Shit," he echoed.

* * *

THE YEAR IS 1988; the day after my high school graduation. The sky is drifting with clouds changing shapes—houses to cars, cars to wheels, wheels to breasts. Mountainous, doughy, with soft areolas and long sugary nipples. I keep tasting them, keep smacking my virgin lips while Konstantin is in the other room, having sex with one of his beautiful girlfriends. He's never at home anymore, comes to sleep occasionally or visits when our mother is out, so he doesn't have to answer her questions: Where are you all day? What do you eat? Where did you get that leather jacket?

No sounds are coming from the room, but as I press my palms and my face, my cheeks, my nose, my tongue, all of me to the wall, I imagine their bodily vibrations, gentle thrusts growing steadier and harder as my penis engorges with blood, about to spill. My hand reaches inside my shorts when the door swings open and my brother's girlfriend appears like a nymph, transparent, draped in air and her long blond locks. Her feet are small, lovely, with scarlet toenails; a thin golden chain coils around her ankle.

As soon as she steps into the room, she's enveloped in sunlight, and I tremble to touch her, such slim shoulders and perfect breasts. She doesn't protest but guides my hands farther along her thighs; her skin mellows under my fingers. She has a shaved pussy, red and tender like her mouth. It opens and closes—a wet, living thing. I come inside her, she arches, buttocks raised, heels pounding at my back when she calls out my brother's name.

"Happy fucking graduation," Konstantin says and grins. In the doorway, his naked erect silhouette looms too far and too close.

* * *

SINCE HIGH SCHOOL I'd dreamed of becoming a radiologist; I was convinced it was the best profession in the world because you were able to see the invisible, to see inside people. But I couldn't afford medical school, or my own apartment, and I couldn't bring myself to ask Konstantin for help because it would have meant that I had conceded to his despicable behavior, endorsed his impudence. I could have never done that, stooping so low, humiliating myself to no end. So I worked long hours at the kiosk, every day and even on weekends, saving what little I could. My mother, however, had lost her job three years into perestroika when it'd become clear that only the young and the dodgy would lead Russia into the twenty-first century. Konstantin was one of them; he possessed no degree but plenty of talent, criminal talent. He had the nose of a bloodhound, he smelled money and fortune, and he chased them to the death. He believed in the imminent success of his clandestine undertakings as other people believed in their government, who kept robbing them of chance and hope, a desire to achieve. Konstantin often said that socialism was about petty theft; perestroika was about grand larceny. One must adjust, and one must share. Years later, reading about ordered killings, which would slowly become routine, I understood that "sharing" had always been unwarranted and through sheer coercion. It was a continuous game of Russian roulette—each lucky, missed shot brought you closer to death.

Little Konstantin had moved into Big Konstantin's apartment and my mother's heart with ease and confidence, without doing much of anything other than curling up on her lap and eating her food—beef cutlets, *rassol'nik*, fried fish. Just like Big Konstantin, he exuded restlessness and was a voracious eater yet remained skinny. Each time my mother picked him up, she worried about breaking him in half. He was five but looked barely three. He was inquisitive and intrusive, and I compared him to a rescue pet too eager to trust any feeding hand. Unlike me, my mother had never questioned Konstantin's paternity and embraced the boy with the kind of selfless love only a grandmother could bestow. And Little Konstantin indulged her, melting under her stroking hands like snow under the sun. He laughed when she bathed him, tickling his feet, and nestled with her on the couch, watching cartoons or an old TV show, *In the World of Animals*. Each day they went out for walks and returned with sweets and toys. They built Lego castles and race tracks, improvised a puppet theater from old gloves, and held imaginary tournaments while deeming themselves great warriors, fierce and fearless, protected by cardboard armor. My mother turned twenty-five again, with a life marked by promise and a kid's touch. She gained weight, grew breasts, and colored her hair chestnut brown; she wore young-women's clothes, tight and uncomfortable, but also low-cut and low-rise, hems dragging across the floor. Even her face filled in and blossomed, a touch of rosy glow on her cheeks. In just a week Little Konstantin was calling her Big Mama.

"Konstantin means constant, everlasting," my mother said once, during supper. She reached to touch the boy's head, his pixie face fondled by long brown locks.

"And Leova?" he asked.

"Bold for his people. Lion," she answered.

"King," I said.

"You don't look like a king. You're too short."

"Sorry." I spooned dressed herring into my mouth, chewing steadily.

"If you have a son," he continued, "will you call him Little Leova or Lion Prince?"

"You think you're so fucking smart."

"You think you're so fucking smart."

"Stop it. Both of you," my mother said.

Little Konstantin focused his soft, woolly eyes on my face; I glanced out the window, at a large icicle that hung low over the sill, threatening to crush against its silver lip.

* * *

THE YEAR IS 1995. It's our mother's fiftieth birthday, and Konstantin has ordered fifty burgundy roses to be delivered to our old flat. A stylist has been hired to pick out our mother's dress and massive chest-crushing jewelry, a calf-hair purse and a matching pair of high-heeled shoes our mother has trouble wearing. She wobbles from the bathroom to the kitchen to the living room, pausing and ogling herself in a dim hallway mirror. A driver in a black Mercedes has been paid to chaperone her to a spa that morning, where she's been transformed into someone with a pompadour and flawless skin.

An Italian restaurant has been reserved months in advance, friends gathered, wines selected and paired with exotic seafood platters and hand-rolled pastas in rich bloodred sauces. In the background a band is playing "Yesterday," and the guy impersonating Lennon shakes his long, stringy hair. Waitresses hover over the table, where our tall, rejuvenated mother resides between her sons. Konstantin pricks a shrimp and spools a forkful of pasta, raises a wineglass. "If you wanted to punish a bad person, what would you do, Ma?" he asks, sucking the pasta off the fork, chewing with applied force.

"Me?" she asks, confused.

"Yes." He dabs a napkin at his lips. "Would you kill him? Or would you make him suffer for the rest of his life?"

"Whose life? Who are you talking about? No one deserves to die," she says; the confusion in her eyes has given way to fear. She blinks and rubs her cheek, her glowing complexion now smudged between her fingers.

"You're too kind, Ma. Always have been—to all of us assholes," he says and downs the wine, beckoning at the waitress, who obliges at once, a bottle of red in hand.

"Speak for yourself," I say. "And stop interrogating our mother, you heartless jerk."

"You heartless jerk. What did you ever do to care for her? What did you give her? I paid for everything, including your fucking suit."

"Money is paper."

"Money is freedom—freedom to do whatever I damn please."

"Steal and murder?"

"Wow, some potent words, little brother. Be careful, someone may hear you."

"Mom, is that true?" I turn sideways. "Did he buy my suit? You said it was your money, and I said I'd pay you back."

She squints, hard, as though one of us were about to hit her. "Why do you always have to do this?" She grinds the words between her teeth like dry buckwheat. "Spoil everything?"

"I spoil everything? I'm the culprit of all your troubles?" My voice escalates, stomach churns with anger. A few guests snap their heads in our direction. "I'll sing," I say and acknowledge the empty stage, the instruments, like dead bodies, scattered on the floor. "It's my gift to all of you." I get up, the wine pulsing through my veins; my mother catches my hand, tries to hold me in place.

"Don't embarrass yourself, asshole," Konstantin smirks.

"Can you pay me *not* to?"

* * *

WHEN, EVEN BEFORE the funeral, the police asked my mother whether she was aware of the criminal activities her older son had been involved in, she shook her head and said, "It's your job to know such things and prevent them from happening. My job is to love and protect my children. And sometimes we all fail."

Oddly, I began feeling like that too. There was sad helplessness in everything I did, an unnerving importunate sense of paralysis, the inability to derive satisfaction from food or studies or even sex, albeit sporadic because I wasn't in a relationship. I had money but no one special to spend it on; I lived in a beautiful apartment but couldn't wait to escape in the morning. Worse even, I no longer desired to become a radiologist. I had lost all interest, all ambition to see inside people. They seemed no more than a compilation of organs damaged by age or disease. They feared death and accidents, the unavoidable and the unknown. There was no cure for them and no hope.

It was early spring in the city, the roads a marsh of snow and dirt. Wet, murky air clung to faces, coated buildings and trees. The river had begun to thaw, and you could see a plexus of cracks sprawling out toward a dark spot in the middle, barely scabbed with ice. We still hadn't heard anything from Little Konstantin's mother, and by the time the big icicle broke off and crushed against the kitchen sill, he'd stopped leaping from chairs or scampering to answer the phone. Occasionally, though, I would spot him by the window, quiet yet tense, his baby palms pressed against the cold, foggy glass. He would stand like that for a while, unperturbed by voices or house noise, a bug frozen in time.

"He's gone," my mother said as soon as I arrived from work that day. She stood by the kitchen window, her coat bunched at her feet. I could tell she'd been crying, her face blotched red, hairs adhered to her puffy cheeks.

"What do you mean? His mother returned?"

She shook her head. "They took him."

"Who took him? What the fuck happened?"

"We were rolling snow, what's left of it. We had to move quickly to cover a larger territory. A taxi pulled over. I turned around and he was gone." She sobbed in my sweater, and I lifted my arms around her.

"We have to get him back," she said and wiped her face with the stretched sleeve. "We have to pay ransom. They called. Konstantin owed a hundred thousand."

"Dollars? No fucking way."

"I can't let them take my baby."

"We go to the police."

"They're all corrupt. And what will we say? That Little Konstantin's mother left him? We have no proof. He'll be placed in a home. I can't let that happen. He's mine."

"But he isn't. Don't you see?"

"No." Her forehead strained in protest. "I love him. He belongs with me."

"What if he doesn't?"

"Don't say that."

"What if the trick is not to love someone so much that he doesn't disappear or run away?"

She stared at me. "Are you making a joke? Because it isn't funny. I've loved you equally, but he was the one who needed me most. Can't you understand that?"

"No. Because in the end it didn't save him but made him do crazy, ugly things. So he could be the man our father wasn't. So he could send you on posh vacations, buy you fancy duds, this apartment—" She slapped me, her hand just as quick and hard as eighteen years ago when I'd told her that I nearly drowned and Konstantin was responsible.

For the next two days we didn't leave the apartment, and we didn't talk, passing a few cautious words like explosives, with nervous fear. On the third day clouds blew over the city, gray like rocks, and it began to rain. The river darkened and swelled and was moving. Large, jagged floes drifted along the snow-fringed banks. Out the window the floes resembled wrecked ships or parts of buildings with remnants of life stuck to their broken surfaces. We waited by the phone. We knew we didn't have that much money in Konstantin's account, and selling either apartment, old or new, would take time, but perhaps we could negotiate about transferring the property over to the kidnappers.

The caller turned out to be an older woman with a scratchy voice who coughed short, incomplete sentences into the receiver: Bring the money. Leave the money. Pick up the kid. No police or the kid dies. Her words penetrated the distance and my ear in quick forced jabs.

"Let me talk to the boy," I said as soon as she stopped. "I want to make sure he's alive."

I heard a few muffled sounds as if someone was wrestling with the phone or conferring in a hurry. I switched to the loudspeaker so my mother could hear the entire conversation, her pale face a tempest of emotions.

"Hello," I said, then louder: "Hello?"

"Big Mama," Little Konstantin said.

"I'm here," she answered. "I'm here, baby."

"Big Papa is—" and the line went dead, an echo of empty beeps spreading through the kitchen.

My mother started at the phone then at me, her eyes wet like river pebbles.

"That motherfucker," I said, spitting. "That goddamned motherfucker."

Twenty minutes later the cabdriver pulled into the neighborhood of shabby, piss-reeking five-story buildings—*khrushchevki*—about to be demolished like the rest. In the yard, as I got out of the taxi,

I spotted a filthy tailless dog scrabbling about a pile of trash. He dragged out a chicken leg, scraps of skin on a dry bone, and began gnawing. I stood watching him, but for just a moment, a heresy of rain and snow in my eyes.

I ran up the steps, I found the door, I rang the bell. I pounded and threatened until I heard a sly shuffle, the chain being lifted, the bolt turned, that sound a wall clock makes when it's about to strike an hour.

As a boy, I must've imagined our meeting many times, only in reverse—I was the one standing behind the door, waiting to embrace the visitor, hoping him to be my father. I never imagined his face but compared him to a healthy tree, thick trunk, shapely outreaching limbs, lush brown hair rustling in the wind. When the door cracked open and was drawn back by an invisible someone, I found myself facing a short middle-aged woman with yellowish skin and frightened eyes. She was like a bird plucked of all feathers, thin, humble, about to die.

"Where is he?" I asked, and she pointed along the dark narrow corridor, where amid the junk shelves and coats I detected something moving, slinking along the wall. It was a man in a wheelchair, Little Konstantin on his lap.

"Lion King! Lion King!" The boy jumped off, scurrying in my direction. I bent down and picked him up. He was warm, soft, and smelled of baked apples. A streak of white crusted on his cheek. He was dressed in the same blue-mohair sweater and jeans as the day he'd disappeared, but the clothes seemed to have been washed, the jeans ironed. "Big Papa said you were coming to get me."

"Oh, yeah? What else did Big Papa say? That he is a thief and liar? A goddamned motherfucking asshole?"

"Stop cussing in my home," the man in the wheelchair said. He was almost bald with a cleft in his prickly jaw. His nose was crooked and his small eyes too close, wincing at the light the woman switched on. He was dressed in a plaid flannel shirt and gray sweatpants stretched at the ankles; he made me think of street beggars, those fetid bums in train stations and subways. I felt no pity toward him and, sadly, no anger.

"I'm Liya, Boris's wife," the woman said, and I recognized her voice, so weak and raspy as though an animal had been clawing at her throat. She handed me the little coat and boots. "We're very sorry. Please, forgive us."

I didn't answer.

"Make a scary face and snarl at them," Little Konstantin said. "Like when you study for your exams and I want to play."

I patted his head then sat him down and began threading his arms through the coat sleeves.

"Fucking assholes," I finally said. "How could you?"

My father wheeled closer, his feet in green corduroy sleepers touched my shins. "He did this to me."

"Shut the fuck up," I said. "You don't get to blame him."

"Konstantin wanted me to go back to your mother. Offered me money and a new apartment. When I said no, those punks forced me to lie on the ground while he drove his car across my legs. She was there," he pointed at Liya, who nodded, fighting tears.

"So you stole his child? That's your piss-ass excuse? The fuck is wrong with you?"

"I need surgery. Abroad. I may be able to walk with prosthetics."

"Did you pay someone to kill Konstantin?"

He shook his head, vigorously. "No, no. I'm not like that."

"How would I know?"

"You're my son."

"Fuck off."

"I sent money, when I could."

"What's my name?"

He didn't answer but cupped his knees; the woman leaned over and whispered something in his ear.

I held Little Konstantin's hand as we sauntered out of the apartment.

"I bet she didn't love you like that," my father yelled. "Did she? Did she?"

I stalled, reached into my pocket, and took out the money, all I had. "Here," I said, turning and foisting a hefty stack into Liya's hand. "Don't buy him new legs though. He might walk away." I laughed, a dry, choked laugh, the kind I imagined Konstantin laughed when the gun fired but before the bullet made it all dark and irrevocable.

* * *

IT'S SUMMER ALREADY. I got accepted into medical school and am veering toward cardiology, the science of the heart. Little Konstantin has been drawing and cutting them out of paper, so that hearts of various sizes and colors are scattered about the apartment—red, purple, deep-orange, the color of the bloody sun pulsing over the city. The Moskva River rushes, meanders along the grassy banks. Every now and then large boats sail by, the water parts and closes, the circles diminish and finally disappear, one inside another.

It has taken a thick yellow envelope three weeks to travel from America to Russia, and I don't show it to my mother at first. But when I do she cries silently, hot tears streaming down her cheeks, falling into the *pelmeni* dough. She continues to roll it out thin, thinner than skin or hair. "We can still visit," she says. "Can't we? The mother won't mind. How hard is it to get a visa?" I shrug and take her warm, sticky hands in mine, and she holds on to my thumbs like a child, with all her might.

The next day Little Konstantin and I are dressed in shorts and old-fashioned *matroskas*, cotton sailors' shirts our mother bought at the market. We look ridiculous but are hesitant to shed a smile or a word, standing low on the riverbank so that our toes touch its wet lip. An armada of birds flies into the trees hooded with foliage. The limbs bounce and sway and finally settle, the birds concealed among the leaves.

In his hand Little Konstantin holds a toy lion he arranges inside a warped black-leather shoe I found in the yard, when all the snow had melted.

"He won't drown?" he asks. "Will he?"

I blink. "No. Of course not."

"Are there lions in America?"

"Yes. Everywhere. Big lions, with thick manes and sharp teeth." I shake my head and snarl at him; he lets out a shy giggle and leaps backward. We are silent, but just for a moment, observing a tremble of clouds on the water.

We lower the shoe into the river and push it downstream with a severed tree branch. We watch the shoe sail, reluctant at first, bobbing on waves and leaning to one side. When it disappears from view, we climb up the bank and continue to watch it drift, straight ahead, unimpeded—oblivious to everything but water and wind.

All of Me

In a bar, at Shakers, I wait for my friend Norma to join me for a drink. I've known Norma for twenty years since I first immigrated to Roanoke, Virginia. I've been meeting her in this bar for over a decade, mostly for gossip and child-free time. We got acquainted at a fitness center, where she taught step aerobics and now takes Zumba classes. In my mind she's hardly changed—the same plump body and lascivious smile. The curves of her breasts and buttocks are taunting. Both Norma and I have been married to our husbands for nineteen years, with two children each, who are about to graduate high school. She has daughters and I have sons, and we've always joked that they should get married, so we can finally be connected not only through spirit but through blood of our future grandbabies.

Other than our age—forty-five—we are very different, Norma and I. She's blonde, blue-eyed, fair-skinned; I'm half Russian, half Armenian with a bale of black hair and skin that looks tan year-round. She's a lighter side to my darker one. Norma loves comedies and Hallmark family entertainment, and I crave the tragic and the desperate. Fellini, Bergman, Tarkovsky. I listen to classical music that can make me weep in the midst of dinner or sex—a Rachmaninoff elegy or a Chopin nocturne, or Scriabin's Revolutionary étude—and Norma favors jazz, nothing too fancy, no Monk or Coltrane, but maybe Gershwin's "Summertime" with Charlie Parker on the sax. "Oh, but how he caresses that instrument," Norma would say. "I could make love to that man all night."

And she would, if she could, but she can't. Norma is married to Jerald, who's tall, silent, handsome. A man with large hands and a befitting penis, Norma brags and brags. I don't share her enthusiasm on the size of her husband's genitals, his tool of sin, but even I get curious. Can a woman love a man that dearly for that long that even his penis size grows proportionally to the number of years they've shared? First it was like this, then it became like that, and now it's the most potent, beautiful magic wand. All Norma has to do is rub it with her hand or stroke it with her lips. Oh, the pleasures of giving and receiving!

Arguing with Norma is a joyful challenge because while I think in dichotomies and absolutes, she prefers shades and semi-tones, watery pastels. Raised in a country that forbade everything but science and servitude, I keep insisting that the world is bipolar, that one cannot know the good without the evil, bliss without agony, but she pinches her soft lips together so that from a distance they resemble a rosebud, then slowly pulls them apart, her mouth blossoming into a full smile. "Not true," she says. "Yes, true," I insist. "In my country, suffering overrules pleasure." "Then all your women are virgins?" she asks, her face now as serious as when she attempts to read a Russian novel on the beach. She has many—by Tolstoy, Dostoevsky, Nabokov, Bulgakov—all gifts from me.

I should mention that Norma's literary palate is much more yielding than mine; she compromises, allows an occasional thriller, mystery, or romance. Chick lit. She argues that if women don't read other women, don't empathize, then it's over, the world has turned Paleozoic. "Back to the womb we go. Can you imagine the darkness?" Norma is an OB/GYN nurse; she spends her days staring at strange vaginas, which, she insists, are gloriously different. In shape, color, and size. She imagines how lost men must feel when they approach what they think is familiar territory, hills and coppices and caves, only to discover a parched desert or a lush steppe, the occasional swampland. Go ahead and conquer that, my dear! Get drowned, get choked between those fleshy thighs. Norma enjoys flaunting her knowledge, partly because she wants me to use it in my stories, partly because there's no one else to tell it to. "I'm a pussy reader," she says and laughs, her open-mouth laugh, the kind of laugh you want to slip in your pocket, like a keepsake.

Other than an occasional shopping trip or a meal on International Women's Day, celebrated all over the world but America, Shakers near Valley View Mall is the only place we socialize alone. It's never too busy to accommodate two women longing for drinks and each other's company. I down the rest of my vodka and beckon at the bartender to order a gin and tonic for Norma. I know that she's entered the restaurant and is approaching the bar because a few single men have stopped looking at the TV. Their heads turn in the direction of the door, where my friend lingers under a globe of light. She's wearing a shrunken T-shirt and a pair of tight navy jeans that accentuate her hips and her ample buttocks, which she swings lightly while walking. Her thighs singing blues, something popular, something from Muddy Waters—"Got My Mojo Working."

Norma's hair is a deliberate mess, waves of honey-gold. She shakes it and shakes it.

"You're earlier than me," she says, leaning to give me a peck on the cheek. "What's wrong?"

"Nothing."

"You've had two drinks before dinner. Spill it."

I love how economical she can be in her demands. How curt.

"So?" she asks, wedging her sweet behind on a red bar stool.

"I don't know where to start."

"Start from the beginning."

"That would be too long."

"I don't work tomorrow."

I laugh, but mostly to acknowledge how good she makes me feel, how secure. I wave at the bartender for another vodka.

"I lost my desire," I say as soon as he turns away to fill a glass.

Norma blinks then tucks a curl behind her ear. John once compared her ears to conches, and now I always think that.

"You mean sexual desire?" she asks. "For your husband?"

"I mean all desire. Writing too."

"Oh, but that's what you call writer's block."

"No. I have no problem imagining shit or putting it down on paper. I just have no desire to tell lies that pose as truths."

"That sounds like your favorite guy."

"Slavoj Žižek?"

"Him. 'I'm terrified of un-freedom that poses as freedom.' He isn't talking about sex though?"

"No. He's talking about this country."

"What does that have to do with your desire?"

"I don't know. You brought it up. But I haven't had sex or written a word in six months. I can't fake it."

"And you're just telling me this?"

"I thought maybe the perimenopause is to blame."

"Have you tested your levels? FSH? Progesterone? Estrogen? Testosterone?"

"Don't only men have that?"

The bartender sets Norma's drink on the counter, and she swirls the ice cubes about the glass before drawing a long delicious gulp. "A lack of libido is common at our age. Hormones are dropping from one month to the next."

"Mine are in my toes. No—the tips of my toes."

"I'll make an appointment for you tomorrow. Let's do some blood work. Until then stop torturing yourself. Be happy."

"A Russian can never be happy unless she's absolutely miserable."

"That's fucked up, really fucked up."

I dredge up a smile.

* * *

A WEEK LATER Norma calls to inform me that my blood work is normal. "Ovulating like crazy," she says and sneaks a chuckle.

"My tubes are tied." I light a cigarette and blow out smoke, ever so gently. She cannot possibly hear.

"Put down that cigarette," she says. "Pick up a pen. Start working."

"I can't."

"What you need to do is to go away with John for a few days. The boys can stay with us. There's nothing like sex in an unfamiliar place. Jerald and I love doing it in big cities, in hotels, on balconies."

"Why balconies?"

"It's exciting."

"It's exhibitionistic."

"So? My nipples are hard just talking about it."

I imagine Norma's large flat pale nipples shrinking implacably against the wind and all the street noises.

"I don't think I can do that."

"Why not? Anyone would love to fuck your husband. *I* would love to fuck John. If we put his picture on Craigslist and try to sell him, we'd make a fortune. Hell, we can have bids."

"That's eBay. And let's not get rich by prostituting my husband." I get aroused, if only for a second, from imagining Norma fucking John. Her body mellowing under his. I know how pathetic and perverse it sounds, but I hang up and rush to masturbate. On our bed, armed only with my finger, I touch myself while conjuring John's penis filling Norma's mouth. I imagine them in a shower, on a dark balcony, in the same bed. John's long white fingers caressing Norma's milky thighs, his tongue sweeping paths between her legs. They are perfect together, my husband and my best friend. In my fantasy I stretch out to touch their bodies, to feel their desire or maybe to apologize for intruding. We achieve orgasms almost simultaneously, and then I feel sick from shame and pleasure.

* * *

NORMA HAS NEVER cheated on Jerald; or if she has, she didn't tell me. When we meet a month later, at a flea market, she doesn't mention my desire but browses through pottery and Native American artifacts. The wind chimes dangle over her head and make the loneliest of sounds. She picks up a pair of earrings, two large feathers attached to silver hooks, and presses them against her cheeks, under her hair. She looks ridiculous yet tender-faced. It's early May, warm and humid, almost summertime, and Norma is wearing a new dress and a straw hat. The dress is blue-and-white polka-dot, sleeveless, flaring at the bottom. She looks softer somehow, blushing from the sun. The golden sandals on her pedicured feet have tassels, and when she walks, they bump against her ankles. She resembles a goddess with her long sun-bleached hair and roly-poly arms.

At another booth she tries on a cowboy hat, of brown felt, broad-brimmed and high-crowned with a buckle ornament on the left side. She appraises herself in a full-length mirror. I stand next to her, a head taller and twenty pounds lighter, less desirable, but more agitated. I'm dressed in a pair of white capris and a black T-shirt that says: *Don't fuck with writers—we'll describe you.*

"Do I need this?" she asks and bends the brims of the hat, so that it rides higher on her head.

"I don't know," I answer.

"And this?" she fingers a dream catcher hanging from the mirror.

"It's fake. You'll have nightmares."

"Maybe I already do."

"What's wrong? Guilty conscience?"

"No, but I'd like to fuck an Indian," she says.

"Why?"

"Just to know what it's like to fuck an Indian."

"That's awful. That's like if someone would want to fuck me because of my accent."

"I bet they would. I bet that happens all the time." She laughs, and a few men turn to ogle her. Norma can be tempting, even in a housedress. It's the hair, I convince myself, the ease with which she drapes it from one side to the other, exposing her fragile, sun-grazed neck. "Are you and John trying therapy?" she asks, her intonation is not that of curiosity.

"Yes. Three weeks from today." I run my hand along the crooked edge of a bowl carved out of burly maple. "This looks Russian for some reason. Or Armenian."

"Buy it. Or I'll buy it for your birthday."

"It's months away."

"Don't use it until then."

"No. It's bad luck. We don't do that kind of thing."

"Such bullshit." She reaches for the money, laughing, but her laughter is strained, an old-joke laughter. There's no edge to it, and no heartiness.

* * *

THIS IS WHAT Norma doesn't know: I started to lose my desire when my sons began to grow pubic hair. There was suddenly their smell, their sweat, their stained underwear. My love for John was still absolute, but my desire so thin, sporadic. I wanted to stay married, I wanted to overcome the notion of incompleteness by having sex with strange men in strange hotel rooms, at conferences and readings, where writers mingle, drink, and forget that they're blissfully married to the most soulful, kind, generous, trusting people.

I have a strange feeling in hotel rooms. It's almost passive-aggressive. All I want to do is fuck and sleep. Maybe that's all you can do. Hotel rooms indulge no emotions other than those of fear and pity. Fear of being discovered, pity of needing to be there, on those strange beds with coffee, blood, and sperm stains eaten deep into the covers. Why would anyone want to do that? Touch the world's filth? Undress in front of total strangers? Expose bodily imperfections, the smells, the scars? Those silent betrayals of the flesh?

(Father,

Father, father, father. I have no memory of you, except one—in a hotel, with a prostitute scooping clothes from the bed. Your voice is so thick, smoky, bitter, unapologetic. Mother has never gotten over your betrayal. She had affairs, perhaps too many; she drank, perhaps too much; she even laughed, though somewhat obsessively, but she's never loved anyone else. Growing up in Soviet Russia, where things continuously disappeared, I don't know whom I missed more—the parent I didn't have or the one who didn't know how to parent. I wonder if sins and desires are passed through blood. If lust is bequeathed. My mother, she didn't know how to pretend or to surrender. Self-sacrifice is still unthinkable. The daughter is her father's child. The abandoned one, the guilty.)

* * *

A WEEK BEFORE initial family counseling, Norma asks if she can attend one of the readings with me at Hollins University, where I graduated years ago. The visiting writer is a famous Native American guy, but Norma has never read any of his books. I'm just as puzzled by her wish to attend the event as when she says she'll drive and let me indulge in classical music. I feel oddly uncomfortable, as though a certain boundary has been breached, my privacy invaded. But I can't say that to her. It's Norma, after all.

We've already had two drinks, so she's tipsy and loquacious.

"Do you know that when my mother came to visit a few years ago and ended up staying with us for five months, my periods were late and spotty, and I began to forget things, just like her? My brain fogged, and my hands shook."

"You're imagining things."

"Ask Jerald. He said that even my pussy smelled old."

"How would he know? He likes to smell old women's crotches?"

Norma grins, shaking her blond mane, then asks, "Why doesn't your mother visit?"

"She hates this country. She hates any country that starts with an 'A.' Armenia too."

"Why? What exactly does she hate? Politics?"

"No. She doesn't give a fuck about that. She hates everything else, starting with bread and ending with medical care. It's all a fake to her."

"And John?"

"She loves John, but mostly because she can't understand what he's saying. Her language skills don't extend past yes or no."

We both laugh, and then we're both quiet, engrossed in music.

After Scriabin's Étude op. 8, no. 12, when it seems that the tragedy rises and falls and your heart is broken ten times within two and a half minutes, we listen to Chopin's Nocturne op. 48, no. 1, which starts achingly slow, with rests and pauses between the lugubrious minor notes. It's like reading a conflicted love story, which will eventually escalate into a fury of smashing chords.

Midway through the piece, Norma turns down the volume.

"I wonder what he was thinking when he wrote that," she asks. "Such passion."

"He was in love with George Sand."

"The bisexual cross-dresser?"

"Yes. She entertained the most famous artists and writers of the time. Flaubert, Dostoevsky, Turgenev, Delacroix."

"She slept with all of them? Was she that promiscuous?"

"Oh, she was indeed promiscuous and daring, but a lot of her affairs are exaggerated. Her literary, public, and domestic lives were full to the brim. She wrote everything. Poetry, fiction, nonfiction. Her published correspondence alone comprises twenty-five volumes. Can you fucking believe that? Writing that much with feathers?"

"Like digging a grave with a scoop."

"She also produced plays, educated children, gardened, enjoyed needlework and jam making."

"Sounds like someone I know."

"Flattering, but no. I don't do shit compared to her. And I don't entertain."

"If you had her money, you probably would."

"Maybe. But the most fascinating thing is that she wrote fiction from personal experience, yet she also tested out possibilities for life that she then lived. Her experiences gave rise to her stories, but her writing also shaped her life. Although I think she was very lonely. As a child she longed to be near her mother, and the need for physical closeness never went away. Perhaps that explains her many affairs."

"Didn't she love Chopin?"

"Not sure about him. One of her great loves was Marie Dorval, a famous Parisian actress. When Sand watched her act, she recognized her own suppressed emotions. The two women were opposites and thus were strongly drawn to each other."

"Just like us."

"I'm not drawn to you sexually. Don't even try."

Norma laughs, her big candid laugh, a laugh you want to swallow because it makes you feel warm and lovable and understood.

"Have you ever cheated on John?" she asks.

I stare at her, the cascade of her golden hair and full pomaded mouth. "Why do you ask? Trying to justify your own sins?"

"No. I figure all writers do that. All artists actually. They seek expression through their work and lovers who inspire that work."

"What if their spouses and children inspire their work and they need no others?"

She shoots me a sly look. It isn't full of mockery but amusement. "You lost your desire. You have to get it back."

"You can't reclaim your desire for one person by sleeping with another."

"Can you ever reclaim it?"

"I don't know. I don't know. I don't know."

* * *

I REMEMBER WHEN I first started writing: during pregnancy, when I was engorged with hormones and even more desire. John and I had sex every day, and the words, the stories grew out of me like my children. I was happy, and I was tired, and I was hungry. I ate voraciously, and I wrote obsessively. Sometimes I did it standing up, positioning a small notebook on the windowsill. Sun tickled the pages, then tree limbs, then snow. I could see it falling in the mountains like tiny weightless feathers.

(My children,

My glorious fortunate children. My Gods. My beloveds. These are the things I should've taught you: There's sex without love, and love without sex, but neither have the right to exist without desire. You will be betrayed, and you will be forgotten. You will forgive. Oh, sweet, gullible, unruffled youth! How lucky you are to share parents who devoted their lives to loving you so much that they at times forgot to love each other. How blissfully ignorant you are of pain, of longing, of want. How unaware and unprepared. How I wish I could warn you, could protect you from what is to come—spring tiptoeing into summer, slipping into fall. Autumn leaves. When I first heard that song, I wanted to sleep with it, to make love to it, to tuck it between my legs like a pillow. I wanted to gather and hide all the leaves.

I'm as good a mother to you as my mother couldn't be to me. She said she was lonely when she held me on her knees. You cannot imagine such loneliness.)

* * *

JOHN IS DRESSED in a linen blazer and a dark-maroon T-shirt, untucked, hanging over the blue jeans. He has a new shorter haircut. It's much more youthful, despite all the gray at the temples. Until now I haven't noticed what he's wearing, although we ate breakfast and drove together and sat in the waiting room, nearly obliterated by snowdrifts of paperwork.

"It'll be summer before we're finished," I joke to the receptionist. "Or fall. Autumn leaves. Do you know that song?"

She shakes her head, the twists of her black hair bouncing on her shoulders.

"How about 'All of Me'?"

"Don't think so."

"*You took the part that was my heart. . . .*" I can see that she isn't particularly impressed by my singing, which my mother once compared to the croaking of frogs.

She gathers the papers and ushers us into the therapist's office. The room smells of coffee and rich burgundy leather. After the introductory banalities, the silence is terrifying. I long for Norma to be present, to start her insouciant prattle. To describe vaginas or what doctors occasionally find in them: condoms, tampons, bits of fruit, and even tweezers. "What the hell are the tweezers doing there?" she'd asked, hands on hips. "No eyebrows grow on pussies."

I can't help but laugh, and both John and the therapist, a middle-aged, silver-suited woman with fake nails, stare with intent, questioning faces: Is everything okay? Are you okay?

I nod, although I have no idea what I'm doing here, how exactly this therapy, this woman, can help resurrect my desire. Jesus! I suddenly imagine the woman putting her wide thin mouth on mine and attempting artificial respiration. With her manicured hands, she gives my heart a few violent pushes then switches back to my mouth.

John is quiet, which for him is a state of being. He's an astronomer; he spends his days calculating and rationalizing, and his nights gazing at the stars. He must find them, must give them names. He fills the charts and constructs elaborate algorithms, a solar maze penciled and stapled to the walls of his study. He fills our sons' lives with dreams and wonder. He exemplifies perseverance. They adore him, of course, that tall brawny man, who hikes, and swims, and lifts weights.

"I think that each of you should voice a personal concern," the therapist says. "And we'll go from there." She smiles, and I'm reminded of a piranha, with its muscular jaw and finely serrated teeth. The fish produces one of the most forceful bites measured in vertebrates.

Neither John nor I speak. I imagine us all fish in a water tank, submerged into the murky depths. We navigate with our tails, not our heads. We have no truths, only instincts. Gills, gills, gills.

"Maybe let's start with something positive," the therapist continues. "A memorable episode. A romantic trip. Something that involves just the two of you."

I want Norma next to me on the couch. I want her to appraise the woman's sex life and erotic vigor just by looking at her hands and feet, as she did that time at the reading by looking at the author's. She made me laugh. She said, "Clean, beautiful, strong hands—passion, tenderness; feet not too large, toes in—insecurity."

I dig through my memories like a child through a pile of blocks. I stack them up. First Meeting. First Date. First Kiss. First Sex. Falling in Love. More Sex. Wedding. Honeymoon. Pregnancy. Writing. Kids. More Writing. The Loss of Desire. Oh, the economy of the trivial! I return to the Honeymoon block. Orlando, Melbourne Beach, Sanibel Island, Key West, where we toured Hemingway's estate that smelled of those fat polydactyl cats reposing in nests of grass. The tall shapely palm trees made me think of penises, and I sneaked my hand under John's shorts. We barely made it to the room, where I could see the sun squatting in its final stroke of heat over the lip of the water.

"Do you know why he killed himself?" John asked, rolling on his side, fingers high in the air, as though he were afraid to smell them.

I shook my head, still breathing his flesh and the ocean.

"He couldn't fuck and he couldn't write. And he knew no other pleasure."

I have no idea why out of all the words John said to me on our honeymoon, all the beautiful, loving, passionate words, I chose to remember those. Although I could speak decent English when I came to America, I wasn't a writer back then, and I was filled with desire like the ocean with fish.

"How can you do this to me?" John asks, and the Honeymoon block falls between my hands, between my knees. "How can you share this stuff with Norma and not me first? How can you lose your desire? After everything we did together? Raising our children?

Building a home?" His jaw is shaking. It's peppered with gray stubble.
He forgot to shave.

(My Dear,

My Darling. The love of my life, the father of my children.

There's nothing in this world I wouldn't do for you, but someone
should've told the newlyweds to cover their nakedness, to salvage
their desire. There should've been rules on the gates of nuptial
bliss: Don't look at each other's naked bodies unless for sex.
Don't watch each other take showers unless for sex. Don't use the
bathroom together unless for sex. When you pull your fingers
out of your lover, don't wipe them on the sheets. Don't wipe
your mouth. Kiss her right after you kissed her; she wants to
know what she tastes like.)

"I'm sorry," I say. "It's awful. I'm awful. You have no idea."

"Fuck you. Fuck, fuck, fuck you."

* * *

THE FOLLOWING week-month-year exploded with changes like a
summer day with thunderstorms. After therapy, after tears, after
fights, after the acknowledgment of my guilt, after the resurrected
and much-anticipated, much-dreaded sex, John and I separated and
then divorced. I couldn't hold on to my love, and he couldn't hold on
to his. (Mother, mother, why didn't you teach me?) Norma confessed
to fucking John in our house while I was away at a conference. She
called it a sympathy fuck, a feel-better-soon fuck, and John called
it a retaliation fuck, a fuck-my-frigid-wife fuck. It's been months
and months, but I still refuse to meet her at Shakers. She calls it my
Russian stubbornness, and I call it the lack of desire. In the summer
my oldest son will marry Norma's oldest daughter, and we'll become
grandparents when the leaves turn yellow.

I do miss them, John, Norma, the children. I search for them too. On crowded streets, in restaurants and strange hotel rooms. On pages of my stories, and others'.

Once I saw my friend in Fresh Market on Grandin. She was picking out meat at the deli and didn't notice me loitering in the bakery nook, squeezing a baguette. She wore black yoga pants and a down coat, tennis shoes. Her hair swept up in a choppy bun. I watched her taste a slice of salami or roast beef—the silent chomping of her jaws.

She was so ordinary, so familiar, so far away.

The Heart of Things

When Leezy phones to inform her that their mother had a heart attack, Carmen is still in bed, on the cusp of sleep, diving in and out of a dream, in which she's being led across the ocean by some unknown invisible force. The space around her widens with each step, and the only scrap of land has long disappeared from view. She wears loose white vestments with a red cape that flickers in the wind. The ringing breaks through her dream in spells; she trips—her robe catching on a stone or a fish, a mossy carapace of a turtle—and falls, sinks through the layers of water and kelp, sea anemones, silt-coated oyster reefs. She attempts to shout, but her mouth fills with algae, which is her hair strewn with limpets and barnacles, baby starfish. To her dread and utter fascination, she discovers her mermaid tail, emerald green, housing a shoal of tiny creatures under the sharp iridescent scales.

Carmen opens her eyes; the room is dark, the curtains pulled shut. The machine blinks with Leezy's message that Carmen replays a few times before getting up and walking to the bathroom, where she splashes her face with cold water until her skin tingles. She imagines her sister returning home from an apothecary and discovering their mother on the floor, her long hair a lake of quicksilver. Their mother has always insisted that long hair is all women have these days to set them apart; their desire to be independent—pantsuits and briefcases—has taken all the femininity out of them. "Cutting off your hair results in cutting off your beauty together with your wisdom," her mother once said, and Carmen didn't argue because the experience of being raised by a stern mighty-shouldered woman who possessed the will of all the men Carmen had dated told her not to waste her time or breath—her mother would not change.

Carmen has been living in the States for seventeen years. She came to visit an American she'd met in Red Square, then got hired by a local dinner theater and stayed. At the theater, Carmen first worked as a waitress, but she was tall and lissome, could sing, dance, and speak decent English. The productions were all musicals—*The Wizard of Oz*, *Oklahoma!*, *Hello, Dolly!*, *The Fantasticks*—so six months later, she began acting too, small parts, group scenes. She left the man who'd courted her and moved in with one of the actresses. Life became exactly what Carmen had imagined it to be. She performed, partied, got high, engaged in euphoric and tireless sex, swooning in clouds of smoke and fog. She woke up in lounge chairs by pools or on private beaches, half-buried in sand, listening to waves slosh ashore while the sun lit up the world.

Unlike her sister, Carmen has never wanted to marry the Prince of Wales. Nor has she longed for a magical someone to walk into her life and sweep her off her feet. Leezy has always been different. As a child she was dreamy and sullen, bone thin. No matter how much their mother tried to fatten her up and turn Leezy into a plump, robust woman a man would want to bear his children—"hips," their mother had said, "it's all in the hips, the woman's strength and passion"—all her efforts failed. Leezy stayed pale and gangly, nose in a book. At forty-five Leezy still hasn't married, and Carmen is swept with pity comparing their childhood pictures to the more recent ones, diligently sent to Carmen by their mother once a year.

There has been a fleet of men in Carmen's life and only one in Leezy's—the guy she dated in her university years. After graduation he left Leezy for her best friend, with whom he did things Leezy refused to do. "What kind of things?" their mother asked. But Leezy wouldn't answer. She shook her head and stuck her tongue out and pretended to gag. Carmen was thirteen then and had a vague idea what her sister was talking about, so she laughed like crazy, spitting crumbs of supper on her plate. Their mother reached out and slapped her on the cheek, which startled Carmen but also infuriated her. From that moment on she felt that the balance had somehow shifted, that their mother would always side with Leezy because she, too, was the abandoned one, the one who needed the most love and care.

They haven't talked for an eternity, her sister and she, and Carmen hasn't seen her mother since that last visit, five years ago. Carmen was thirty then, still working at the same theater, which her mother failed to acknowledge. Real theater was only in Moscow, as far as she was concerned. And what her daughter did—jumping on stage in tight tops and short ruffled skirts that looked like cheap lingerie—was not acting or even performing. It was vulgar entertainment for a certain kind of clientele who didn't know any better. They quarreled—a lot—about food, movies, books, clothes, which was nothing unusual, but at some point Carmen phoned her sister to tell her that she'd be putting their mother on the first available flight from Miami to Moscow. Leezy didn't answer but hung up.

* * *

ON THE PLANE Carmen sits next to a man whose white starched shirt and shaved face suggest that he must be an office worker. Carmen guesses him to be forty or a bit older. He has no ring on either hand. As soon as they are offered drinks, the man introduces himself as Josh and asks for a beer while Carmen prefers cognac.

Josh is American with a Russian ancestor on his mother's side—the reason for his two-week trip. "To dig for roots," he jokes. "You?"

"I have no roots," Carmen says. "Just bloody relatives."

Josh laughs. When she inquires what he does, he's hesitant for a moment then says, "I'm a doll maker."

"You mean like Barbies?" she asks, even more puzzled. "Really?"

He shakes his head. "Old dolls, like Pinocchio, Petrushka—theater puppets. I work for a European company."

"I was born in a theater," Carmen says, well aware of how odd it sounds.

"Your mother is an actress?"

"No. She used to sell tickets. But she loves theater more than men." Carmen grins, adding, "She was already in labor and refused to leave the opera. Hence my name." She takes a sip of cognac then asks, "What does *your* mother do?"

"Don't know. I grew up in an orphanage, been to a few foster homes. I was a mean child, got into fights constantly. No one kept me long."

Carmen doesn't know how to respond to such honesty. When she first came to America, the man she was staying with warned her that "How do you do?" was a rhetorical question and demanded no answer other than "Fine, thank you." Her actress roommate told Carmen not to elaborate on any personal illnesses or dramas, not to pry into people's private business, even if they were willing to share. In America an expression of sympathy was brief and polite, never overbearing. Life was not a Russian novel; here people weren't so much into eternal suffering, and your interest in someone's affairs should not extend past a glass of wine and a warm, insouciant remark: "Really? Sorry to hear that. You don't say."

And yet Carmen can't help her next question. "What did it feel like to grow up without a mother?"

"Like you're the oldest person in the room." Josh pauses to refill his cup. "You're your own ancestor. You feel exposed, unprotected. And you're always looking, always speculating. She could be my mother or she, or maybe that lady with tattoos and a cigarette hanging out of her mouth, or maybe that one on TV, who drowned her six children and I was the lucky one, the one who got away."

"I'm sorry," Carmen says. "It's terrible."

"Yep. But it could've been worse. I could've been aborted." He gives Carmen a shy smile and waves at the flight attendant for another beer.

They begin serving food, and the cabin fills with greasy smells, but Carmen isn't the least bit hungry. She peers out the window at the vermillion sky. It seems as though they are flying through the heart of the universe. She remembers how during the two months that her mother stayed with her, in a cluttered one-bedroom apartment in Miami Beach, she insisted on buying groceries and cooking since restaurants were so unjustifiably expensive, and Carmen subsisted on protein shakes, chips, and salsa. Once, however, right before her mother's return to Moscow, the two of them ate in a narrow, bullet-shaped diner converted from an old trolley cart in the Art Deco district, where buildings resembled stage decorations or movie props. The food was cheap and all-American—turkey, stuffing, mashed potatoes, gravy. To Carmen's surprise her mother devoured everything on her plate. On the way back they bought ice cream, strolling along Lincoln Road, waffle cones in hand, recalling the taste of a Russian *plombir*. As they reached the beach, they took off their shoes and stepped on the warm sand, skirting around a few roped-off turtles' nests, tracing the shoreline, their footprints filling with water, washing away. The sun was red, like pulp of a watermelon, glowing low in the evening sky. Her mother stopped and eyed a mangrove, with its massive aerial roots bogging in the sand, and then peered into the glazed depth of the ocean, cocking her head, squinting. "The water is always the same," she said. "Always beautiful."

* * *

AT DOMODEDOVO AIRPORT Josh helps Carmen with the luggage, offering to share a cab. But Carmen declines, on the account that they'll be heading in opposite directions, although it isn't entirely true—she could've dropped him off at his hotel and then proceeded home. She does write his number down, out of courtesy.

Riding in the cab Carmen notes new buildings cased in glass, mirroring one another in the afternoon sun. They are liquid, mercurial structures, not much different from the ones in Miami. She drives by billboards flashing with the same beautiful mawkish faces, birch groves and farmers' markets, kiosk stands, where you can buy any ridiculous thing at any godforsaken hour. Despite some of its recent remodeling, the city looks crippled; the older, poorer districts lie gutted at her feet, their entrails exposed on the hot, dust-caked asphalt. She thinks of Miami, which is so unlike Moscow—a perpetual holiday, a feast of scantily clad bodies and tanned shimmery skin, life's eternal glow.

At some point during her mother's visit five years ago, Carmen drove her to the mall, although her mother insisted that she needed nothing, except maybe bras. So they shopped for bras, which was just as exhausting as anything they did together. It took her mother hours to wade through the Macy's lingerie department, Carmen dogging after her. She'd seen her mother naked countless times; she'd know it was her mother's body even if it had no head. Carmen shuddered at the thought. But standing behind her mother in the dressing room, looking in the mirror—her parched breasts bared under the harsh fluorescent lighting—Carmen grew aware of how much time had passed since those summers in the country, as well as of how much time had passed between them. In the mirror her mother's body was a display of years and gravity, her withering nakedness a testament to Carmen's own age, suddenly making her uncomfortable, filled with pity. She pressed her hands to her chest, as though shielding herself from an invisible someone in the mirror.

Her mother had picked out five bras but couldn't decide which one to buy, and Carmen, without even looking at their prices, paid for all of them.

* * *

WHEN CARMEN ARRIVES at her old flat, it's still daylight, but the hallway is tomb-dark, and as soon as she steps across the threshold, she has sensed it—the change in the air, the frigid permanency to it. Leezy doesn't come out to greet her, so Carmen prowls along a narrow corridor, discovering her sister in the kitchen, kneading dough for pierogi.

"The funeral is Saturday," she says, not so much to Carmen but to herself. "I have to make all the food. The neighbors will help with the rest. We need to find another pallbearer. Maybe you could call one of your old boyfriends." She sweeps her gray hair away from her face, but it falls back, the tips brushing the dough.

"Where is she? Which morgue?" Carmen's lips barely move, just parting wide enough to let the air pass.

"She's here, in her bed. Yesterday I tried to convince her to go to the hospital. But she refused. It just happened this morning. I called twenty morgues—no one has any space. It's been very hot. Lots of deaths." Leezy continues kneading the dough.

"So she's going to lie here for two days?" Carmen asks, the words falling from her mouth like beach pebbles, hitting the floor.

"I called a private mortician. He'll be here in a few hours. We'll have to wash and dress the body." Leezy frees her hands from the dough and wipes her cheeks with their mother's old apron tied loosely around her waist.

Only now does Carmen notice how flushed and puffy Leezy's face is, wet from tears, sweat. Two deep lines encapsulate Leezy's mouth, her skin sandy-yellow. She hasn't gained any weight but seems thicker, heavier. There's something irrefutable in her expression and fragile too—a shell pried open. She's her mother's daughter, but also her own self, with limited experience of life and men, of anything really, except books.

"Can't we pay the mortician to wash her?" Carmen ventures to ask. "I mean wouldn't that be the smart thing to do? Natural?"

"Natural?" her sister repeats, stretching the syllables.

"In America funeral homes take care of everything."

"We aren't in America, so you can drop your fancy. I'll do everything myself."

"How are you going to get her to the bathroom?" Carmen pulls the chair out and sits down. She feels tired and jet-lagged, starved too. Her mother's absence hasn't yet affected her, become irrevocable, solidified. She keeps turning her head toward the door, expecting their mother to sail into the kitchen like a cruise ship.

"Not *her*, but our mother, Carmen. Our mother. The one who gave birth to you."

Carmen raises her eyes. "I thought she only gave birth to you, and I was the afterbirth. A defective condom. An accident."

Leezy picks up the dough from the table, squishing it through her fingers. "Why are you so—"

"So—what?"

"Unrelenting. Unaccepting."

"What's there to accept? That she loved you more than she did me? That she protected you, petted you, worried about you?"

"She worried about you too, Carmen."

"Not so much."

"You're the one who left."

"And you're the one who stayed. I'm the bad guy, and you're the good guy. Glad we settled that." Carmen gets up and stomps out of the kitchen, through the dark hallway, past her bloated suitcase and the old coatrack, where her mother's cape still hangs by the entrance door.

Half an hour later, having smoked a few cigarettes, Carmen creeps back into the apartment. From the hallway she can hear Leezy filling the tub while talking to her mother, as though she were still alive. She is cooing almost, describing in a soft confident voice what she's about to do and why she has to do it, like a parent preparing her child for the inevitable. Now she's taking off the soiled clothes, and now she's lifting her up, and now she's placing her in the water, and now she's going to wash her—here and there, everywhere. She says she'll be gentle and fast and thorough, all those things her mother taught her.

Leezy cuts off the water, and Carmen hears a small splash, a low wave crashing ashore. She stands in the dark, head against the wall, imagining her mother's body sunk to the bottom of the tub, eyes closed, chin low, hair wavering like seaweed fingers. She imagines Leezy picking up a coral-shaped sponge and lathering her mother's arms, one at a time, her caved-in chest, and under the breasts, small, shriveled, fitting in the cups of Leezy's hands, and then the heavy slopes of her mother's stomach, her thighs tracked with veins and stretch marks.

* * *

AT NIGHT CARMEN can't sleep. She curls on the living room couch surrounded by shadows that creep over the walls and the tall sagging bookshelves. What kind of books are they? How many? Has her sister read them all? Carmen remembers how as children they spent their summers in the country with their grandparents, staying at their dacha—a small cottage painted blue and constantly being worked on. How they lay awake, listening to crickets chirp behind an old woodstove or gazing at the full moon like a gorgeous pendant suspended from a limb of an aspen tree. They made crazy wishes with serious, adult faces: "When I grow up, I'll marry the Prince of Wales."

"And I'll become a ballerina and dance at the Bolshoi." When Leezy turned eighteen, Carmen was eight, but most of the time Carmen felt just as tall and smart as her sister. She even tried to read her books, flipping through pages of romance novels packed with forbidden love. Carmen didn't quite understand what it meant—if it's love, why was it forbidden?—so she kept searching for words or scenes that would explain to her the mystery of a broken heart, which, too, made little sense. If it's a heart, how could you break it?

Their mother came every weekend; their father didn't come at all. After the divorce his visits shrank from once a month to none. When their parents lived together, they fought and often in front of the children. Their father accusing their mother of being too controlling and stubborn, impossible to live with; their mother repeating the same question over and over again, "Who is she? Who is she? Who?"

At the dacha all those fights had seemed far away, replaced by thunderstorms and the crackling of logs in the woodstove. Carmen ran wild through meadows and coppices, fields of prickly wheat, while Leezy sat on a blanket by the river, reading books. On occasion Carmen tried on Leezy's bras, stuffing her small fists inside the cups to make them look full, Leezy turning red, snatching her bras out of her sister's hands. Sometimes Leezy played tricks on Carmen, burying her dolls in a pile of manure behind the house. Carmen, in turn, tore and burned pages from Leezy's books, the pages that seemed to have important dialogue or scenes, without which the reader would never get to the heart of things. "Things aren't supposed to have hearts," Carmen told Leezy. And Leezy said, "You are the one without a heart. Why did you have to destroy those books? Go away and don't come back. You aren't my sister anymore."

Leezy's words had tortured Carmen to no end. Once she woke up in the middle of the night and tiptoed to Leezy's bed, peering at her sister's face that was so unlike Carmen's, long and pale and freckled. "I'm still your sister," she whispered in Leezy's ear then slunk back into bed and toiled to go to sleep. Outside trees shivered in the wind. Their tangled limbs scraped the glass, reminding Carmen of witches' hands, bony and crooked, with curved purple fingernails. She thought she saw a woman's face pressed against the window, her hair a collage of leaves soggy from rain. Lightning flashed and the face dissipated, leaving a trace of fog on the glass.

* * *

THE FUNERAL IS a small, private affair, attended by a few neighbors and relatives. As it turns out, their mother didn't have many friends, most either died or were too sick or too old for such joyless gatherings. To find another pallbearer, Carmen first wanted to phone their father, but Leezy rejected the idea on the grounds that their mother would have never allowed the man who didn't love her in life pity her in death. Carmen abided; she knew her mother's pride and her will, which could have forced waters to part open and fish to swim backward. She resolved to ask Josh, despite her initial reservations and uneasiness of imposing on a total stranger.

He arrives at their flat thirty minutes early and is dressed accordingly—a black suit, a white shirt, and a gray-and-white-striped tie. He's freshly shaved, but still has a beach smell about him, a hint of grain and salt, although very fine. Carmen can't help but admire his posture and promptness, the way he carries himself in the face of grief and foreign circumstance. His manners are businesslike, calm and focused, and yet there's a welcoming softness in his expression, the implied understanding of loss beyond sentiment. He hugs her, and he gives her flowers, a bouquet of five white lilies, from which Carmen plucks one, breaks off its head, and inserts it into the slit of his lapel.

"The number of flowers for funerals has to be even," she says in English, fitting the lilies in a vase. "And odd for all the other occasions. Not that you need to remember that."

"I do, if I want to see you again."

His honesty isn't new or disarming, but pleasant; an extended invitation to which Carmen doesn't have to respond until much later, if ever. He speaks very little Russian, so he can't communicate with anyone except through Carmen, and she introduces him to several relatives and her sister. Leezy wears a black sleeveless dress that turns her skin pallid white and exacerbates the deep lines around her mouth. Her hair is braided and arranged on the back of her head in an intricate old-fashioned style, like the one their mother wore. As always, she has no makeup; her cheeks are pasty, the eyes two dark wet pits. Freckles crowd her nose and her shoulders, and Carmen is surprised her sister still has them.

"Thanks for coming," Leezy tells Josh, and Carmen translates.

"No problem. Of course. I'm honored your sister thought of me." Again Carmen translates, but Leezy doesn't let her finish and strays into the kitchen, leaving Carmen to pause midsentence.

"She's upset. Too much on her," Josh says.

Carmen nods as her gaze switches to an older couple on the couch holding hands. They sit too close to each other as though pressed for room or air, which is hot and stiff, heavy too, weighing on Carmen's shoulders like rain clouds, years and years of arguments that must turn to water and then to dust. Suddenly an image surges—her walking through the woods with Leezy and their mother. Carmen must've been ten or eleven, they were gathering wild mushrooms for soup. They strayed too far, the dachas were no longer visible, and no sound could reach them but the birch trees catching limbs and shedding leaves that twirled about as Carmen tried to grab a few. She tripped over a cluster of roots and fell, twisted her ankle, thrashing and wailing, inconsolable. It was getting dark, the air humid, the sky swollen with clouds. The storm was gathering above the village, and far in the distance, through a thicket of tall slender trees, they could see a crack of lightning splitting the horizon. They took turns carrying her on their backs—Leezy and their mother—Carmen's spindly arms and legs wrapped around their hunched bodies. She would ask them to stop, to rest, to wait until someone came by and helped them. But their mother would not. "You're as light as a feather," she'd say again and again, adjusting Carmen higher on her back. "A small, beautiful, graceful feather."

Carmen experiences a peculiar tightness in her chest, and then a sharp pain and a thickening of air. She breaths in and out, unbuttons her blouse, revealing a triangle of tan skin below the sharp collarbones, a thumb-wide space between her breasts. She presses on it and massages clockwise and then reverses the direction. She steps closer to the window, which is open, the sun rays sneaking through tree branches. The leaves are still green, with threads of purplish-red, like veins on her mother's hands. Carmen's throat is parched, scratchy. She misses Miami—the lights, the beach, the ocean. All its immeasurable vastness and depth, the feel of wet shifting sand under her feet.

Josh walks up to her and stands right behind, his hand on her shoulder. He squeezes lightly, and Carmen reaches up and pats it. His fingers are strong, smooth, with round, almost feminine fingernails. Carmen has the urge to hold on to those fingers, to feel them touch her body in a dark room, with nothing visible, nothing at all. The sun, the heat, is making her dizzy, and her skin blazes under the makeup. She's garbed in a black shirt and a matching pencil skirt that ends right above her knees. "Too short," her mother would've said. "Too short, and too tight."

The casket is at the far end of the room, placed on their ancient dining table, with pleats of red fabric gathered around the base. Next to the table, the lid, also draped red, leans against the wall, with a large three-barred cross stitched in golden silk. The casket is a simple delicate construction and doesn't resemble the formidable American versions Carmen encountered in Miami, but it's the fanciest, most expensive arrangement they could find on such short notice, and Carmen paid for it. As well as for the mortician, the flowers, and the crematorium services. They decided against a preacher since their mother never attended church or believed in any omnipresent force or will stronger than her own. Leezy tried to share the expenses, but Carmen wouldn't oblige—it was the least she could do. A frown on her sister's face became a scoff, all melting into tears, torrents of incoherent mumble.

"We have a problem," Leezy whispers in her ear. Carmen trembles and shifts her head.

"What is it?" she asks.

"It's too hot, and she's begun to thaw."

"To thaw?"

"The makeup on her face has melted, and you can see the bruises, where she fell, but also some bloody discharge from the mouth and in the corner of one eye. I don't know what to do."

Carmen twists her hair at the roots, musses the bangs. "Shit," she says. "Shit. Shit."

"What's wrong?" Josh asks. He continues to stand beside Carmen, but his hand is off her shoulder.

"Our mother is a snow maiden, melting under the sun," Carmen says, perhaps a bit loud. "Do you know that story? There's an opera too. Rimsky-Korsakov."

"I haven't heard the opera, but I read the story."

"Shit," Carmen says. "Where will we find another mortician now?"

Josh pinches his chin then rubs his thumb up and down his lips. "What kind of makeup do you have?" he asks. "Perhaps I can help. I know a lot about faces."

Carmen rushes to translate each word to Leezy, who offers to ask the neighbors for more cosmetics.

In a short while the mourners are being ushered into the kitchen while Josh arranges tubes of concealers and foundation, tinted moisturizers, small cups of cornstarch and white flour on the table, next to the casket. Carmen delivers primers and two types of blush, powder compacts and a bronzer, lipsticks, glosses, brow pencils and eye shadows. A set of weathered brushes in a jar. Their mother is dressed in a beige linen suit and a white satin shirt without a collar but two diaphanous strips of fabric tied into a lush bow. Her face hasn't changed much, yet it does appear hard and brittle as though carved out of glass. She has no jewelry on except for an old gold watch she rarely took off while alive. Neither Carmen nor Leezy wanted to keep the watch, and Carmen regrets it. She'll probably never wear it, but the thought of taking the relic to Miami along with half of her mother's ashes mingles into a feeling of unexplained comfort and longing.

As Josh shrugs off his jacket and rolls up his shirtsleeves, the sisters stand on the other side of the table, with wads of tissues and cotton in their hands. Carmen thinks they look like nurses assisting a plastic surgeon, who's deft and impassionate and determined. Josh smooths the hair away from their mother's face and tucks a few snowy strands behind her ears, exposing a large bruise above the right temple and another a bit lower, on her jaw. He examines the rest of the face and under the sharp chin. His movements are swift, feathery, almost imperceptible, as though he isn't tending to a dead body but an ungoverned spirit that Carmen imagines hovering about the room. Both she and Leezy don't breathe a sound as they watch Josh work, carefully, meticulously, touching and retouching the dead flesh, massaging the stiffened folds, patting, stroking, buffing, bringing a warm glow back to the lifeless cheeks.

For just a moment Carmen is distracted by the tree limbs swaying behind the window, a pandemonium of leaves. There's also a face, a child's face, looming through a plexus of branches and sun rays. The girl's lips press against the glass, open and close silently, like those of a doll. She is telling Carmen something—a tale perhaps—something sad and beautiful and unknown.

A Lullaby for My Father

I dreamed of my father's lungs. They flew into my room, sat on my bed, and started singing in Armenian. I, of course, couldn't understand a word; the language of my ancestors, so beautiful and so sad, buried with them. My father's lungs were massive bean-shaped organs, clear of tumors or perforations. The right lung had three lobes, and the left only two; each lobe was lined with tiny air sacs, where the exchange of gases took place. I could see it happening right there, in front of me, as my father's lungs sang and sang. I reached out and touched them, drew them to my chest. I hugged my father's lungs and felt them hug me back. It was the loveliest and the scariest of feelings. I woke up panting, bathed in sweat.

A dull hammering sound echoed in my ears, so I got up and shuf-fled to the window. Outside my father had a few boards stretched across a workbench. He pounded nails into the wood, his tool belt sagging below his gut. He was a short heavy man with dark skin and massive hands and a snowdrift of curly hair. He ran his fingers along the sanded boards the way I imagined he'd once run them along my mother's body, with love and grace.

Before he came to live with me in Virginia, my father lived in Brooklyn, and before that in Yerevan, where he built caskets. He'd been God among the undertakers. The Funeral Jesus. He could coax a soul out of dead wood, the way he touched it, sanding it off to the texture of skin. He carved in ornaments too—rosettes and vines and birds, crosses and cherubs. And inside the caskets, he burned in the names of the deceased, words from favorite songs, or a line of poetry. He built caskets for his grandparents, his parents, his friends and lovers, and one for my mother, although she was still alive at the time. But he wanted her to admire her last wooden garment and critique his skill, while she still could.

Now, in my backyard, surrounded by dead birches my Russian mother had insisted I plant and my American ex-wife insisted I killed with the pine fertilizer, my father worked with the frenzy of a man who knew about death and didn't wish to be caught unprepared. He stopped every few minutes, interrupted by a chaffing grainy cough, but as soon as it would subside, he'd return to tending the wood with his indefatigable hands. I was amazed how much power those hands still held, even after he'd been sick for almost a year.

"What are you building this early in the morning and with such zeal?" I asked, raising the window all the way so that only a screen and few tufts of grass separated us.

"Noah's ark," my father said. He still spoke Russian with a slur of an accent.

"I'm sure the neighbors are loving it, on this glorious Sunday morning."

"They're all at church, unless they're Turks, and we don't give a shit about those."

"Turks are people too," I said.

"Not in my book."

"That's discriminating."

"Tell it to the dead, Boris. All the thousands they butchered with daggers and hatchets."

"Don't start with that again."

"It did happen."

I knew that when it came to the Armenian Golgotha, as my father described the slaughter of his people by the Ottoman Turks in 1915, there was little to be discussed. Opinions were irrelevant, just like his doctor's death warrants regarding smoking. My father never listened and never gave up the habit. Over the years he had to give up so much and so frequently—my mother, me, his job, his land, his country, his Brooklyn apartment, his freedom—he refused to part with a single cigarette, not even a charred stump. He chewed on it until it shriveled, soggy.

"Such a nasty habit," I said.

"I'm a nasty man," he answered. "But I was thinking, you know how we say a cobbler is always without shoes, well, I don't want to be like that. I'll build me the smoothest, roomiest, most comfortable coffin, so I can rest in peace." He grinned and began sorting through a tin jar of nails I'd collected while being married to Nancy.

My sons and I, we'd always tried to build things: a tree house, a sandbox, a dog's shack. But I was artless with hammers and saws. So artless that at one point I'd questioned my paternity, but then I walked to the mirror, where, after a moment of breathless lingering, I contemplated my tan, hairy, grim reflection. Even if I were to shave off my eyebrows, I couldn't have denied the obvious—my father's blood, and that of all the massacred Armenians, as my mother had once pointed out.

I wished I could have called her, could have held the phone to my father's ear so she could have yelled at him to stop being ridiculous, to quit smoking, to do chemo and radiation, surgery. To fight the cancer.

"I'll come and help you," I finally said.

"Good. Maybe I can still teach you a few things."

We worked for hours, measuring, sawing, sanding, nailing. My father told me that dead bodies shrank, but you still had to allow extra space. He told me that even though my Russian grandfather had lost both legs in World War II, my father still had to build him a full-size coffin, to honor in death what the man missed in life. And then I remembered my mother's funeral and how long it took my father to pick out the interior upholstery for her casket. He wanted pure silk, and he wanted it eggshell-white, and he wanted it not glossy. "Death gives meaning to everything," he'd said. "It gives each living moment its beauty and its horror." Before they nailed the lid, he held my mother's face between his hands as though he were about to kiss it. She looked so beautiful, her features unharmed by the failures of her heart.

I pressed together two immeasurably long boards while my father hammered nails into them. My hand jerked, and my father missed, cussing.

"Goddamn it," he said. "Remind me again why you stopped playing piano?" He bent to pick up a crooked nail then tossed it on the trash pile.

"Do you remember what I was doing when I graduated from the conservatory?" I asked and passed him another shiny nail.

"Of course not. It was decades ago. You lived in Moscow, with your mother."

"Mishka and I—we couldn't find any jobs. We played in restaurants. Early nineties. The collapse of the Soviet Union. No one gave a fuck about classical music. We ate hotdogs year-round."

"When I die," my father said with an impervious face, "I want you to play that piece you played when you were fifteen or sixteen. I loved it. My heart sobbed each time."

"The Chopin nocturne?"

"Yes. Start practicing, will you?"

Even as a child I rarely laughed at my father's jokes. They were too grim, too absolute. There was only one way to understand them—his way. But now I actually thought he was funny, and I laughed so hard my ribs hurt. I loved my father to the point of pain.

* * *

AT NIGHT MY father choked with cough. I got up and made him chamomile tea, as my mother used to do, with a touch of honey and mint. He drank it obediently, letting me hold the cup to his trembling sweaty face. It was strange to see him like that, humble and weak, with a patch of gray hairs on his wrinkled chest. I touched a tissue to his face and his chest, wiping the perspiration. And another one to his mouth; I noticed a smear of blood as he pushed me away. "Just don't wipe my ass," he said.

When my father went back to sleep, I groped in the dark until I found his cigarettes, then stepped outside. In late May the air smelled of grass and dirt. The night was breathless, a graveyard of stars above my head. My mother had compared them to dead souls. Now she was one of them. I lit a cigarette and stared hard at the sky, trying to guess which shiny cold thing was my mother. I wondered: When my father died, would he, too, have to share the sky, the universe, with my mother? Would I have to share it with Nancy?

I blew smoke into the darkness. It'd been two years since my wife remarried. Our teenaged sons lived with her and her new husband in Brooklyn. Bob made promises he never broke. It was a beautiful thing. He insisted that most of his American friends were just like him—they kept their word. I was exactly the opposite. I broke every promise I'd ever made—to my parents by promising to love them equally, to Nancy by assuring her that I would love her forever, to my children when I left their mother because I could no longer make love to her. I hadn't seen my sons since Christmas, when I stayed alone with them in Nancy and Bob's new beach home in Riverhead. We ended up watching the water the entire week. They had adjusted. They enjoyed their stepfather's predictability and their mother's smile, which never left Nancy's face when she was with Bob. My sons felt safe and nurtured, and I felt happy and heartbroken, which was like unrequited love—a confluence of pain and desire.

I had rescheduled all of my students' piano lessons and taken a few days off at Brewin' Around, a local coffee shop, where I worked when I didn't teach. We'd agreed to drive to Johns Hopkins Hospital in Baltimore the next day because my father had an appointment with a pulmonologist at their cancer center. In the morning he looked pale and listless. His habitual boisterousness replaced by a silent stare. He hardly ate anything, but kept drinking coffee as though it were a magic potion that would dissolve his tumors.

When we finished eating I loaded the dishwasher, packed our bags, and scoured the house for his hidden stashes of cigarettes. I checked all the closets, and under the beds, and inside the kitchen cabinets and the pantry, pulling out cans of soup and jars of pickles. I emptied trash baskets and dipped my hand inside crockpots and vases. I ransacked all the shoe boxes and coat pockets and gloves, where he sometimes slipped the last cigarettes from a pack. I wanted a clean house, a fresh start for him. I was convinced that when we got back from the hospital, my father would be scared into quitting. I believed that a world-renowned pulmonologist would have more authority in the matter, and his words, as well as his voice that I imagined low and firm, with a comforting softness, would impact my father in a way that neither I nor his family doctor could.

My father had never driven in America; he didn't speak enough English to pass a DMV test. In the past year he'd depended on me to take him to the grocery store or the bank for the lack of public transportation in Harrisonburg, Virginia.

"It's a dump, this town," he said.

"I like it here. It's safe."

"Of course, it is. There are no people."

"There are people. And there's James Madison University. It's a good school."

"It's a dump."

"Okay. I got your point. You don't have to stay here. You can live in Brooklyn."

"Also a dump."

As we drove past the university, the impressive sprawling campus, my father was silent. With a cigarette stuck behind his ear, he reminded me of Mishka and our old conservatory days, when we used to bum smokes on the streets. We were that poor. But also full of vigor and laughter. Mishka used to joke about our instruments, my piano and his violin, that they had tiny cameras built into them. They watched us all the time. He distrusted everyone, especially doctors, surgeons, and anesthesiologists, because he'd been convinced that someone would implant a camera into his eye or ear and record all that he saw or heard.

I said, "Mishka died because he didn't want to be put under. His appendix ruptured. He was paranoid about doctors committing crimes."

"Don't blame him. Who knows what they do to you on that table. They could shove a finger up your ass—or worse—and you wouldn't know."

"Don't be ridiculous."

"It's true. Your mother met Peter at the hospital."

"Peter was on call that day. She had a miscarriage, and you weren't there."

"You weren't there either."

"I had to stay at home. I was twelve. They wouldn't let me come. But I was the one who called the ambulance. I was the one who washed her feet and clipped her toenails that night because she couldn't go to a hospital with such feet."

"Your mother—a perfectionist."

"You should've stayed when she asked you to."

"I had to deliver a casket."

"The dead can wait, but a baby—"

"What do you want from me now? An apology?"

"I want you to admit it."

"Admit what? That she couldn't have any more children because of me?"

"No. That you allowed her to grieve so much, her heart gave out."

"She was happy when she died. She was married to Peter."

"You fucked around. She never forgave you."

"Maybe I haven't forgiven myself. But you can't know that, can you?"

The sun finally broke through the rags of clouds. My father pulled the cigarette from behind his ear and cracked open the window. I gazed at the mountain ridges, a broken line weaving in the distance.

* * *

LAST CHRISTMAS, when Nancy and Bob had left for their anniversary cruise to the Bahamas and I stayed at their beach house, I grew restless. One night, while my sons were asleep, I crept into the master bedroom and rummaged in the closet and the chest of drawers. I had no idea what I was looking for. I discovered that Bob wore briefs and argyle socks and that Nancy's bras and panties had deeper, sexier cuts, lace and pearly beads. I stuck my hands under a pile of her T-shirts, where she'd always kept her "pleasure" toys—a tiny rabbit with long vibrating ears or a rubber bear that shook its raised paws—and found nothing. I lay on their bed and buried my face in their pillows. I inhaled. I imagined Bob making love to my ex-wife, caressing her body the way I used to. I imagined her holding his angry penis close to her cheek the way she'd done mine. I imagined my sons walking in on them, horrified by the smell and proximity of two naked bodies, all that heaving, sweating flesh. I almost cried. I missed my wife, with whom I could no longer sleep, and I missed my children, with whom I could no longer wake up. For a moment I even missed Bob, who'd made a promise to love my family and never let go.

My chest swelled with longing. I wanted Bob and Nancy to be my foster parents and surround me with love and promises and the smell of just-baked turkey. I wanted to try on Bob's briefs and see if they fit, if my dick was bigger than his. I wanted to crawl under their bed and listen to them fuck, all honey-skinned and wild-eyed, with beach sand in their hair. I wanted to know why Bob desired Nancy and I didn't, the kind of things she did to him that she didn't do to me. Half of me wanted to punch him in the face. The other—to get punched.

I left the next morning, a few hours before they were supposed to return. I'd made breakfast for my children—fried eggs and sausage and the leftover asparagus that would make their pee stink for days. They tried to hug me in their teenage awkwardness, holding their pimpled virgin faces away from my sullen, scraggy one. They said: "We love you," with the same lazy nonchalance they ate vegetables or played games or watched TV. And I told them that I loved them too, more than they could ever imagine, my heart folding in my chest for the thousandth time since I'd left their mother. I thought how privileged they really were, born in this country, raised by three devoted parents, speaking English without an accent, never stumbling for words, not having to prove their worth to anyone. I thought how they would never have or want to be Russian or Armenian, or anyone other than American, and that they would only have one life as opposed to my three.

* * *

MY FATHER AND I had decided to spend the night in DC because my father wanted to visit the Spy Museum and the Holocaust Museum. When I asked why, he said that those were the two closest things to Russian and Armenian cultures: spies and genocide. He refused to look at the monuments. In his opinion there was no greater monument than a man's life lived in honor and tradition.

The city traffic was merciless, and my father wondered when people worked. He also marveled how many people walked or rode bicycles. In Armenia bicycles had replaced donkeys.

"We used to deliver everything that way—fruit, cheeses, even wine in small wooden barrels. Once I had to transport a casket tied to a donkey's back," he said.

"That's ridiculous," I said.

"Life is ridiculous. Only death is perfect."

We rode in silence a few more miles, patches of clouds and sun in the windows, when my father asked, "Remind me again why we're seeing this doctor?"

"For a second opinion."

"So he can postpone the inevitable?"

"So he can advise us on how to proceed."

"How can one proceed if one only has a few months? Let's get Viagra and call some prostitutes."

"My mother was right, even on your deathbed that's all you think about—sex."

"I'm horny, I can't help it. My Armenian blood boils when I think of pussy. Yours should too."

"Mine has been diluted by revolutions and snow. It never reaches the boiling temperature."

"Funny. Is that why you left Nancy? You couldn't get it up?"

"It's complicated. But yes, that too," I said.

"You could've found someone else to screw."

"No, I couldn't. I didn't want to cheat. I didn't want to hurt her like that. I didn't want my sons to find out and hate me forever."

"Right. Like they don't hate you now. Like you don't hate me."

"I don't hate you. But we have nothing in common, except for the last name."

"And the eyebrows. Don't forget the eyebrows—your Armenian heritage."

"I don't feel Armenian. I've never felt Armenian."

"Do you feel Russian?"

"No. Not really. I feel disconnected from everything and everyone, my children too. I feel crazy, like I don't belong, like if I died tomorrow, no one will ever notice. No one will come to the funeral. There won't be a funeral."

"Oh, for fuck's sake, Boris." My father began to cough. His ashen face tightened, and he gripped his chest, reaching for tissues.

"What's wrong? Are you in pain?" I asked.

"No," he wheezed. "Not compared to you."

As we were about to cross the Potomac, the traffic stopped, all six lanes. My father lit another cigarette, and I pulled down the window and leaned out. The Memorial Bridge appeared congested. The police cars on both sides flashed blue lights. I couldn't see anything else because of other people who'd stepped out of their vehicles, gazing into the clouds. A few people walked up the bridge, so I got out too.

Several feet ahead I saw a tall man standing on the railing, towering over the mossy-green water. Or maybe he just seemed tall because he'd dared to do such a thing—climb a fucking bridge and stop traffic. He wore a blue suit over a white shirt and had long black hair but no shoes. His feet loomed large and brown against the pale stone of the railing. The man shouted something, but I was too far away to understand it.

"Some crazy Indian," a woman said. "He wants his land back. His tribe and his salmon. Cops can't do a damn thing, afraid he'll jump." She regurgitated a smile, and I felt sick to my stomach.

Walking back to the car I kept turning my head, kept watching the guy's hair mussed by the wind, kept noting the onlookers recording his act of defiance on their phones. I felt like a coward next to him. I couldn't have done such a thing. I couldn't have argued. I could never bring myself to do that. I couldn't even admit to Nancy that what we really had was the Cold War: we observed appearances and exchanged courtesies, but the animosity, the misunderstanding seemed eternal. I couldn't tell my children that Bob was a good man, a man who could keep a promise and they should honor that. I couldn't tell them that I couldn't visit more often because seeing them made me want to stay.

My father grew restless in the car, clouded in smoke. I climbed back in but kept the door open. I sprinkled water on the windshield, the wipers viciously smearing the dust.

"What's the matter?" he asked. "You look like you've spotted a ghost."

"Maybe I have."

"Of the past?"

"Of the future."

"No worries then. I won't live to see it." He grimaced, his parted lips revealing his crooked nicotine-stained teeth.

* * *

HE FLEW. The Indian. A flash of his hair like a black feather against the milky sky. Neither my father nor I could see it clearly, but the crowd and the police all rushed to that side of the bridge.

I vomited on the pavement, my father yanking a tissue out of the box and handing it to me.

It took an hour or longer for the traffic to start moving, but we had no desire to proceed with our plan and visit the museums. When we finally arrived at our hotel room, in saturnine silence, we didn't want to leave it, not even for food. We took showers and ordered in—roast beef sandwiches and tomato soup, which my father couldn't finish. He said it looked, smelled, and tasted like blood. He stepped outside a few times to smoke while I lay in bed and watched the news, where no one mentioned the dead Native American guy. But then I thought that perhaps he didn't die but turned into a fish and swam away. I was convinced they could do that, Native Americans. There was no death in their culture. I laughed because my father would have been out of business had he lived among them. But he would have still made caskets because work gave him pleasure while mine brought me sadness, a nugget of dissatisfaction, a realization that I could have been so many things but remained what I was.

When my father returned, he said, "Goddamn that Indian. As though one death could prove anything."

"One life can't prove anything either."

"The hell it can't. Your Armenian great-grandfather. He was a pastor. He led his people through the desert. He gave them hope against all hope."

"It was his duty," I said. "To resurrect Jesus in every prayer. Otherwise, what's the point?"

"The point is that you believe that you'll survive, and you will."

"Then believe that you'll survive. Let's start the treatments."

"Why? Why do you want to prolong my misery?"

I gave him an intent stare. "Because you're my father. Because there's no one else."

"Is that why you chose to live with your mother after the divorce? You left me."

"But I brought you to this country."

"And I'm still trying to figure out why."

I reached out and switched off the bed lamp, pulling a pillow over my head.

That night I dreamed about the Native American guy, who walked into the room and sat on my bed and touched my forehead with his enormous thumb. In the darkness all I could see was his smile, two rows of healthy bone-white teeth. He leaned over, his face so close, his teeth rubbed against mine. He had fish in his hair and a drum in his hand. He pressed the drum into my naked chest, and I felt my heart beating wildly against the scuffed hide. The moon walked out of the cloud, allowing me to glimpse his face, which was so much like my father's—dark, proud, with impressive brows. I touched his cheekbones and felt stories folded into his thick lined skin.

When I woke up my father wasn't in the room. His shoes weren't by the door, his clothes missing from the hangers. In the bathroom I discovered bloody tissues wadded into the basket. It was almost nine, and my father's appointment in Baltimore was at one. At first I thought that he went out to smoke, but when he didn't return in twenty minutes, I dialed his phone. It rang in the room, stowed in his bag, which sat next to mine. I felt helpless. I had no idea what to do. I couldn't call anybody else, and I couldn't file a missing person report, not until tomorrow. It seemed ridiculous to wait that long. It also seemed out of his character to just disappear. I told myself that perhaps he'd gone to get coffee and was lost, had no phone, and could've forgotten the name of the hotel. He spoke poor English and knew no one in the city.

I rode the elevator to the lobby and asked the receptionist, who shook her head in response. I talked to the doorman, who remembered an older coughing man dressed in all gray catching a taxi, but he had no idea where the driver took him. On the streets I walked empty-minded and heavy-hearted, pondering, replaying our latest conversations in hopes to determine my father's trail of thoughts, which could lead me to his whereabouts.

Finally I stepped inside a restaurant and sat at the bar. The TV was on, and at first I didn't pay any attention. I ordered coffee to go. And then—a shot of vodka. I heard my mother saying in her mournful voice: "Way to go, Boris. How Russian of you."

"I'm Russian," I said out loud, and the bartender said, "Oh, yeah?"

"I'm Armenian too. My family survived the genocide." I dumped the vodka into my throat.

He nodded. "I've heard about it. You need another vodka?"

"Cognac. For my father. He left me."

"Sorry, man. How long ago?"

"This morning."

The bartender laughed. "You're funny. Didn't know Russians could be funny. You people are kind of grim. Don't blame you. The hell you had to crawl through. Putin—he's worse than what's his name? The guy with the huge mustache?"

"Stalin."

"Yeah," he said and poured the cognac. "Shit, man. Would you look at this." He pointed at the TV. "Some crazy-ass dude is on a hunger strike in front of the Turkish Embassy. He demands the Turks acknowledge the genocide. Isn't that odd—you were just talking about it?"

I swallowed the cognac, left a fifty on the counter, and ran out of the restaurant.

By the time I arrived at the Turkish Embassy, a crowd had gathered. Reporters, cameramen, police, ambulance, sympathizers. The traffic slowed, and the cabdriver let me out on the opposite corner of the street. I gently maneuvered my way through a beehive of people until I was confronted by two policemen, who asked me to show my ID when I told them the protestor was my father.

"Did you know about this?" they asked. "Is that why you came here? All the way from Virginia?"

"No. No. We came to see a doctor. He has lung cancer."

"He's been here for two hours. Can you talk to him?"

"I can try."

They let me pass, and just steps away I discovered my father sitting cross-legged on the pavement, right under the Turkish flag. It snapped in the breeze like a bloody tongue. For some reason my father had taken off his shoes, exposing his shriveled vein-streaked feet. Also, on the pavement, right in front of him, someone chalked "ARMENIAN GENOCIDE 1915" in large bold letters I didn't dare to cross. They resembled bones against the dusty gray asphalt.

My father looked thin and stern, haggard, darkness in his eyes.

"What are you doing?" I asked as I approached.

He raised his head. "I couldn't sleep, but I figured out why we came to this country—to protest."

"To protest?" I almost screamed.

"Yes. When we protest in Armenia, no one hears. We can't protest in Turkey because they'll throw us in jail or club us to death. But here—people care about horrors and torture and racism."

"It's only news. Tomorrow it'll be replaced by some new horror."

"Maybe. But today and every day until I die and begin to rot on this pavement, the world will listen. More people will listen."

"Do you know how crazy this sounds?" I asked.

"And do you know that when Armenians were forced to leave their homes, they weren't allowed to take anything with them—no food, no clothes, no water? They swallowed their jewelry. After the massacres, the Turks roamed for days among those thousands of corpses, slitting their guts, digging for gold and diamonds."

"Stop it, Dad. Please."

"They raped our girls. They crucified the women, and then they raped them too, dead, dragging them off the crosses."

I closed my eyes and bit my lip, petrified by his words, but he continued.

"They burned our babies and made their mothers eat the ashes. They buried us alive in the desert. The earth moved—for months— oozing blood."

He retrieved a folded paper from his jacket and passed it to me.

"Here," he said. "Read it out loud. I copied it this morning from—" He coughed and coughed and coughed. I saw blood in the corners of his mouth.

I held the paper in the palm of my hand. I hesitated. More people gathered around us, more police cars, more cameras. Several boys snapped our pictures; a few raised their phones overhead. I wondered if they could hear and record our conversation, if someone could understand our choppy broken speech. Half of me wanted to call my children and say: "Don't believe everything you read or hear. I haven't left you. I could never leave you." The other half wanted to let them go, to let them be Bob and Nancy's kids, to let them never eat borsch or read Russian novels or talk about the Armenian Genocide.

"I can't do this. If my sons find out, they'll be terrified. Embarrassed too. They won't speak to me again."

"They need to know, Boris."

My heart pounded in my chest. I stood silent for some time before finally sitting down next to my father, taking off my shoes and socks, and crossing my legs. I unfolded the paper. It was a poem by Grigoris Balakian, "Lullaby on the Way to Zor."

> *Oh, lullaby, lullaby, my baby, lullaby,*
> *Expelled they're taking us toward Zor,*
> *You don't have a cradle for me to rock you,*
> *To give your little body a rest there.*
> *My helpless orphan, we're left in fate's*
> *Cruel hands, ridiculed by all,*
> *I found a dirty rag as swaddling clothes for you,*
> *Black grief gnaws at my heart, the fire of my life.*

The poem had three more stanzas, which we read together, in rattling accents, each stanza louder than the one before. When I paused to look at my father, he seemed to have frozen on the pavement. His skin ashen-white, his hair too, his enormous hands as though carved out of ice, everything except for his eyebrows, like an extended bridge, connecting one's past to one's future, joys to sorrows.

Half of me wanted to climb the railing, the other—to walk away.

Heroes of Our Time

When I was eighteen and my grandfather Rudik was still alive, I often stayed with him on spring weekends, while my grandmother and my parents went to our dacha to plant a garden or prune the apple trees. There wasn't enough room in the car for everyone, with all the food and seedlings and clothes. Our dacha was located just outside of Moscow, but to travel there by train or bus could be a sweaty, laborious undertaking neither my parents nor my grandmother wished to endure. Though not in terrible health or entirely helpless, my grandfather had been a double amputee for the better part of his life. He spent his days in an ancient rickety wheelchair because prosthetics were too painful; they chafed my grandfather's skin to blisters, which resembled a growth of tiny red grapes in place of his knees. Another thing I should mention is that my grandfather had lost his legs in

1915, crossing the desert of Der Zor, when the Ottoman Turks had forced Armenian families to leave their homes. My grandfather used to tell my friends that he'd left his legs buried in the snow, the only part of him that stayed forever with his parents.

That spring in 1991 my grandfather was recovering from bronchitis and didn't wish to be driven to the dacha at all. I was a first-year student at Moscow State University and had to study for the upcoming exams, so I gladly agreed to watch over him instead of digging dirt or spreading manure under the fruit trees. I hated yardwork. And I hated being bossed around by my parents, who despised the idea of a young man becoming a writer, or worse—a poet. My responsibilities included running a bath for my grandfather, helping him dress, dispensing medicine, and serving his meals. In my family, food was God and God was food. We worshipped bread and herring and pierogi, dolma and baklava. My mother and grandmother usually cooked enough to feed all the once-starved Armenians from Yozgat to Boğazliyan to Kayseri. Even though the variety of staples had shrunken to a minimum during perestroika, my grandmother could devise one hundred recipes for old, shriveled, purple-eyed potatoes. She was Russian, and she knew hunger as she knew death. In 1942, during the war, she'd peeled bark off trees and boiled it with resin and mice. She had eaten snow, ash, and dirt.

When my family left for the dacha that Saturday, my grandfather sat on the balcony and watched the leaves shiver in the breeze. The lilacs shed purple cross-shaped blossoms on his hands, which were large, brown, and cracked, like two parcels of desert land. From the kitchen window I saw him pat a flower with his crooked finger then bring it to his mouth. He shook his head, chewing. He had an enormous head with a blizzard of white hair; from the back his head resembled an iceberg wedged between his shoulders. His skin was tan, his features prominent—a massive nose, wide cheekbones, earthy eyes, and opulent charcoal brows.

"Are you hungry?" I shouted.

"No," he shouted back.

"Then why are you eating flowers?"

"I want to know what spring tastes like. I'm too old to remember."

I walked out of the kitchen and into the living room, where the balcony door was wide open, inviting in a light breeze.

"You want to get out for a bit?" I asked, now standing next to his wheelchair. "The weather is nice."

"It'll rain."

"How do you know?"

"My feet are aching," he said and laughed.

I laughed too, although with a slight delay. His caustic sense of humor still took me by surprise.

Another thing I should mention is that my grandfather often made people uncomfortable with his jokes. He didn't discriminate between men or women, children or adults, rich or poor. For him telling a bawdy joke was like farting in public—a completely natural thing. "We're all people," he'd say. "We all love a good laugh and a good fart." All of his long, not-so-fortunate life my grandfather shocked and argued, and many of our holiday gatherings resulted in fights and tears. He never apologized. He'd touched death, and it had made him unafraid of pretty much everything: the Ottoman Turks, the Nazis, Stalin, the Gulag, nuclear and hydrogen bombs, hunger, perestroika, the upcoming collapse of the Soviet Empire. What was an Armenian man but a confluence of pride and pain?

"You want something to read?" I asked.

"What do you have?"

"Goethe's *Faust*?"

"Why are you reading Germans, Mikhail?"

"Why not?"

"Your grandmother won't approve. What's it about?"

"Well, it's in two parts. The first part is about Faust selling his soul to the devil, who helps him seduce a young woman—"

"Stop right there," my grandfather said. "I want the same deal."

"With the devil?"

"With you, in the role of the devil."

"A small favor."

"I have money saved. It's in that vase your grandmother never uses because it has a crack."

"Money for what?"

"For a prostitute, Mikhail. If you help me find one, when I die—and it won't be long—I'll go to hell and ask the devil to grant you immortality."

"I don't want immortality."

"Of course you do. Isn't that why you write poems? To keep on living? I'll ask the devil to inspire you with the most beautiful and tragic verse. Because what good is beauty without horror and suffering?"

I studied my grandfather's face, which I didn't recognize at the moment. He smiled, devil-like, and I was tempted to part his thick hair and examine his head for small sharp horns. I finally pulled the wheelchair back into the room and shut the balcony door, afraid that someone might hear us—an old habit bequeathed to me by my grandmother, who still shuddered each time someone rang the bell, especially late at night.

"Where am I supposed to find a prostitute?" I asked.

"Don't you have any friends?"

"Yes. Nice friends."

"Prostitutes can be nice."

"I can get arrested, you know."

"The country is gutted. People don't know what they'll eat tomorrow. I doubt anyone gives a shit about horny business." He laughed, but this time I didn't reciprocate. I was mute with shame. For him, as well as for myself. To be having such wretched conversations with my heroic ancestor, who crawled through the Syrian Desert and chewed rocks to stay alive.

"I've been faithful to your grandmother all my life," he said. "And I couldn't have run around even if I'd wanted to. But just once, before I go, I'd like to smell pussy. Young, healthy pussy. I can't do anything else, but these hands—" He lifted them in the air, and I could see his thick blue veins undulating like snakes. "These hands can still be of use. They can feel a woman and make her feel things too."

By then I was convinced that my grandfather was just as serious as Mephistopheles, who made a bet with God to deflect his favorite human—Faust—from his righteous pursuits. Just like Faust, I had no say in the matter, my fate owned and defined by those two omnipotent, omnipresent figures. I was doomed to help my grandfather commit adultery but also allow him to experience one last mortal pleasure.

* * *

EVEN IN DARKER Soviet times, during the Cold War, there were a few hotels in Moscow visited mostly by foreign guests. Those were also the places where top-dollar prostitutes nested in bars and restaurants. Cops knew them, doormen knew them, waiters and maids. The women paid generously to be known but also unnoticed. They were supposed to be clean, well educated, and gorgeous. They all spoke English. Some said that a few of them worked for the KGB, supplying secret information their drunken, lascivious clients divulged in bed. Others said that the women hunted future husbands to take them to America, where the prostitutes joined the CIA. It was never about sex or money, but spies and secrets. From an early age, in schools and at home, my friends and I had been warned about visiting such hotels or approaching such women, no matter how stunning or affordable they appeared.

Hotel Intourist, a skyscraper at the very end of Gorky Street, stood gray and sullen. A doorman guarded the entrance. He was tall, square, in a suit, and had the face of a wrestler. His imperviousness was frightening. His massive feet in black dusty shoes resembled rocks. Not a mouse or a roach could slip by those feet. So, to go to the bar or the restaurant, I had to either wait for him to disappear, which could never happen—he'd lose his job along with his head, for leaving the space unattended—or try and bribe him. For a moment I contemplated telling the truth and admitting to my grandfather's senile lust, but then I rejected the idea. They could arrest him on grounds of immoral behavior: contributing to the delinquency of a minor. Barely eighteen, I was still considered an immature, vulnerable creature, susceptible to craziness and dangerous influences. I thought of my grandfather being wheeled into a prison cell, where no one would give him baths or help him to the commode. He would shit his pants and sit in them for hours. I felt sorry for him, for the ridiculousness of his desire, and the stupidity of my own actions.

Just then I spotted a voluptuous young girl strutting through the hotel doors. She wore platform shoes, a tight denim miniskirt, and large butterfly sunglasses. Her lips were glossy and her hair a black silky shawl. She lit a cigarette and sat on a bench under a Coca-Cola umbrella, next to an outdoor grill. The smell of smoke and meat teased out my hunger.

Tentatively I approached and asked for a cigarette.

She reached inside her miniscule purse and produced a Marlboro. I stuck it in my mouth, and she flipped a lighter.

"You live in the city? Or just visiting?" I asked, sitting down.

She stared at me, and I wondered about the shape and color of her eyes, which I couldn't see.

"Why do you want to know?" she asked. Her voice was thick and sticky and sweet, like my grandmother's gooseberry jelly. It was also a sleepy voice, as though she was bored to death with such questions.

I decided to switch to business.

"My grandfather is a cripple. He has no legs. He's also very old." I paused and looked around to make sure that no one could hear me. "He wants to have sex one last time before he dies. Do you have any friends who'd be willing to do such a thing for a considerable sum of money?"

"How considerable?" She scooted closer and spurted smoke into my face.

I whispered the answer in her ear. She laughed and bit her lip, coughing.

"I didn't mean to make you choke," I said. "Sorry." I tapped on her back with my hand.

"Do you have the money with you?" she asked. "How do I know you aren't lying?"

I took out a hefty stack, let her hold it, then, just as quickly, stuffed it back in my pants. "It's half. The other half afterward."

She bent down and scraped the cigarette against the pavement; her skirt pulled low, baring a strip of golden skin. I felt heat spreading through my chest like fire through dry straw. Despite her slim figure, she had large doughy breasts heaving under her half-buttoned shirt. At eighteen, I was still a virgin, but I imagined losing my face in her cleavage, between those plump orbs, holding them in my hands as she straddled me and took me deep inside. I imagined her flesh grinding into mine until her sweat dripped in my mouth.

I swallowed and crossed my legs.

"Where do you live?" she asked.

"Kuzminki."

"Shitty neighborhood."

She laughed, loud and vicious, which made me think of Mephistopheles and the absolute pleasure he took in baring men's faulty nature, their greed and pettiness and lust.

"What's your name?" I asked.

"Frida," she answered.

"Is that a real name? Or a work name?"

She took off her glasses and bestowed on me a look in which the entire Russian history came to life—all the bloody wars, the revolution, hunger and depravation. She seemed older than what I'd imagined, and smarter. She lifted my hand, which was dark like buckwheat compared to hers, and studied my fingers. Her touch was so gentle, I felt shivers running all the way from my heart down to my hairy balls.

"Are you a pianist?" she asked.

"No. I used to play when I was little. Now I'm a poet."

"Oh, but that's even better. More useful. Words have power. Words kill."

"They do?" Never before did I think about words being murder weapons. Although it was true that many Russian poets had ended their lives tragically—Pushkin, Lermontov, Yesenin, Mayakovsky, Mandelstam. So there was a traceable connection between poetry and death.

Frida folded her lips in thought then slipped her hand through the mass of her hair. "Do you want to go to a party?" she asked.

Her question surprised me. "What party?"

I conjured half-lit rooms filled with smoke, booze, drugs, and loose, dangerous sex. Perhaps I should have gotten up and walked away, but I didn't want to admit my insecurities to a gorgeous woman. What was a man but a struggle of lust and will?

"You don't have to go if you don't want to," she said and fitted her sunglasses back on her nose. She scooped up her hair and swept it over her left breast. Slowly I leaned in to kiss her cheek. Her face was warm and a bit sticky. It smelled of smoke and flowers. She didn't protest but remained affably permissive. I kept thinking that she didn't act or smell like someone with a past, someone who allowed her body to experience what her soul didn't. But then I remembered my grandfather's latest wish and thought that perhaps there was no true pleasure in the world other than physical. A man didn't exist outside of his body, bound and confronted by its ceaseless urges. A body had to be touched just as it had to eat or piss.

"I'll go to the party," I said. "For a little while."

* * *

IN THE TAXI I longed to break the silence but didn't dare. Frida still had her glasses on, although it was rather sunless in the back of the car, where we both sat. Her legs seemed unfathomably long compared to mine, and so soft—I had placed my hand close to her thigh and touched it inadvertently each time the car swerved in traffic. We drove past Red Square and down the Moscow River quay, a glimpse of Kremlin stars in the distance. I marveled at all the foreign names, shops and restaurants emerging in the city. And for a moment I felt like I was in America or England, in a capitalist heaven as opposed to the post-Socialist hell. With an exotic beautiful woman by my side, whom I could love and who could love me back.

The ride was short, and I offered to pay. When we got out I searched for street names or road signs, any small quaint shop, a bakery or a haberdashery to orient myself. But all Moscow Soviet-style neighborhoods looked the same—a conglomeration of gray concrete boxes with washed laundry flapping on balconies, making me think of ghosts. Yet I was certain that I'd never visited that part of the city. It appeared too quiet and too clean, the streets running in perfect symmetry. I followed Frida to a twelve-story apartment building and up the stairs, even though there happened to be a working elevator. I heard it descending as we climbed up. The green walls smelled of fresh paint and felt sticky when I touched them with my finger. All the flats had the same doors, brown or black, also just painted, but no numbers, which I didn't even notice at first, not until Frida took out a long, jagged key and slipped it into the hole.

The flat was crowded, submerged in smoke. At first not a single person paid attention to us, although they acknowledged Frida's presence, squeezing her shoulder or her hand. A few gave her a hug. They ignored me altogether; I was her shadow—dark, mute, invisible. Or perhaps they were used to seeing her with different men. I had to admit, it was not like any party I'd attended with my friends. Except for the clouds of tobacco smoke that swallowed words and faces, it was the opposite of a party. No one laughed, and no one danced, and no one argued. I couldn't hear any music or singing, of which Russians were so fond. Men didn't scream or cuss but conversed in conspiratorial voices, cigarettes pinched between their lips or fingers. Women didn't huddle in the kitchen, chopping kielbasa or stirring salads. Neither did they ogle men in hopes of taking one home. Dressed in casual clothes—jeans and T-shirts—they spoke with mournful intensity. Some had short hair; others ponytails or braids. They didn't look like prostitutes; nor did they look like girlfriends or wives or lovers. They looked like comrades. Stern, focused, uncompromising, bound by a secret mission. I had a scary feeling of walking into a dream, where things were always done to you and not by you. For whatever reason I thought of my grandfather as a ten-year-old boy, his feet pulp and bone, clawing a grave for his parents inside the frozen desert.

A short, stocky guy with a large bald head came up to us. He hugged Frida then asked, "Who's this? Where did you find him?"

"He found me. He's a poet."

"You can't bring no damn poets here. He'll rat us out."

"He won't. He has money, and he can write speeches and declarations. Record history. We need him. Get him a gun."

"A gun?" I asked. "I don't want a gun. I don't know how to use one."

"We'll teach you. Such are the times," Frida said.

"What times?"

"Where do you think you are?" the man asked.

"Some crazy party?" I answered in a tone that didn't convince even me.

He laughed and lit a cigarette. There was something so malicious in his smile, my heart caught in my throat. I coughed and coughed, and Frida's fist jabbed at my back. It hurt, but not as much as when the bald man grabbed my hand and squeezed the life out of it.

"What's your name?" he asked.

"Mikhail," I answered.

"We'll call you Lermontov."

"Why?"

"So no one can reveal your identity to the militia if arrested."

By then I understood that I was no longer in a dream, but sucked into some other version of reality, which promised to be grim and painful.

"Yes," Frida said. "Everyone here has a different name. This is Lenin," she pointed at the bald man. "He's the mastermind, of course. And there, by the window, the guy with the black hair and bushy beard—that's Marx. He grew up in Socialist Germany, but his parents are Russian."

"Who's that?" I pointed at a tall man in round glasses.

"That's Trotsky. He isn't entirely reliable, but he has a hiding place in Mexico, where we'll join him should things go wrong."

"Things? What things?"

"An uprising. A revolution. We want Mother Russia to be what it once was. In Chekhov's time."

"You want the monarchy back?" I asked.

"No," Frida answered. "We want everyone to be free. To travel abroad without visas. We want to reverse history, to take this country away from peasants and workers and give it back to the Decembrists, the aristocracy."

"Where are you going to find those? They're all extinct by now."

"There're still a few left, believe me."

Things seemed real and unreal at the same time, frozen in their predictability. What was Russia without snow and revolutions?

Their idea seemed insane to me, but I also knew from my grandfather that most wars had been started by lunatics with aggrandized ambition. There was no cure for it and no salvation. Sadness washed over me like rain over a window. I didn't want those people to be damn revolutionaries but ordinary horny people. I wanted them to strip off their clothes and fuck right there on the floor, in a mad ceaseless orgy, because I wanted to join them, all of them, those bustling hands and lips and tongues. I was much younger, and I was convinced that only love could save the world, not tanks or guns or bombs.

"What were you doing in the hotel?" I asked Frida.

"Meeting important clients. Foreigners who can help make this country strong again."

"I need to get back to my grandfather," I said. "In case he wants to shit. His wheelchair won't fit into the bathroom." I cracked a smile, turned around, and pushed my way toward the door, my heart sinking lower with each step.

I knew that at any minute someone might point a gun at my back or head and shoot me dead, execution style. I knew that a man, one man, couldn't do a damn thing to save humanity or his own life. Still, I kept walking, hands in pockets, a little swagger to my step, a little shudder.

* * *

AFTER RUNNING DOWN the stairs as fast as I could, I was joined on the street by two men in black-leather jackets. They asked me where I was heading and whether I had time to take a quick ride in their car. They insinuated that perhaps I'd seen or heard something I wanted to share. They called on my honesty and my Soviet duty. They blew smoke in my face, and I raised my eyes, scanning the apartment building, in hopes to see someone's face, someone who could at least witness me being whisked away. Most windows were dark, however, and I discerned no signs of life on any floor.

The street lay deserted. The sky thickened with clouds, and trees shook with new fragile growth. The men's clothes were tight, and so were their smiles. I imagined a long sweaty ride in the back of their car, a dark building full of dingy narrow rooms, in which people like me had been held captive for years. I imagined my parents never knowing the truth, the ugly fate that had befallen their only son, and my grandfather shitting his pants each time my name was uttered, blaming his horny ass for my disappearance. I suddenly knew how my story would end, how all such stories ended.

"If you show us where they are, we'll let you go," the men said.

I hesitated. I wished I hadn't gone there, hadn't met any of those people. I wanted God or the devil to intercede and take the blame.

"I don't know which floor," I finally said. "We took the stairs. And the door had no number."

"What are their names?"

"Lenin. Marx. Trotsky."

One of the men raised his hand, about to hit me, but the other stopped him.

"Are you fucking with us?" he asked.

"No," I said. "That's what they—"

"Lermontov." I heard Frida's voice. "Wait."

She ran up to me and grabbed my shoulders, her face so insufferably close to mine. There was fear in it and also hope. I wanted to push her away, to pretend that I didn't know her, that she'd mistaken me for someone else. But then I thought that perhaps she saw me being interrogated and came down to save me. Or herself. Or all of them.

The earth fell away under my feet. I saw hell's fire and huge black cauldrons and naked men boiling in them. I touched her face, skimming my fingers along her cheekbone.

She leaned in and kissed me then, full mouth, teeth and tongue. Clumsy, slobbery, passionately, the way I'd imagined it, the way people kissed in books and movies. The way you could only kiss someone for the first time and only once.

* * *

IN THE CAR I would bribe the men with my grandfather's money, and they would let us go, dropping Frida off at one subway station, me at another, but I would never see her or any of her friends again. There would be a coup in August of that year, and the country would collapse like a pyramid of wooden blocks. We would finally become free, allowed to travel, to trade cities, countries, motherlands. But during those few hot, terrifying days, while my parents worked and my grandmother stayed at the dacha, my grandfather and I would turn on the TV and watch the protesters in Red Square and the tanks on Moscow streets, in front of the White House. And then we would turn the TV off. I would heat his food and pour his vodka, and he would be slow chewing his cutlets and then telling me how, when his parents had been executed by the Ottoman Turks, he lived in the forests of Injirly or the tunnels of Amanos, eating anything he could find: leaves, twigs, roots and tree bark, any dead animal.

In late evenings, after my grandfather would fall asleep and right before the curfew, I would sneak outside and wander about the city, gathering words for my poems, trying to find the flat where the revolutionaries had convened that afternoon. But even though I could finally locate the street, I failed to identify the building. They all stood alike, gray and faceless in their uniform anonymity.

For years I would think about Frida, how brave and passionate she seemed, devoted to what she believed was the right cause, dreaming, perhaps in vain, to resurrect, rebuild, our tempestuous Motherland. I fantasized about her too, while crafting poetry or making love to other women, a flow of her gorgeous hair, a sway of her breasts and hips. Like that time when I'd first met her, she appeared both real and imaginary, close and distant. Once, while smoking a cigarette in front of Hotel Intourist about to be demolished, I thought I'd spotted Frida getting into a taxi. I scurried after her, shouting her name and waving my hands, but before I could reach the car, it pulled away and swerved around the corner. Still, I kept running, as fast as I could, my heart racing, my feet slipping on the icy pavement—bursts of snow in my face.

Simple Song #9

Boy meets Girl.

At a farmers' market, where he sells tomatoes as large as his heart. Girl is pale, tender, and smells of spring. Of those first crocuses that poke their stubborn heads through a scarf of snow. Boy can't say that to Girl, can't compare her to flowers growing in his yard. A college student, she seems smarter, older, with her red hair twisted in a choppy bun and her dragonfly glasses perched high on her nose. In her hands—a Virginia Woolf novel Girl describes as a maze of characters linked through imaginary tunnels. All Boy knows is the earth; he can grow anything from just a tiny seed.

Their first kiss is sloppy. It reminds Boy of the way slugs attach themselves to one another on the walls of a garden shed. He doesn't say that, of course, but lets Girl slip her tongue inside his mouth, her hands deeper inside his shorts. Her fingers are strong, cool vines crawling up and down his penis. Boy wishes he could keep them there always, but Girl laughs, warns him about the messy nature of such interludes. By then she's on her knees, and it seems to Boy that her tongue is that of a lizard unfurling with great speed. Boy is in Eden, where he and Girl disobey all earthly rules.

By late fall Boy plants an apple orchard, and Girl moves into his house. She brings her cat, Septimus, and fits Woolf's novels next to Boy's gardening books. Girl studies arts, which one day she'll master. All of them: literature, painting, music, dance. There's so much to do! Planet Art is amazing, isn't it? Boy shrugs, "Planet Life is too." While Girl takes classes, Boy tends to the farm. He feeds chickens, spreads fertilizer, digs up potatoes, chops firewood. Girl calls Boy, not without tenderness, Mr. Tin Man. "Yes," he murmurs, glancing at the book on her nightstand, "Mrs. Dalloway."

Two things are of crucial importance to Girl: buying flowers and educating Boy. In winter she makes him read all the literary novels she studies in college. Woolf, Duras, Atwood, Morrison, de Beauvoir. What is Boy to do with all those names? All those women—in his house and in his bed? The novels are living things, Girl insists. They evolve with time, grow deeper, like trees through the earth. It is as though one were to walk into the future without having to live through the present. The feeling of ordained triumph one can only experience at eighteen. A waft of sharp ocean air. A slap of a wave.

Boy desires Girl.

That's all he thinks about when she's around, shaking her copper mane in his face. He imagines Girl's tan slim body coated in beach sand he'll lick off her grain by grain. Off her nipples, off her vagina, off her asshole. Her coarse pubic hairs.

It has been three years already. A few apple trees are in bloom. Boy plucks off the blossoms. Too much growth can exhaust the roots. He and Girl talk about marriage the way they talk about anything else, morning coffee or afternoon rain. They ought to enjoy it. They ought to send out invitations, reserve a venue, order a cake, plan a honeymoon. To one of those faraway lands Girl dreams about. They ought to think about a baby.

Girl refuses Boy.

She has no intention of getting fat, of sharing her body with some unknown reptile; she's terrified of pain, epidurals, needles in spines. She wants no scars on her belly or inside her beautiful vagina, no engorged leaking breasts, sweatshirts crusted in vomit or stained with pee. "No, no, I'm not Mrs. Ramsay," she cries. Boy wants what Girl wants, so he says, "Of course not. You're smarter than her. You're that other woman, the one who paints. Lily?"

To stay with Boy means to sacrifice her art for his bed and his kitchen. Not that Girl cooks. But every time he does, she feels insecure, as if she's supposed to reciprocate by presenting him with a new poem or a drawing. She has to justify her art, her creative search, which Boy supports but can't possibly understand. Somehow his tenderness makes her feel guilty, even in bed, even when he sweeps his tongue between her thighs. Even when he calls her names, those ridiculous vulgarities that used to fuel her desire. Girl stops giving head. She finds it demeaning even though it makes Boy so vulnerable, so weak, at the mercy of her mouth. Even though she loves to watch him come, his eyes glassy, as though pooling with tears.

The smell of tilled earth is too sour in the fall. Girl moves to London, Milan, Paris, Barcelona. She's received a grant and peregrinates like a bird in those foreign lands Boy can't help but trace with a finger on a faded map. He counts days, weeks, months. He trades coats and cars, ventures to see a movie. It's a story of a pregnant teenager, who gives her child up for adoption. Because how could she raise him alone? Teach him anything meaningful? She needs to finish high school, go to college, enjoy life. There's an alcoholic mother, an abusive stepfather, and three other siblings smoking pot and playing video games. No one tries to convince the heroine to keep her son. When he leaves the theater, way before the movie ends, Boy feels as though he's been pushed inside a cave, the opening sealed off with a rock. He can't see a thing, not even the tips of his fingers. Boy is small, outdated, a fossilized insect, a seashell. He imagines being found on a beach by Girl, who'll bring him home in a pocket of her dress.

At the house Septimus the cat is speaking in tongues: of hunger, weather, loneliness, the neighbor's dogs. Together they eat chicken in the dark.

Boy misses Girl.

He counts in garden seasons how long since he last saw her—five. How long since she last wrote—four. How many words—three.

Girl meets Man.

Boy gets a gun.

He shoots groundhogs digging tunnels through his orchard.

Another year goes by, maybe two. Septimus dies, and Boy buries him under an apple tree. He places a jagged stone on a hump of dirt.

Boy doesn't tell Girl when she calls, her voice stretching halfway around the globe. Girl sounds too educated, worldly, unsentimental. For her, life is infinite and ineffable, like the ocean, one breathtaking wave after another. Nothing has the right to exist but Art. She refuses to get married. She thinks marriage is an impediment to personal growth. An artist has no responsibility but to her work, which can't be ascribed or categorized. Otherwise it has no meaning and no right to exist. Girl is happy as she's never been. She can tell this to Boy because they, too, were happy once. Because he listens. Because he isn't a writer, like Man, who turns her life into stories, where every woman is her. It is as if she lives in a room full of funhouse mirrors. Each part of her reflecting at odd incomprehensible angles on opposite walls. She doesn't ask about the cat. She praises Italian wineries, French bakeries, and Spanish architecture, the guy named Antoni Gaudí, who, Girl insists, was visited by extraterrestrial beings. Otherwise how could he have created such unfathomable structures? Those Martian galaxies? They, too, are living things; they have souls. Girl wishes Boy could see them, but he's afraid of flying, of crossing the ocean, of getting lost. Besides, he can't leave the farm: his coop, his garden, his orchard. His empire apples, those succulent crisp red jewels of autumn.

Boy loses Girl.

In the following years he spends nights reading Man's stories on the internet. They burst with female characters who aren't Girl. They're grotesque imitations of other girls Boy has dated. Vain, boisterous creatures with small breasts and big mouths, who talk about life as though it were a farmers' market—everything is seasonal and everything is for sale. Man knows nothing about Girl, Boy concludes. Nothing that matters, nothing of great substance. He knows nothing about family or children either. He writes about them as though they were tomatoes rotting in his garden, of which he has limited experience. Boy is sure Man has never grown a plant from a seed, never fingered a seedling into warm, tilled soil. Still, Boy is jealous of Man, of his proximity to Girl and his skill of erecting small heartless words into love-hate pyramids.

Boy never cries. It's rain lashing at the trees in the dark.

More winters drag into springs, more snow melts into the earth. Memories fold one into another. Boy's hair sprouts gray; a hump of a belly under his shirt. He replaces Woolf's novels with nursery rhymes. He grows tomatoes as small as a baby's toes. Boy is a father and a husband, with two sweet daughters, who climb him like garden vines, and a wife, who plants flowers and bakes pies. Together they own a dog, two cars, more land. They never argue or refuse sex.

One summer they spend a week at the beach, where the salty air is sticking to their skin. Waves heave, roll, and smash ashore; gulls screech and dive low. A lighthouse blinks in the distance. Boy is thankful to Wife for all she's given him: her hips, her hands, her heart. Those apples she churns into butter and songs she croons at night.

While the family builds a sandcastle, Boy fingers out small chipped shells. He remembers Girl calling them ocean tears. It's been only a few days since her last message—about coming back, about Art being a heartache, a deception, about Gaudí dying before finishing Sagrada Familia, about Woolf killing herself, about poor old Septimus and all the things Girl left behind; Boy's broken heart she still holds dearly, like a favorite novel.

Girl loves Boy.

Boy loves Girl.

But what are they to do about it now? Him hiding the shells in his pocket. Wife asking, "What is it? What?"

Nepenthe

Fall has settled in the mountains, their fissured backs patched with colors—pumpkin orange, amber yellow, cranberry red. Shades upon shades of green. From the distance it seems as though the mountains have been draped with quilts, shielded from rain and impending cold, the weather. It won't snow for a while, and when it does the mountains will appear taller and wider but also farther away. Irene finds them enduring yet vulnerable, and so heartbreakingly female. She and John used to argue about it. He would say: warriors in stone armor, knights, crusaders, guards. And she would say: wombs, earth bearers, mothers, wives, girlfriends.

On the dining room table Irene has emptied two large tin boxes of old buttons gathered over the years—a life's worth of buttons. She recognizes some of them; others she swears she's never seen or held before. Irene can't bring herself to clear them off the table. Somehow the sight appeases her, fills her days with substance, and even provides odd moments of pleasure. She loves slipping her hands through heaps of cool, manifold plastic, or stacking up the buttons like coins. She may gather fistfuls of buttons and watch them fall through her fingers, or she may sit still and gaze for hours, trying to discern something small, something insignificant—a quiver perhaps, an oscillation, a wavering of sorts.

When the phone rings Irene has just spotted a knot of a button she assumes is hers. It's brown-green, woven, thick, pointy, almost like a small cone or a berry. She twiddles it in her fingers as she walks to the kitchen and picks up the receiver.

Irene is pretty sure she doesn't know the caller, but the caller knows her or rather her name, which is listed as the emergency contact for one of their patients, Ms. Vera Rudskaya. Although the name is mispronounced and then pronounced again, this time a bit faster and clearer, Irene experiences a slight trepidation in her chest and arms and nearly loses the button on the floor. The voice is telling Irene that Ms. Rudskaya is a cancer patient at Johns Hopkins, and that she's undergone a serious surgery; soon she'll have to take chemo treatments and possibly radiation. The doctor thinks much will depend on the postoperative care and the family. And since there doesn't seem to be any—just Irene—the nurse has been asked to contact her.

Irene feels compelled to say something at once, but finds it impossible, her vocal cords constricted.

"Hello?" the voice says, calm yet urgent. "Is there any way you can come to the hospital? Any way at all? How far do you live?"

Again Irene finds it impossible to answer. How far is far? she wants to ask. Are we talking miles or hours? Days or years? Forward or backward? How far can she really go? The nurse is following orders, but Irene, of course, is under no obligation to come or do anything else—the patient doesn't expect any visitors.

It takes Irene less than an hour to pack for an overnight trip—she could never stay longer—and she's on the road by 8 a.m. the next day. She has no animals to worry about, and her plants won't need watering for a week, as cool and damp as her house stays. Her refrigerator contains very little food since she dines out every night, usually at the Bistro on Main, at the table by the window facing McCampbell Inn, where eight years ago she'd gone to have an affair.

The Bistro is always crowded; many students eat there, young women who haven't really known failure, blooming with optimism. Irene can't help but listen to their insouciant, often inept, conversations and marvel at their youth. Not so much their age, but the excitement of all things possible, still ahead.

Last night, at the neighboring table, a few girls ordered scallops, and Irene heard the waiter claim they'd been delivered fresh that morning from Maryland, which was when Irene decided to make the trip. It will take her approximately five hours to drive from Lexington to Baltimore with stops and traffic, but she's in no hurry either; she might even spend an afternoon in DC browsing through the Smithsonian. She's heard there's an ancient rug expo in one of the pavilions.

* * *

VERA ARRIVED AT their home in Virginia on a sweltering, dusty August day in 1992, making Irene think of the Russian steppe, miles and miles of uninterrupted grassland. The girl carried nothing but an old trunk of sturdy, painted-brown cardboard held together by two leather straps. Her name was printed in white across the front. Vera was a scrawny teenager with short dandelion hair and dark eyes, the color of loam. Not so much a pretty face, but a pert one. She was dressed in black leggings and a satin turquoise-blue tunic cinched around her waist with a wide black belt. A flat silver cross dangled on her neck. She appeared considerably smaller in frame than Irene's children, Mike and Zoe, and somehow older, even though all three were the same age, not quite eighteen. John taught history at Washington and Lee and thought it to be a marvelous opportunity to host a student from the former Soviet Union. "Just think what she knows, what she can share," he told Irene. Irene shrugged, but did agree that perhaps it would be interesting, if not beneficial, for her children to live and socialize with someone from that other, darker and much forbidden, part of the world.

In her trunk Vera had very few personal belongings: a dictionary, two pairs of underwear, socks, a toothbrush, and an oversize T-shirt she later gave to Mike. The rest of the space was taken up by an Oriental rug, folded and sewn inside a sheet.

"To you. Gift. From home," she'd said, hefting the rug with as much effort as her slender arms allowed. Irene couldn't help but reach for it and then drag it to the living room, where John ripped the sheet open with a knife.

The rug was large and frayed around the edges, the colors faded into the richness of hues glowing in the afternoon sun. It had ornaments of leaves and vines and blossoming flowers with curlicues of different lengths and thicknesses. The rug gave the room an inviting, homey look, lying like patches of dyed wool on the hardwood floor. They ended up keeping it there, replacing the one they'd bought at an outlet years ago and that seemed cheap and crude next to its Russian contender.

Vera spoke decent English and laughed freely, with a child's ease and explosiveness, sometimes at things or situations Irene perceived as less than funny. She had a heavy accent John found exotic, but Irene deemed harsh, irreparable. There was a feeling of distinction about her, however, in her manners and the way she said, asserted, things, commanding the room to her attention. The day Vera had arrived, she'd asked for chores, so she could earn some pocket money to buy burgers, Coke, and Marlboros—the three things American. She also asked for old clothes, anything they could spare, until she could find a job that paid cash because with her student visa she wasn't allowed to work, just study and experience the culture.

Irene didn't know what to make of the girl, who was so unlike her own children, so independent, mature, assiduous, self-sufficient. During the eleven months Vera was staying with them, Irene had never heard her say no to anything: food or clothes or errands or homework, or any of the family activities Mike and Zoe spurned as boring or ridiculous. Vera welcomed picnics, hiking, biking, fly-fishing, cooking, cleaning, washing dishes, or doing laundry, and Irene often wondered who the girl's parents were and how they'd managed to raise her that way. Were deprivation and a totalitarian regime the key to successful parenting? Was everything they'd been told about the Communist aggression wrong? Was America really a better place? Irene wondered and even shared her concerns with John, who laughed and then asked, "What are you saying? That you want our children to go and live there? Among all those zombies?" And she said, "Vera isn't a zombie. She's so alive, I almost feel dead next to her."

And that's when things started to change—Irene knows it now—when she began feeling dead, uninspired by her home, her surroundings, her own children. The lack of vigor in her life, and even purpose, some larger, unattainable truth one was supposed to discover at midlife, something that was meant to prepare you for old age, to carry you through all the heartbreaks and disappointments, grave illnesses, the inescapability of death. Irene felt deprived. She possessed no such knowledge, no such truth, a realization that some-how became more prominent, more astute when Vera was living with them. Irene grew restless, mostly because she couldn't share her thoughts with anyone, and because they were just that—thoughts—random, incoherent, a skein of speculations she toiled to understand herself. If her life was a dream, Irene would have never questioned her actions; they would have seemed logical and necessary, even with no beginning and no end, just the middle, the prolonged continuous tense—her running someplace, chasing someone, searching for her children, her husband, saving a kitten or putting out a fire, filling her pockets with beach sand.

* * *

BY NOW IRENE has already passed DC. The traffic is merciful, and Irene hasn't stopped but once to use a restroom and get coffee, which she leaves unfinished in her cup.

Twelve years ago, when John was first diagnosed with type B aortic dissection, they both quit drinking alcohol or coffee and tried to adhere to vegetarian diets, with an exception of one burger on Sunday. They bought their produce from a local co-op, and in the summer Irene even tried to grow a vegetable garden. It turned out their backyard was mostly clay, so she carried bags and bags of potting soil mixed with a fertilizer. Irene was never a petite woman; she was tall and big-boned, with a sturdiness to her hips that had gotten wider and heavier after the birth of her children. Her weight not so much a burden to her, but an asset. She had a cloud of hair, shoulder-length, so curly and stubborn and all gray. She wore no makeup and no sunscreen, just a moisturizer, her face smooth and tanned. She had large feet and hands, and her arms were long, robust, delineated with muscles. She dressed in loose skirts and favored calm, earthy tones—greens and browns, an occasional russet, never red. Irene worked in the garden all summer, tending to the vegetables the best she could, but except for a few cucumbers and a bushel of tomatoes, nothing else took. Her carrots looked pitiful, her eggplant refused to turn purple like its picture on the seedlings cartons, and her peppers and zucchinis were malnourished dwarfs compared to the healthy, taut ones she bought at the market.

After John's exigent surgery five years ago, when the damaged area of the aorta was replaced with an artificial graft, Irene decided to plant an apple orchard because she'd heard all her life that apples were a poor man's medicine. Not that she and John were poor, but they were contemplating retirement. Their children had long gotten their degrees and respective jobs and lived on their own; neither was married or had offspring. At seventy John still taught part-time at W&L, and Irene, being ten years his junior, continued to work as a teller in a local branch bank and trust. By then the whole family got together only once a year, for Thanksgiving or Christmas, although since John's illness, the children did call more often.

Their property to the side of the house—a large, abandoned, brush-ridden lot, which they'd bought separately a few years after they'd moved in, hoping to put in a pool or a pond—allowed for seven trees spaced eighteen feet apart. When she finally picked out seven apple varieties—yellow transparent, Lyman's large summer, liberty, freedom, Virginia's beauty, Victoria Limbertwig, and Granny Smith—Irene had taken into consideration several factors: the ripening time was important, pollination if a tree was not a self-fruitful variety, and climate; Irene also had to make sure all the trees would withstand scorching summer heat, as well as occasional winter blizzards.

The trees' resistance to diseases was one of the determining factors too. Apple scab, for example, manifested itself in black fungal lesions on the surface of leaves, buds, or fruits and underwent sexual reproduction in the leaf litter around the base of the tree over winter, producing a new generation of ascospores the following spring. But the disease rarely killed its host, although caused significant damage, reducing fruit yields and quality. Fire blight, however, was often transmitted by honeybees, birds, rain, and wind, and under optimal conditions was capable of destroying an entire orchard in a single growing season.

Irene chose to plant three-year-old semidwarfs because they were easier to manage and they could produce fruit earlier than standard-size trees. However, since apple cultivars are usually grafted onto different rootstocks, some of the trees could still have poor root anchorage and require additional support. From various online sources Irene had gathered the following facts: grafting is the practice of attaching one plant to another in such a way that the two pieces bond and become one plant; the plant selected for its roots is called the stock, the other selected for its stems, flowers, leaves, or fruits is called the scion; there's a thin layer of tissue sandwiched between the bark of a tree and the wood, known as the cambium layer, which is comparable to the circulatory system in a human's body and responsible for transferring water and nutrients from the roots to the top of the plant and vice versa; when grafting, it's extremely important to bond the cambium layer of the stock to the cambium layer of the scion; it's also important not to cut too deeply, and into the wood; both tissues must be kept alive until the graft has taken; joints formed by grafting aren't as strong as naturally formed joints, so a physically weak point often occurs at the graft.

Generally an apple tree could start bearing fruit in four to five years, but some could try after just a year or two. In that case, Irene was told by a young farmer she'd hired to help her plant the orchard, she must clip off all the buds. Because fruit production requires so much energy, a young tree might be easily stunted by it, its root system weakened.

Now, in late October, most of the apples are on the ground, except for the Granny Smith. Irene doesn't know what to do with all the apples, and her children live too far away to worry about picking them. So Irene takes her apples to the co-op, bags full, and leaves them by the door.

* * *

IN BALTIMORE IRENE doesn't go to the hospital right away, but decides to eat lunch at one of the restaurants overlooking the harbor. It has transformed greatly in twenty years—the shopping, the dining, new hotels and businesses—all that glass and steel, reflecting, corrugating in the water. The day is warm and sunny, and Irene chooses to sit outside, gazing at the magnificent ships docked all around, and then at the way the water oscillates, pinpricks of light on its dark, silky surface. There's a bit of a breeze coming from the harbor, and Irene wishes she hadn't left her jacket in the car. She orders a crab-cake sandwich and a small salad, dressing on the side. And also tea—hot tea, she corrects the waitress.

Somewhere, not too far away, a tour guide is gathering a group of people to sightsee in the city and visit Poe's grave. The man holds the writer's portrait high above his head. Irene cannot see the face on the portrait in great detail but knows it to be weary and sad, with feverish eyes, sharp jawline, and black moustache over the thin, pencil-etched lips. She remembers memorizing a portion of "The Raven" in high school though cannot recall a single line, just some words and the mood, so somber, so cumbersome, the strike of a hammer in each *nevermore*. She says, "Nepenthe," out loud. And then again. She has no idea what it means.

* * *

DAY BY DAY, word by word, Irene watched her children grow to adore Vera and revere her opinions. They ate everything she ate, including beets and cabbage and raw onion, and even chicken liver Irene had to procure and fry. Her children wandered outside barefoot, even on the coldest of days, and took rain baths, guffawing in the yard, drenched to the last hair. They even started reading those heavy Russian novels Irene could never bring herself to check out of the library and mimicked Vera's facial expressions and also her speech, acquiring some sort of an accent, which sounded unbearable to Irene's ear.

To celebrate Memorial Day the family had decided to spend a long weekend at the beach. Mike, Zoe, and Vera clamored in the backseat while John drove and Irene marveled at the Francis Scott Key Bridge they were crossing. It was like crossing into the future, into the unknown, water all around them. Irene felt liquid herself, unmoored, flowing in the directions of great ships and a few smaller boats buoyed in the distance. Oddly enough she succumbed to peace when they traveled. Or perhaps it was all the distraction, the complete and utter abandonment of everyday duties, of the nagging realization that somehow her life was exactly what she'd wanted it to be and yet not what she desired.

John and the children seemed to have enjoyed the beach, basking in the sun and even swimming, as cold as the water was, but Irene had trouble relaxing or falling asleep. One night she stood on the deck of their rented house, picking up a pack of Marlboros and a lighter Vera had forgotten on the lounge chair. She lit a cigarette and took a few drags, her college days suddenly in her mouth, all the random night-long fests, cold stringy pizzas, unlimited booze. There had been sex too—nervous, sweaty, immature, often interrupted, but free. Free from everything but the pleasure it offered. The ocean crashed in the distance, the water black like oil. A tusk of a moon above. On her way to bed, Irene was passing the girls' room when she stopped, halted in the dark. The door was not shut tight, and she touched it, barely, pressed her fingers to its slick surface. Even before she'd stepped into the room, she became aware of things, fleshy things, things that mingled, grew, bred in her home, under her motherly gaze, things she'd allowed her children to do, to be a part of. As she tiptoed into the room, her eyes adjusting to its conspiratorial darkness, she saw all three spooning on the floor—Zoe inside Vera inside Mike. It was hot and damp in the room, the window opened, the shutters raised. The air salty, sticky, grains of sand under Irene's bare feet. She stood, not moving, her eyes isolating the pieces of underwear—a cami, a pair of briefs—next to the bed. Under a white sheet rolled down to their hips, her children were naked, as they had been inside her, their skin pale and silky, a soft curl to their brown hair. In the middle, Vera was tan and blonde, glowing like a lantern.

"They were just sleeping," John assured Irene the next morning.

"Naked? Naked?" she asked.

* * *

AT THE HOSPITAL, at the Kimmel Cancer Center, Irene learns the following: Ms. Vera Rudskaya has stage 2 lung cancer; a thoracotomy was performed two days ago and the affected section of the lung was removed, along with the lymph nodes; the patient has a chest tube to allow the fluid to drain; the cancer hasn't spread to other organs; she will begin external radiation as soon as she has healed from the surgery; the radiation will have to be five days a week for three weeks; it may harm the esophagus, causing problems with swallowing; the radiation will most likely be given together with chemotherapy for a more aggressive treatment.

Irene has a stack of medical brochures huddled against her chest; in her other hand she holds a large tote filled with apples. The center is impressive and accommodating, and has all the standard smells: chlorine, sanitizing alcohol, reheated cafeteria food. Irene imagines Vera asking for borsch or *pelimeni*, the large sickle-shaped Siberian dumplings the girl made for them on Thanksgiving. Vera has just been moved from an IC unit on the third floor to an inpatient private room on the fourth, and Irene lingers in the hallway before pushing the door open with just the tips of her fingers.

Once in the room, Irene is extremely quiet and also careful, so as not to wake the patient, whom she cannot recognize, no matter how long and hard she stares. On the bed, inside a cocoon of sheets and hoses, tiny poking tubes, lies a middle-aged woman, gaunt and pallid, a wax figure with graying hair and skin like dead leaves. At first Irene thinks there has been a mistake, and somehow this woman, whom Irene doesn't know, got her name confused. She thinks she did all that traveling for a stranger, for someone who perhaps is also alone, like Irene.

"I knew you'd come."

"Me?" Irene asks, startled. She's amazed at how much softer Vera's accent has gotten, but also how dry her voice sounds as though short of vowels. She wonders how much air she's able to draw into her pared lungs. "I didn't know where to come," Irene says, apologetically. Vera's eyes are directed at her, and Irene notes them to be much darker, almost black.

"Here're some apples," Irene says and fetches a few out of the bag. "I grew them. They are quite good. I give a lot of them away." She regrets she said that. She doesn't want Vera to think she brought the apples because she needed to dispose of them.

"Thank you."

Irene unloads the apples on the tray table, so conveniently tall, on wheels. Now the room smells like her orchard on a warm, windless day.

"What kind are they?" Vera asks, whispers now.

"Freedom, Virginia beauty, and this is Victoria Limbertwig," Irene says, pointing at a gorgeous fruit of purple color. "It'll keep all winter." Picking up the brochures from the table, Irene stows them inside the empty tote.

"You leaving?" Vera's cheeks are a bit flushed, perhaps from the effort. Irene knows she must not talk; both of them must not talk.

"I'm staying the night," she says. "I'll come back tomorrow. You need to rest."

"Which hotel?"

Irene shrugs. "I haven't booked one yet. But I saw plenty around the hospital. Lots of sick people here." Again she regrets she said that. She wishes they could just use telepathy, like aliens, transporting their thoughts silently through their eyes, or dipping in and out of each other's minds, retrieving all the pertinent information, a scoop of years, the lacking episodes.

"Stay at my place. Not far. Stay as long—" Vera wheezes and attempts to cough, and Irene rushes out to get a nurse.

Irene has Vera's address copied from her driver's license onto a piece of paper, Vera's keys in her purse. In the lobby, at the info desk, Irene was able to obtain a city map and jot down a maze of directions.

Perhaps she should've stayed at the hotel, and she still can, but she will at least take a peep at the place. She feels brazen, alone in the city, doing something spontaneous and inane, something John would have disapproved of. Some days she's replete with sentiment and longs to talk to him, so she calls his cell, which she keeps charged and turned on at the house. She listens to a short greeting message, his old crackle of a voice, followed by a sharp beep, and then she says things into the receiver, silly things, trifles really, like how windy it has gotten and cold, how she should have worn a heavier jacket and made hot cider to drink on the road, how gorgeous the leaves are, flying at her in great sweeps, throwing themselves against the windshield. Now she also tells him about Vera and that she is going to stay at her apartment overnight and perhaps dust it a bit for when she comes back from the hospital, although it looks like it may be awhile. She wants to add that she forgives him and that he must forgive her too. All it was—a visit, a trip to a hotel room, an unresponsive touch of unfamiliar flesh, a chain of mountain ridges curving black against the dusk-red horizon.

Irene is surprised at how easily she's able to locate the street and the apartment complex and the apartment itself, on the eighth floor above the parking garage. Irene wonders how much it costs to rent such a place in the heart of the city. Surely Vera doesn't own it. The apartment is small though, with a narrow strip of a hallway that leads to the kitchen and the living area combined. There's a balcony partially overlooking a brick-paved courtyard, with a wrought-iron bistro set and a clay flower pot in the middle. When Irene steps out and peers inside it, she discovers several half-smoked cigarettes crushed at the bottom. The city booms down below, indefatigable, people scurrying places, the streets clogged with afternoon traffic. She imagines Vera sitting here at night, alone, smoking her Marlboros, squinting at the streetlights, their blurry reflections in the dark office windows.

Vera's apartment is clean, much cleaner than Irene's house, which she's been neglecting in the past months, confining things to piles and stacks on the floor—magazines, newspapers, clothes, empty grocery bags, socks and shoes. The apartment has very little furniture, new hardwood floors, and only one bedroom and one bed. Irene hasn't accounted for that. She inspects the living-room sofa and is disappointed to learn that it doesn't unfold. The kitchen cabinets contain almost no dishes but some food: tea varieties, honey, cubes of brown sugar in a bowl, a handful of shelled walnuts in a Ziploc bag, sea salt, dry lentils, wild rice, organic pasta, a full bottle of sunflower oil, and oatmeal. In the refrigerator Irene finds nothing except fish oil capsules and probiotics, soft ice packs in the freezer.

Irene opens the dishwasher and begins to transfer the cleaned, dried dishes and cups to the cabinets, placing them anywhere there's room.

* * *

MIKE AND ZOE dismissed Irene's questions about that night on the beach, brushed off her worries like bread crumbs from the dinner table. They just shrugged and made puzzled faces and even suggested that Irene had imagined things, dreamed them up.

Then Irene's mother fell and broke her hip, right after the children's graduation, and Irene drove to Ohio to help her father. When she returned, however, ten days later, her house, her husband, and even her children felt foreign to her. Try as she might, she couldn't find the cause of her unrest. Everything was in its place, exactly the way she'd left it. And yet things had shifted, acquired a strange inimical light, a concealed meaning. The dishes had been returned to the china cabinet, the cups and glasses to the cupboard, the silverware gleamed in the drawer. But Irene couldn't bring herself to touch any of it. Everyone seemed happy to see her, but then John asked if she would have to travel back soon. Mike and Zoe would be leaving for college, but Vera was offered a year of study at W&L; she could take over the housekeeping, at least for the summer. In her bedroom, even before Irene undressed or unpacked, she began pulling the covers and sheets off the bed, tossing them in a pile, which rose like a snowdrift on the floor.

* * *

AFTER INSPECTING THE master closet, the contents of Vera's drawers, and the bathroom cabinet, Irene has deduced the following: Vera is not married, and even if she was once, it was a long time ago; she doesn't seem to have any children either; she works in an office, judging by all the gray pantsuits; she doesn't waste money on expensive shoes and prefers cotton underwear and wireless bras; she isn't anywhere near menopause unlike Irene, who stopped menstruating right at forty. Also: Vera reads a lot, and she misses home. Three full bookcases are lined against the wall, mostly novels, some poetry. Russian souvenirs clutter each shelf, as well as the TV cabinet, the dresser, and both nightstands. Irene's fingers travel from a set of nesting dolls to the amber animals to a beautiful jewelry box carved from tree bark— birch, she assumes. Irene pulls off the lid and contemplates Vera's old silver cross, thin and delicate, with curving edges, like the blossom of a dogwood tree. Irene takes the cross out and holds it on her palm then tries to fashion it around her neck, fidgeting with the clasp. She unbuttons her shirt in front of the mirror and touches her hand to the cross, too small, too humble on her age-mottled chest.

Irene longs to call her children, to tell them: I've found her. Come back, come back home.

* * *

VERA LEFT, vanished from their house, the morning after Irene's return from Ohio, the trunk gone from under the bed. Irene and John reported to the school's International Student Council and the program coordinator, but remained brief in their statements. There was no mention of the fight between the spouses the previous night, or of the children's infatuation with their Russian guest, or of any suspicious behavior that could have led to the girl's disappearance. No one blamed Irene, but no one paid much attention to her either, disregarding her genuine worries, her attentiveness in the matter. And even though she'd wanted the girl to leave, she didn't mean for her to disappear. Irene felt disconcerted at first, and then guilty, and then distressed. She imagined Vera vagabonding about the world, trunk in hand, bumming rides, sleeping in trailer parks, strange cars, or mice-crawling basements. She imagined the girl locked in a filthy house or kept in a tent in a backyard, a covey of babies by her side.

Mike and Zoe bristled against Irene and gradually stopped communicating with her or John altogether, holed up in their rooms, locks turned, music blaring. They grew polite and aloof and switched to the farthest of colleges, the remotest of places. They almost never called, and she and John saw them less and less. Each time they visited, Irene wanted to take them in her arms and say: I'm sorry. I was protecting my home, my family. When you have your own children, you'll understand, know, and perhaps forgive. But she didn't say it, and they didn't come to her, didn't let her offer any explanations, mend the way.

After the children had moved, Irene and John were suddenly confronted with age and time—years' worth of time—all that togetherness so insufferably drawn out, augmented by the empty house. There was no urgency and no fear, but silent contemplation of life in passing. They tried going on trips, but that, too, brought no relief and even deepened the discontent, their marriage too old, too desperate—a boat left in the open, beaten to smithereens. And then John fell ill, and they no longer had the option, Irene nursing him through getting better and then through getting worse.

* * *

ONLY IN THE morning, lying in Vera's bedroom, does Irene realize the odd thing about the apartment: there are no pictures anywhere and no photo albums. Jolted out of bed, Irene squats on the floor and bends, groping under the wooden frame. The trunk is there, at the stretch of her hand. Irene turns on the light and sits back down, examines a throng of her fingerprints on the dusty cardboard. Inside the trunk she finds nothing but a frayed baby quilt and one photo—that of Vera, somewhat younger and fuller in the hips, next to a teenage boy, who looks a lot like Irene's children when they were that age. Irene stares at the picture that says many things, none of which she can quite articulate. There's an air of familiarity to the people in the picture, as well as suppressed tension, a disappointment too, their faces austere and tender at the same time. On the back of the picture, she reads: *Ralph, 2006.*

At the hospital, an hour later, Irene is told to wait while the nurse is dressing Vera's scar and changing the bandages. The weather has turned rainy overnight, and the city is glazed with mist, slick wet surfaces everywhere, the reflection of headlights on the cobalt-black asphalt. Irene hasn't had any breakfast except for a cup of tea, but she doesn't feel hungry. When the nurse finally beckons her in, Irene has learned from the wall posters in the hallway almost as much information about the lungs as she did about the heart after John's surgery. She's also made a fascinating discovery: lobes are sections of the lung—the right lung has three lobes, and the left only two; respiration is controlled automatically in the medulla of the brain, so that a person doesn't have to always think about having to inhale and exhale; it's the same type of automatic process that keeps the heart beating.

In the room Vera is sitting up on the bed, the robe loose around her bony shoulders, the blue hospital gown showing. Her cheeks are revived with color, and her hair is combed and tucked behind her ears. But she still looks emaciated, drained of the energy Irene once envied. The IV machine has been unhooked and the chest tube removed earlier that morning. The room carries the aroma of apples piled in a bowl and moved next to the sink.

"Do they need washing?" Vera asks.

"Sure." Irene walks to the sink and turns on the water, places the whole bowl under a cool stream. "They may be too hard to bite."

"There's a plastic knife somewhere."

"I see it." Irene turns off the water and picks out a garnet-red apple and also a wad of tissues she places on the tray table. She fits into the chair opposite the bed and starts peeling the apple in one long drool. As soon as she finishes, she cuts the fruit in half, cores and slices it, handing a pink-fleshed piece to Vera. She holds it between her fingers gently, making Irene think of a rodent, small and skittish, and so frustratingly helpless.

"Fragrant," Vera says and brings the apple to her mouth. "Almost like in Russia." She chews with care, and Irene does too.

Her head swarms with questions she wishes she could just swat at or dart at Vera, like: Where are your parents? Do they know about the cancer? Why did you leave us? Where did you go? What became of you? Did you marry? Have a child? Who's Ralph? How old is he? Are there any apple trees in Siberia?

"Do your parents grow apples?" Irene surprises Vera with the question, who studies Irene's face for a moment.

"No. They don't grow anything."

"But didn't you say they were farmers?"

Again there's a slight pause, a weight to Vera's silence.

"I grew up in an orphanage. I was left there when I was just a baby, on top of a rolled-up rug."

"The one you brought to our house?"

"You still have it?"

"Yes. Of course. It's a bit worn, but lovely. The colors are all blurred." Irene passes Vera the rest of the apple, and they spend the next few minutes chewing. Irene fetches another fruit from the bowl. "You need to eat as many apples as you can. I have a trunk full. And there's plenty more at home."

"How are Mike and Zoe?" Vera relaxes against the pillows now, her eyes closed, her chin tilted up. Only her jaws are slightly moving.

"Okay. They are okay. Zoe, she runs marathons in California. And Mike is somewhere in the Arctic Circle, chasing the aurora borealis."

"John?"

Now the silence is all Irene's, and Vera stops chewing; her eyelids tremble, but she doesn't say a word. She looks tired, drifting off.

"You know," she finally says and then swallows. "Aurora is really a girl. A girl in love. Sometimes she's happy. Sometimes sad. Sometimes lonely and furious. But also stupid." She pauses, managing a weak smile. "And that's when the light is the most luminous."

* * *

IT'S HALLOWEEN NIGHT a week later. Irene has carved a pumpkin and placed it on the bistro table. When she lights the candle inside the gutted, hollow vegetable, she acknowledges that one eye is wider and much lower, which gives the face character. On other balconies neighbors have done the same, placed lit jack-o-lanterns on tables or on the guardrail. Anywhere Irene looks, she sees orange faces grinning in the dark. Earlier today, when she hauled groceries from the car, she noticed a monument across the street, a bronze statue dressed in a knee-length cape, a wig, and a red bowtie, with a large black bird on the shoulder and a head-size pumpkin in the crook of the bent arm. Now she can spot the same statue from the balcony, the cape billowing, the pumpkin aglow.

Vera has stuffed a whole chicken with cut-up apples and dried apricots, and Irene places it in the oven. She has already baked an apple pie this morning. She's also bought a collapsible bed and set it in the living room, where Vera is lying in front of the TV, sharing an occasional comment or an observation. On Irene's advice, to minimize the risk of infection, she doesn't venture out much and wears only loose T-shirts and robes so as not to aggravate the scar. They haven't yet shaved her hair, but they practice breathing exercises every day and adhere to the coughing technique.

"Scientists think that at one point, the entire observable universe would've been about the size of a sand grain," Vera says. "Can you believe it?"

Irene shakes her head and passes Vera a cup of warm cider, which Vera makes an effort to reach even though it hurts to lift her arm.

They are starting treatments on Wednesday, but today is only Monday, and the kitchen is still a workplace, still thriving with hearty smells. Irene knows that sometime, in the future, they'll have to invite the children, Mike and Zoe, and Ralph too.

Also: there are months ahead of them, and possibly years.

Beloveds

It's Maslenitsa, and the orphanage smells of butter and fruit preserves that volunteers brought in last Friday, along with secondhand clothes, books, and old CDs. We stare out the windows at the other side of the street, where trees will soon swell with tender green leaves. We dream about beautiful homes and perfect families—mothers, fathers, kids. Everyone is happy and cozy, snuggled in wool, lolling on couches or gathering for meals. Men read newspapers or paint walls; women bake pierogi or knit scarves, hats, sweaters. We dream our mothers still love us and that one day, not too far into the future, they'll be knocking on our doors with armloads of toys and candy. Most of us don't remember what our mothers look like, but when we draw them, they appear tall and thin, dressed in white or pale-pink gowns, angels without wings.

Also, we aren't exactly sure how we got here—from a dark closet to a car to this building crowded with other scared, silent children. It's a mystery we must solve before we grow up and forget each other's smell, as we did our mothers'. Was it the smell of strawberries or meat cutlets or lilacs? Or was it that of vodka, cigarettes, or herring? We don't know. We don't remember. We don't remember our family names or what our mothers called us, what songs they sang or bedtime stories they told. We don't remember if we had beds before these hard, metal ones with frayed cotton mattresses that reek of fish and other leftover food we hide underneath, squashed against the rusty springs of the bed frames.

We're all girls on this floor. Russian, Ukrainian, Belorussian, Moldovan, Armenian, Georgian, Uzbek, Kazakh, Tajik, Turkmen, all or any combination. Our age is approximate—we measure our life not by birth years, but by the amount of luck that has befallen us since we were discovered: on a deserted street, in a car trunk, in a city dumpster, digging for food or just lying there, swaddled in bloody sheets or plastic bags, staring at the night sky. Or was it dawn already? A spring morning filled with birdsong and the smell of young leaves swaying over our puzzled newborn faces? We wish we knew.

Or maybe we don't, because we like to imagine. Our mothers' hands, for example, how they touch our cheeks or brush our hair or give us a bath, all foam and bubbles. We imagine those hands large and soft, like scarves enveloping us, or small and chafed, grazing our shoulders. We try to catch them, to hold them in place, but they slip away like water. Sometimes we imagine our mothers as birds with large useless wings like those of peacocks or ostriches. They live on a faraway farm but can't get to us, can't make such a strenuous journey on those flat, skinny feet. We want to help our mothers; we want to pick them up and carry them home, wherever that might be. We want to wash their hair and clip their toenails and sit them at a table and cook them a meal. But all we really want is to touch them, to know that they're real.

Try as we might, we can't imagine our fathers. We think of them as something volatile, fickle, inconstant. We think of them as March weather: rain, snow, wind. Even those of us who've seen them refuse to describe what they look like.

Once we get lucky, we get picked. We move to America, where we're adopted after years of paperwork. We live in a two-story house in Ohio, Maryland, Tennessee, Virginia. There's a porch. There's a swing. A dog tied to a fence. Our foreign mother isn't at all what we imagined. She owns a truck and a turkey farm. She's big-boned and plump, wears loose shirts, jeans or sweatpants, scuffed boots. Next to her our foreign father isn't really visible. But he reads newspapers, makes coffee, feeds the dog. He drives to school and then to work and then back home. He washes dishes and laundry and throws steaks on the grill. He paints, he vacuums, he hangs lights and pictures. On Sundays he orders pizza, which he shares with us while watching basketball. He doesn't get drunk or beat our mother or piss on the floor. He solves crosswords in bed. Occasionally he massages our feet or rubs sunscreen on our bodies, inspecting them for suspicious moles or sores that won't heal. We try to stand still as his fingers skim our shoulders, belly, back, the cheeks of our ass, where an old burn blossoms like a rose. He tickles us, and we giggle and poke him in the ribs. We know happiness when we feel it, and we describe it in our letters, which we mail diligently once a month.

Back home, in the communal kitchen, our supervisors read the letters out loud. They're all women—married, single, with or without children. They curse with verve and intention, bark orders, and slap our hands when we reach for more butter, sugar, or gooseberry preserves. They demand things of us: ironed sheets, scrubbed floors and commodes, washed windows. They steal from us too, cigarettes or candy, cute trinkets they find in a box of secondhand rubble: a hair clip, a brooch, a baby spoon. They're as close to mothers as some of us will ever know. We're fifteen, sixteen, seventeen, past the adoption age. We can't compete for love against our younger sisters and won't ever see America, but we're closer to getting out, to finding a job, a partner, a home. If life is a circle, we want ours to be as perfect as a blin on a hot skillet. We flip the blin with our bare fingers, then butter it and drizzle it with honey donated by a generous hand. We imagine that hand touching our hair, combing and recombing it, separating our locks and then braiding them together. We imagine our braids as beautiful as the stems of ripe, golden wheat on the old Soviet posters that hang on the walls, masking leaks and dirt. We pretend those stains are patterns drawn by artists, those who got away. We trace the patterns with our eyes and fingers because sometimes that's all we can do to entertain ourselves when we aren't at school, where we often get into trouble.

We aren't expected to enter colleges or universities but to become janitors, street sweepers, factory and construction workers, waitresses, dishwashers, saleswomen, hotel maids. It isn't that we're dumb or lazy, but we might not memorize as well or count as fast or understand the sentence completely—what's written and what's implied—and sometimes, when we're forced to recite poetry, we don't recognize our voices; words garble and drag and fade. Echoes fill our heads, as though we're being knocked against walls. We're trying hard not to faint.

Oh, but we're brilliant too! We know the multiplication table by heart and can duplicate Mendeleev's periodic chart in our sleep. We can add and subtract thousands, solve elaborate equations, all without paper. Once, in a school library, we discovered Gödel's incompleteness theorem. We brought it up in class; we were the only ones who understood the complexity and simplicity of the premise, that *anything you can draw a circle around cannot explain itself without referring to something outside the circle—something you have to assume but cannot prove.* Like a line that can be extended indefinitely in both directions or having parents while being an orphan.

After supper, after the last blin disappears from our plates, we gather in front of the TV to watch our favorite show, a Brazilian telenovela,

Slave Isaura. We sit on the edge of our chairs, empathizing with the smart, slender, petulant girl, her day-to-day escapades. The show is dubbed, but we can still catch those blissful foreign words slipping from Isaura's lips and floating about the room like tiny warm clouds of breath. We dream about being transported to Rio de Janeiro, to the house of the *comendador*, his kitchen, his bedroom, those silky sheets Isaura presses and stretches with her obedient hands. We've only watched eleven episodes, but somehow we know that after great suffering and injustices, Isaura will be saved and rewarded with a lifetime of happiness. We're convinced that in the end, those years of loss, grief, and servitude will be replaced with eternal freedom, with the love of a man who will break down the stone walls that keep her prisoner.

Or maybe she'll run away.

Like us.

One morning, we pack what little we have—a toothbrush, a clean T-shirt, panties and socks—and take off for the city, for the new life we hope to start on the streets. We walk in parks, smoke on benches, share crumbs of bread with mobs of pigeons. We go in and out of stores to get warm and to bum change. We are hungry. We are thirsty. At the mercy of strangers. We find a bar, a restaurant, where men buy us beer and vodka and viscid, spicy liqueur. Before long our age is questioned. "Eighteen, nineteen, twenty," we lie and are ogled with cheerful suspicion, then patted on the cheeks, shoulders, between the knees. We feel smarter, taller, older, but also soft, like butter over hot blinis. We let men buy us food and pour us more drinks. We let them feel under our shirts, tug at the hooks of our bras until our breasts spill into their hands. Men hold our breasts like delicate, fragile orbs, eyes closed, lips pursed. Men give us money, clothes, makeup. They invite us to restrooms, cars, elevators, a dark flight of stairs in some apartment building on the outskirts of the city. They call us darling, baby, beauty, beloved, girl, and we shiver and moan in response. We've never been called so many kind names or been touched in so many sweet places. We know love when we feel it, deep inside, a dusting of tiny petals.

Days blur into weeks, dusks into dawns. Spring fades into summer. We find an empty basement, a construction site, a rooftop. A restaurant that stays open all night. We learn how to smoke weed, fake an orgasm, rip off a condom with our teeth, fall asleep on a commode. Once, in a public restroom, we discover a book, a novel without a cover. It's the story of a mother who loses her children to war and soldiers. She wants to be buried alive on top of her daughters. She refuses to part with them, to give them up. We feel tears drip from our eyes. We keep repeating the mother's name: Viktoria. Viktoria, the mother of Elena, Marina, Olga, Nina, Galina, Inna, Maria, Tatiana, Svetlana, Luidmila, Alina, Lailo, Karina, Polina, Natasha, Kristina, Sofia, Klavdia, Anastasia, Ella, Ekaterina.

We avoid the militia, although we know no one is looking for us. But we're underage, and we'll be punished for running away, for working the streets, for gathering city dust in our hands and mouths. We'll be forced to return to school, to prove the unprovable theorems, to read more books. Something by Tolstoy or Dostoevsky, something interminable and illuminating, lifelong.

One evening, as we're waiting on the corner of a busy intersection for the traffic light to change, we feel someone's eyes piercing us from a distance. It's a woman, stooping low, with a woven tote filled with empty milk bottles. Her hair stands in clumps, her face—a shriveled apple. She has a bruise on her cheek and a scratch on her neck; one of her front teeth is missing.

"Beloveds," she says and rushes toward us. "It's been so long. I thought I'd never see you again."

She opens her arms, and, stupefied, we reach to hug her. We remember being told that all things happen for a reason, that when something has been taken from us, it's for a greater good that will reveal itself. We have to be patient, hardworking, sincere, for our mothers to return, to want us back. But as young girls, women, lovers, we also understand how tricky everything looks in the waning summer light, how unreliable, that if we'd had homes, beds, mothers, we wouldn't have been standing in the middle of a street, searching for a glimpse of recognition in a strange woman's face. We feel tired, in need of a shower and sleep, the touch of cool sheets against our nakedness.

We sleep for days, weeks, in a place that's no bigger than a closet and as dark as a womb. We sip hot broth made from cow bones, scratching out the marrow with our pinkies. The woman brushes our hair while we eat, smiling her toothless smile. We know she isn't our mother, but we can't admit that; we oblige her hunched back and her crooked, arthritic hands. She tells us stories that all begin, "When you were little—"

"Like that?" we ask and point at the walls, at the black-and-white pictures of a girl—three, five, seven years old.

"Yes, like that," the woman says. "When you were little, you loved to stand on the balcony and wave at people."

We nod, conjuring an image of a happy little person with braids and freckles. "What happened to us?" we ask. "Where did we go?"

The woman shrugs. "No idea. You disappeared. I came back from work, and you were gone."

"You left us alone while you went to work?" we ask, angry-like. "How many times? How often? You stupid old hag. We could've found matches and burned ourselves. We could've fallen from the balcony. Opened the door to a stranger. We could've been stolen, raped, killed."

"But you're alive," the woman says. "You've been returned to me. And I won't let you leave. You're mine, mine, mine." Her voice is soft, softer than rain that slithers down the window glass. She cries, and we feel pity—for her, for us, for the girl on the wall.

Time passes, but we don't know how much. Our beds are warm, and our bellies are full. We've stopped screaming in our dreams. We dust the shelves, wash the sheets, sweep the floor. We wear the old woman's clothes from back when she was young: short, square dresses with large collars and shoulder buttons, patent-leather shoes, high platforms two sizes too small. We apply her lipstick and her perfume. We smell like gardenias and look like our mothers, what we imagine they looked like before they had us. Every night the woman reads to us—Marshak, Chukovsky, Mamin-Sibiryak, Kipling's Mowgli stories—and we imagine ourselves naked, shivering inside a cave, or running through the jungle amid a pack of wolves. We listen to her voice that stretches through the darkness pressing hard on our eyelids. We make her stop by pulling the book away and skimming her face with our hands. Her skin is tree bark against our fingers.

Finally it's New Year's, and the woman drags a half-dead pine into the living room. It sheds snow and needles on the floor. The snow melts and turns to puddles, which we try to wipe with our socks. She's out of breath, and we're out of cigarettes, so we throw on her old coats and felt boots and scurry out to the store.

In the yard all is white and merry. Trees are wrapped in snow as though in gauzy shawls; icicles like old men's beards hang off buildings. Children are rolling a snowman or sledding down an ice hill; a few are tracking the ground with their baby skis. The mothers hover close by, chirping and calling out the kids' names. Everywhere, holiday garlands sway and blink with lights. The roads are scraped but slick, and we slip a few times, fall and get up. As we turn the corner, searching for a grocery store or a cigarette kiosk, we peep in windows, behind which families have gathered for a festive meal. Everyone talks, laughs, eats, pressing starched napkins to warm mouths. For a moment we stand still, mesmerized by these tender exchanges, these simple, uncomplicated ways.

It has gotten dark outside, streetlamps casting mean shadows on the snow. As we're paying for the cigarettes, pushing a wad of rubles through a narrow plastic opening, two militia men walk up to us. "What are your names?" they ask. "Age? Where do you live? Do your parents know that you smoke?"

We nod and feign innocence, raise our eyebrows, bat our frosted lashes. "Over there," we say and point at a dingy building of flats in the distance. "We live over there. The cigarettes are for our parents."

"You're lying," the men say and grab our elbows, the sleeves of the old woman's coats.

"We're lying," we say. "Or not. The phrase is paradoxical. Since if it's true, then we're lying, and then it's false. But if it's false, and we aren't lying, then it's true. Gödel's theorem. It's neither provable nor disprovable. It's outside the logic system."

They slap us, pinch our cheeks, twist our arms.

And then we're running.

Through the snow, through the backyards, through the trees.

We're running.

Through strange streets and busy intersections, in and out of underground crossings.

We're running.

Past buildings of flats, playgrounds, ice hills, holidays markets, bars and restaurants.

We're running.

Past grocery stores, banks, post offices, and old churches, where sparrows huddle for warmth under hollow awnings.

We're running.

And when we stop, it's Maslenitsa again, and the orphanage smells of butter and fruit preserves that volunteers brought on Friday. In the kitchen blinis slouch in tall stacks, while on TV the *comendador*'s son offers Isaura to either become his mistress or work on a plantation, cutting sugarcane. Sadness spreads over our hearts like batter over hot skillets as we continue to stare out the windows and wait for tender green leaves to unfurl on trees. Somewhere, across the street, is a perfect home, a perfect family, a perfect kid.

Somewhere—is our mother.

The Suicide Note

I'd been living in Brooklyn for a few months when I met Sarah. She came to shop at Fresh Market on Myrtle, where I worked six days a week, from noon to midnight. It was early December, the city dusted with snow. Garlands of lights looped around windows and lampposts. My coworkers and I had just finished decorating a small artificial tree by the entrance. It appeared lopsided, with flimsy paper ornaments caught in a swirl of wind each time a customer walked in or out. An angel sat crooked on the very top.

In her knee-length fur coat, Sarah stood in front of the tree for a moment before raising her cane to adjust the angel. To my surprise she was able to reach it without much effort, but now the angel leaned to the other side. She kept fussing with the cane until the winged creature appeared dead center.

"That's better," she said. "Whoever put you up there didn't try hard."

That "whoever" was me, but I didn't volunteer the information. Instead I offered her a shopping cart someone had abandoned in the aisle. She asked if she could order a fresh turkey.

We had turkeys, frozen though, but she shook her head.

"I need fresh. My son is coming home for the holidays. I want to cook up a feast."

As half Russian, half Ukrainian, I occasionally had trouble pronouncing English words or hearing them correctly. So I asked, "You're cooking a beast? Animal?"

Sarah wrinkled her forehead. Her skin resembled recycled parchment paper, creased and thin. "Where are you from, young man?" she asked.

"Russia."

"Thought so. Your accent."

She had a sharp nose and dark solemn eyes. Slouching over her right ear, a black beret covered all of her head, so it was hard to guess what color her hair was. Her eyebrows were painted brown, one longer than the other. She looked slim under the lustrous bulk of her coat, with delicate wrists and glossy maroon nails. She must have been eighty or older, somewhere close to the lip of eternity, as my mother would have said.

"I'll ask about fresh turkey and let you know in a day or two, if you leave your phone number," I said.

She nodded, and I spent the next fifteen minutes following her around the store, reaching for various staples on higher shelves. She kept her feet wide apart and moved slowly.

"I had both hips replaced, in case you're wondering," she said. Her husky, crackling voice made me think of trees, dead trees.

"Oh, wow. Does it still hurt?" I asked.

"No. But my marathon days are over."

I gave her a compassionate look. "Sorry."

"Don't be. I hate marathons. At least there's no pressure now. My son, on the other hand, always runs places."

When she said that, I thought of my father constantly rushing out, always late—for work, for gatherings, and even for my grandmother's funeral. How I'd almost missed my plane to America because he'd been late driving me to the airport.

When Sarah finished shopping, her cart brimmed with produce: fingerling potatoes, avocados, asparagus, pomegranates and persimmons, artisan cheeses, smoked fish, milk, cranberry juice, crackers, a stick of salami, chocolate-chip cookies, and vanilla gelato. One would think she had a house full of famished guests. I suggested delivery.

"Will it be you or somebody else? I'd rather it be you," she said.

"I'll ask the manager. If it isn't too far."

"No, just across the road. Bridge Street."

I wrote down her address on one of the bags, and she left, unhurriedly climbing up the ramp.

Late in the evening the store was empty. One of the cashiers yawned while scrolling down on her phone; the other devoted her attention to a peeling strip of her fake nail. They were my age—twenty-nine—also immigrants, but, unlike me, they had their naturalization papers in order. They were half Mexican, half Puerto Rican, with glowing skin and thick ropes of hair. One had a scar above her eyebrow; the other a parrot tattoo on her shoulder that stayed naked even in the winter, her sweater pulled low.

Out the window the girls showed me Sarah's building. She lived in BellTel Lofts, an art deco tower originally constructed as the headquarters of the New York Telephone Company. I needed a cart, since I didn't own a car or a bicycle.

"If you run away with our cart, you're in deep shit," the girl with the scar said.

"What would I do with it? Sell it to Target?" I joked, but they didn't laugh. Yet again I thought how hard it was to make someone laugh in a foreign language. And if you couldn't laugh together, how could you live together? In that sense America remained a mystery to me.

"Oh, and when she talks about her son," the other girl said, "pretend that you don't know he's dead."

"He is dead?" I asked and felt the weight of Sarah's bags in my hands.

"Yeah."

"Cancer?"

"No," the girl with the scar said. "He killed himself."

"Drugs," the other said.

"Overdosed?" I asked.

"Yeah. On purpose. He left a suicide note."

"What did it say?" I asked.

They both shrugged.

"Don't know. There used to be a guy here. He and Sarah's son, they were buddies. He mentioned the note."

"You took his job," the girl with the tattoo said. "He wasn't illegal or anything, but he sort of broke down, started drinking and doping."

"I do neither," I said.

"No, Vlad. Vladimir. You're more dangerous. You invade countries and hijack elections."

They laughed, and I felt a prickle of needles in my spine.

* * *

THE STORE CLOSED at eleven, but I always stayed later to clean up or restock the shelves or just stretch Glad wrap over sliced deli meats. I washed floors too, wiped foggy, fingerprinted coolers, took trash out, and plastered food advertisements over the windows. I also replaced lightbulbs, sorted and discarded rotten produce, swept tables and benches in the back of the store. In short, I did anything the manager asked me to do and for as little money as he could pay an illegal immigrant.

No, I didn't cross the Mexican border on foot. Nor did I enter the country in the belly of a giant ship, hidden amid barrels of dead fish.

My arrival was more prosaic and less strenuous. I entered America legally, on a three-month tourist visa, and then I ended up overstaying it by nine years. I'd brought some money with me, from counterfeiting Levi's jeans and selling them in one of Moscow's markets. I couldn't afford much, but it was enough to carry me into another year until I found a job that paid cash.

When I'd first arrived, I lived with a former classmate in DC. He was a student at George Mason University, a tall, dorky twenty-year-old virgin with Stalin's moustache. We were getting along beautifully until my roommate fell in love, and his girlfriend, a short, plump American from southwest Virginia, insisted he give up his former life for his future one. Vodka, pickles, and black bread for hamburgers, Coke, and apple pie. She moved in, and I moved out, and my classmate stopped speaking Russian, even to me. Still, I didn't want to return home and listen to my mother accusing my father of stealing her youth. Or my father accusing my mother of stealing his country, of forcing her Russian-ness on his Ukrainian-ness. I preferred distance and virtual love. Skype visits.

As I pushed the cart toward Sarah's building, it began to snow again, the flurries landing on my cheeks and lips. A taste of home in my mouth. Across the street, crowned with a red star, a giant Christmas tree stood wrapped in lights. I remembered the last New Year's Eve before I left. A scrawny pine my mother and I had tied to an old sled and dragged through the snow. My father, drunk and asleep in the bathroom. I thought of Sarah, and how bizarre it was that she spoke of her son as though he were still alive while my mother referred to my father as though he were dead. She always mentioned things in past tense, and at some point I stopped correcting her.

When Sarah opened the door, I hesitated for a moment because the person in front of me was almost entirely bald. A few strands of remaining hair were held back with bobby pins. Her apartment smelled of melted wax and a hint of incense. Yet I saw no candles. In fact her home was cold and dark like a cave. I noted no ceiling lights anywhere, which was something I'd encountered in DC and other American cities. It puzzled me because I'd always thought it was a Russian thing—to keep people in the dark.

In the kitchen I placed the grocery bags on the counter. On the other end of the room a petite square table and two chairs sat next to the window. A few large ships stranded in the distance, a shimmer of lights along the shore, the jagged outline of lower Manhattan, like a pop-up Christmas card.

"Wow," I said. "What a view. The Statue of Liberty is over there, right?" I pointed between the two skinny buildings.

She shrugged. "Whoever thought of putting it there."

Her home was larger than expected in a city this crowded. I saw no decorations though, and no tree. Oriental rugs covered the floors. The oak furniture seemed old, frayed, and heavy, yet somehow befitting the apartment, the tall ceilings and soundproof windows. For the first time since I'd arrived in New York, I couldn't hear a shrill of sirens or the hum of exhaust fans. I was entombed in silence. The apartment had three bedrooms, although one without windows, and for some reason I thought that it must have been the room where her son had killed himself. His pictures were displayed everywhere, but they were mostly baby pictures, and a few of a teenager with crooked teeth and red clown hair.

Pointing at the two of them in a gaudy piazza, ambushed by pigeons, I asked, "How old is your son in that picture?"

"Eighteen. We went to Europe right after his graduation. I wanted to show him the other side of the world. I'm German, you know. My parents fled the country right before the war."

When she said that, I felt a pang of resentment. I was three generations removed from the war, but like most Russian-born citizens I grew up celebrating Victory Day and watching military parades in Red Square.

"And your husband?" I asked. "Is he also German?"

"No. American. He died of cancer when Robert was ten."

"Do you ever go back to Germany?"

"Not once. I didn't learn the language either, although my parents spoke it at home. I understood everything, but I refused to speak it. When my mother picked me up from school, I insisted she didn't talk. Robert, on the other hand, took German in college."

"What does he do?" I asked, marveling at how easy it was to pretend that Robert was alive because nothing in Sarah's home contradicted her lie. My question, however, caught her off guard, so she paused, adjusting her turtleneck sweater, pushing the sleeves down and then up, all the way above her sharp elbows. Her skin was white like snow and also translucent. A plexus of veins crawling up her arms.

"Robert is an artist. A painter. He lives in California," she finally said. "Come, I'll show you."

In the corner room with triple windows, the floor was protected with an old stained sheet. Everywhere, against the walls, drawings and paintings leaned in no particular order. Nudes and landscapes, a still life with apples and a dead bird. There was nothing remarkable in those paintings, as far as I could tell, except maybe for the aggressiveness and juxtaposition of colors, fiery orange against seaweed green against rowanberry red. I remembered that in his youth my father also wanted to be an artist, but my mother always said that he had no vision. He could mix paints and knew technique but lacked imagination. He ended up being a mechanic and worked on trains.

Brushes lay on the floor, used rags and tubes of paints. I stepped over them, walking up to a small desk cluttered with colored pencils, erasers, and notepads. I viewed a life-size hand carved from a pale chunk of wood and, next to it, a face cast in white plaster, a kind of a death mask. Eyes shut, lips too, the rest of the features smooth and perfectly delineated. Staring at it made me uncomfortable. I knew it couldn't be her son's face, although did I?

I switched to the easel that displayed an empty canvas initialed at the bottom. There was nothing else on it, yet I kept thinking that I could see something if I looked hard enough.

"It's called '4'33.' After John Cage," Sarah said.

I turned my face to her. "Who?"

"An American composer. Taught at The New School, here in New York. One of his pieces has no notes and lasts four minutes and thirty-three seconds. A performer just sits in front of a piano and does nothing. We're forced to listen to the sounds around us. It's a kind of rebellion against social norms."

"That's a lot of—" I was going to say shit but said, "emptiness."

"Well, it's part of the automatism movement, when the artist wishes to remove himself from the process of creation to achieve higher truth. Because self-expression is really nothing more than an infusion of the art with the social standards to which we've been subjected since birth. Nothing original can come from that. My son says that about painting too—how light touches a blank canvas, baring its irregularities, darker or lighter threads, perhaps even an occasional defect or a shadow. We're forced to study a pure, original form the artist can't control in any way. It's the art of seeing."

I stared at her; the ardor with which she spoke about the blank canvas and her dead son commanded respect. In my family no one spoke of anything with such veneration. My mother cursed profusely while gossiping about her coworkers, their many sex scandals; my father drank on weekends and watched political talk shows, which my mother called impotent or sterile.

I walked to a tall bookshelf in the far corner of the room. I guessed them to be books on painting, and some of them were, as well as on famous artists—Klimt, Schiele, Kandinsky, Magritte, Munch—but most of the books were literary epics. *Moby-Dick*, *War and Peace*, *Grapes of Wrath*, *A Farewell to Arms*, *To the Lighthouse*.

"These are Robert's," Sarah said.

I pulled out the last book, with a woman and the sea on the cover. "Is this one good?"

"Yes. Remarkable."

"Is the author still alive?"

"Virginia Woolf drowned in 1941 in London. During a bombing raid, I believe."

"She went swimming while—" I was going to say Germans but said, "Nazis bombed the place?"

"No. She killed herself. Filled her pockets with stones and walked into the river. Can you imagine the strength?"

"Maybe she was murdered," I said. "Happens in my country a lot."

"I doubt it. There was a suicide note."

"What did it say?"

"I have no idea. Google it."

There was a moment of silence between us, so I said what my mother often said, "Strange how the echo of that war is still here, still haunting us."

"Yes," Sarah said. "It's hard to fathom sometimes."

* * *

THAT NIGHT I read Woolf's suicide note. Addressed to her husband, it started with *Dearest* and ended with *I don't think two people could've been happier than we have been.* I didn't cry of course, but I felt as though I'd been stabbed repeatedly in the chest with a dull knife. She'd loved him not only in life but in death. He was that import-ant to her. I couldn't think of any such person. I loved no one, and no one loved me. Robert left his paintings and one blank canvas. Woolf—the literary masterpieces. All I could bequeath to the world was a pair of fake Levi's.

I called my mother. It was an early morning in Moscow, so I caught her before she left for work. She was a hospital nurse. She hated her job, but she earned good money, more than she could have ever dreamed of earning during the Soviet regime. Although most of that money came from the patients' relatives, who placed cash envelopes in her pockets so she could provide extra care or painkillers. My father used to joke that he needed some too, to spare him from the pain of living with her.

I told my mother about Sarah, and she explained that it wasn't uncommon for people who lost their children to remain in denial.

"When you left for America," she said, "I didn't wash your sheets for a month. I napped on your bed too. But when you didn't come back, I took all your things to the church."

"What? Why did you do that?"

"Why did you drop out of Moscow State and start counterfeiting jeans? You could've become a doctor or a professor. You loved studying."

"Is there anything of mine left in that room?" I asked.

She was silent but then said, "Yes. A book on English grammar."

That book wasn't even mine. She gave it to me before I left, but I never got to study it. I learned everything by ear. "How's Dad?" I asked.

"How the fuck would I know?" she answered.

"Doesn't he call?"

"Where from? Maidan?"

"That's mean."

"What's mean? He left me for his country."

"Why can't you forgive him for being Ukrainian?"

"Why couldn't he forgive me for being Russian?"

I didn't answer; I didn't know what to say. All our arguments started and ended the same way—with a rhetorical question. We both knew the vague, pointless nature of such questions, but we couldn't help ourselves. Our relationship, just as our culture, fed on rhetoric, which didn't contradict the existing order or leadership.

"For once, why can't you pretend not to hate him?" I asked.

"Because. Because he didn't need me to. It was easier for him to fucking hate me if he thought I hated him too. There was no moral dilemma that way: wife, country; country, wife." She sighed. "You aren't coming back, are you? I need to know because I'm thinking about renting out your room. It'd be nice to have some company for the holidays."

I swallowed her words. They fell somewhere deep inside me, where all her words fell.

"Go ahead," I finally said. "I'm staying here."

* * *

A WEEK PASSED, and I finished reading *To the Lighthouse*. Half of it I didn't understand, but the last line tied a knot in my throat. The lengthy ruminations on the meaning of life reminded me of Tolstoy, but the novel was so slim, so delicate. I felt as though I'd entered a new city, its maze of streets and hidden alleys, the mystery, the joy of discovering them one by one, while Tolstoy's novels, as grand as they were, often reminded me of entire countries being under siege.

I hadn't seen Sarah since that evening. She didn't come by or answer my calls. I kept leaving voice mail about fresh turkey, and on Friday afternoon I decided I'd deliver the bird to her. Perhaps she'd caught a cold and couldn't go out or talk on the phone. I also wanted to return to her apartment. I was still curious about her son. On Christmas Eve the store closed early, and I had no place to be. The cashier girls had invited me to a gathering in Queens, but when I imagined riding for a miserable hour on the subway that looked and smelled like a bomb shelter, I abandoned all festive dreams. I thought I'd rather burrow into my rental, a room on Brighton Beach, and gorge on Russian movies from the Revolution to the present day, all the Soviet epics once vetoed by the regime.

The snow fell in large, formless, sticky clusters, the roads turning to mush. The neighborhood felt deserted, except for a group of young people skidding past me. I smelled alcohol and marijuana, its thick, sweet incense. I thought of the night when my father had left my mother, how she stood on the balcony, sucking vodka out of a bottle, cussing him and the rest of the goddamned impotent world. The neighbors called the police. She was so drunk she couldn't even button her shirt, and I ended up doing it for her. Her large naked breasts pressing against my fingers. She smacked me, and smacked me again, then started hitting me in the chest and shoulders, and anywhere she could reach. Her face was awash in rage and tears as she continued to hit me because my countenance and my silence resembled my father's, and also because, just like him, I didn't know how to stop her.

I entered the BellTel Lofts building, rode the elevator to the eleventh floor, and followed a long, dark corridor, which ended at Sarah's apartment. I brushed my coat, stomped and wiped my feet twice before ringing the bell. Sarah didn't answer, so I pressed my ear against the cold gray surface of her door. With a fifteen-pound turkey in three layers of paper bags, I knocked, then rang the bell again, then touched the handle.

The door yielded with a squeak.

"Hello?" I said. "Sarah? Are you home?"

There was no response.

Slowly I stepped into the darkness of her flat. "Sarah, it's Vlad. Vlad from Fresh Market. Hello?"

Stripping off my shoes and jacket, I walked down the hallway. I peeped inside the rooms and turned on the nightlights. Everything seemed in order: the rugs, the furniture, her son's pictures. The books slouching on the shelves, the paintings displayed on the walls. The third bedroom was closed. I remembered that it was the one without windows and that I hadn't seen it.

I knocked. "Sarah? Are you in there? It's Vlad. I brought fresh turkey."

I pushed the door open and at first noticed nothing but a bed or a couch pulled out into a bed. It was low, draped with blankets, under which a body lay motionless. The room smelled of unwashed clothes, but nothing else, nothing putrefying or decaying.

The turkey weighted down my arm, so I set the bag on a chair. I could now see that, unlike the rest of the apartment, the room was in disarray. Sheets flung about the floor, sweaters, pants, underwear. A heap of T-shirts in the corner. A tennis shoe, a soccer ball, a stack of newspapers, which must have come from another century because who read newspapers today? As I approached the bed, I halted, not sure if I was ready to experience death in close proximity. At my grandmother's funeral, the open casket had terrified me.

It was Sarah's body under the blanket. I recognized her sharp profile, her beak of a nose and bald, ostrich-egg head. Her eyes were shut, and no matter how hard I squinted, I couldn't tell whether she was breathing. I smelled something earthy, like moss on trees. My throat tightened. I could hear myself swallow thick pockets of air. Before getting any closer to the bed, I searched for a floor lamp. I found none and took a few steps backward, pushing the door wider.

Sarah opened her eyes, but otherwise didn't move.

"Oh, good," I said, exhaling. "You aren't dead. I was afraid you were. I knocked, but you didn't answer."

She closed her eyes, and I thought that maybe she'd had a stroke and couldn't talk.

"Are you okay?" I asked.

She blinked twice then stared at me, still saying nothing. Her eyes were cold and glassy, as though frozen with tears. My discomfort rose. My ears burned. A tingling sensation in my arms and legs.

"Sarah, please, can you say something?"

I walked to the bed and squatted, placing my hand on hers. It felt lifeless, the skin chaffed and scaly. On the floor, near the foot of the bed, I spotted a piece of paper and picked it up. Somehow I thought it was a suicide note. I flipped it over. The paper was blank on both sides. I flipped it and flipped it again before dropping it. I didn't know what else to do. I studied Sarah's face, so calm and pale like a mask. Her wrinkles barely visible in the dark. Her lips folded, a large mole on her neck.

The apartment filled with silence.

I imagined being submerged underwater, sinking to the bottom of a river, the weight of stones in my pockets. I imagined my mother's face as my body would be discovered weeks later, the things she would yell at my father, him dumbfounded against the wall. I imagined never seeing them again. Them never seeing each other. Not a word passing between us for eternity.

"Sarah," I said. "Please get up. If you don't get up, I'll call the police. And they'll call the paramedics, who'll pronounce you 'incapable' and sign you off to some guardian, who'll take charge of your apartment and your life. You'll be placed in a nursing home, where they'll keep pumping you with drugs until you die."

She ignored me.

"Okay, then, I'll ransack the apartment and steal jewelry and set the place on fire. Everything will burn. You too."

No response.

I finally stood up and shuffled to the corner room and dragged back the easel and the blank canvas, brushes, paints, and a heap of crusted rags. From the living room I transplanted a floor lamp and plugged it in. The place illuminated with a halo of light.

With the corner of her eye, Sarah watched me squeeze a thick layer of rusty paint on a flat-tipped brush. I raised my arm and paused, waiting for her to stop me.

She didn't.

"This painting isn't finished," I said. "It needs shit. Like family, sea, a fucking lighthouse."

In a single bold gesture, I touched the brush to the canvas.

"No!" she yelled. "Don't ruin it. It's perfect."

I drew a crooked line in the middle just as she rose from the bed and grabbed my hand. "Don't you dare touch his things. You, you"— her lips quivered—"why did you come? What do you need? Why can't you leave me alone?"

"Because," I said.

"Because why?"

"Because I'm hungry, and it's Christmas, and I brought turkey, and I have no place to cook it."

She dropped my hand, and I dropped the brush. It landed on my foot, coloring my sock.

"I'm not cooking any turkey for you," she said in that same husky voice that reminded me of dead trees. "I haven't cooked in ages."

"What about Robert? Don't you cook for him?"

"Robert?" She hesitated, as though recalling a long-forgotten face. "Robert died years ago. And before that he never visited. Not even on Christmas. He hated me."

Her eyes pooled with tears. Her shoulders trembled, her chest heaved, her whole body convulsing, one silent wave after another.

I felt the need to embrace her.

I remembered how my mother always accused my father of never feeling sorry for her. How all she ever wanted was for him to pity her—when she had her periods, when she worked night shifts, when she'd gained weight, when I left for America. But he refused to succumb, and he refused to pretend. Instead he demanded pity from her—because he'd lost his independence, his country, his desire, his masculinity, because he'd abandoned his dream of becoming an artist.

I inched closer to Sarah and placed my hand on her shoulder, slowly wrapping my arms around.

"Robert hated me," she whispered, her voice soft and cold like snow.

"No, he didn't," I said, also in a whisper. "He only pretended. Sometimes we all do."

She sighed, a chestful of air, then shook her head, but it seemed that she was nodding too.

I suddenly felt extreme fatigue, as if I'd just crossed the ocean in a small boat, smashing through storms, whipped by rain and wind. I didn't know who I was, who my parents were, or why I'd left home. I remembered being hurt, stubborn, the feeling of absolute freedom and absolute powerlessness. Years, places, experiences, all blurred together except for one. One evening. A Christmas Eve in some old woman's home. A room lit by a floor lamp. A smell of paint. Two people, amid rags and brushes. The way the shadows lingered on the wall.

Second Person

Do not reply.

Do not say something you will regret later. Pretend you didn't hear. Pause for breath. Sip the air. Imagine being a fish. Swim away. Hide in the water. Do not return. Stop feeling guilty about things you can't change. Start changing the things you can. Shake off fear. Smile. Make peace. Move on. Think of the times you shared. Of the years you spent together. Of the happiness you brought to each other. The intimacy. The longing. Forgive and forget. Embrace the sadness. Let go of grief. Let go.

"Don't just sit there, Peas, ogling the dessert menu, playing deaf. Say something."

Stall for an answer.

Contemplate the flimsy greenish paper in your hands. See above the lines. Watch her pull a lipstick out of her purse then slide the black cap off and twist the tube and dab pink shimmer in a mindless gesture against her broad, pulpy lips. Do not get distracted. Focus on the menu. Read in the brackets. So what if it's the last evening, the last dinner, the last conversation between you two as a couple. Keep your head up, your eyes down, your hands on the menu.

Say, "Death by Chocolate looks good."

Curt.

Nothing personal. Nothing to regret later. Polite. As always. That's your downside. Your flaw masked as a merit. Your petit bourgeois upbringing. Your mother's hopeless smiles and coiffed hair. Your father's gray double-breasted suits and stiff-collared shirts. Cultured tea roses in your family garden. Pathetic yellow. Shameful red.

"That's it? That's the best you can do, Peas?"

Need to ask her not to call you Peas again. You no longer like that name. It feels small, uncomfortable. It doesn't fit.

"Peas?"

"What?"

"I asked you a question."

"What was the question? I'm sorry."

Have to stop apologizing for something you didn't do. You possess many faults. Forgetting is not one of them. It simply does not run in your genes, in your family, where children have been taught discipline and the word "mine" from the moment they latched on to their bottles.

"Are you okay?"

"Define okay."

"Now you're being spiteful."

No answer.

Nothing to say. Isn't that how all of your conversations ended in the past few months? She asks a question for which you don't have an answer. For which no one has an answer. Because they aren't really questions—they don't end with a question mark but a period or three dots. It reminds you of playing soccer by yourself. You can't lose. You can't win. But toss a ball around a field of green, kicking and running after it. Need to stop feeling sorry for yourself. Pull together. Put the goddamn menu down. Face your partner. Your ex-lover. Your long, drawn-out spring. Your well of happiness and pit of misery. Face the girl she no longer is.

Say, "I'm okay. I'm better than okay. I'm fine. Yes, fine."

Too many words. You're a writer. You should avoid repetition. Should know better. She taught you that. You owe her the clarity that you possess. The pulse your stories have now. The beat.

"No, you're not. I can hear it in your voice. You've never been a good liar."

True. Your mother taught you that if you lied once, you would always have to remember that lie. And nobody can do that. Not even your father. One lie begets another, until your whole life is nothing but a web of stories you pass around as your own. But isn't that what writers do? Spin stories from lies? Weave hope into an otherwise hopeless existence? Try to make sense where there is none?

Watch her shake her head, spilling copper-streaked hair over her shoulders.

You love this hair.

And this loose curl caressing her perfect ear adorned with a diamond star. You gave her that star five years ago. You even put it in, screwing the gold post through a tiny hole in her earlobe. Should have given her a baby instead, the baby she always wanted, dreamed about. You could have adopted or conceived in a lab. She could have carried it to term. You could have watched her give birth. But you bought her a diamond star and went back to writing a book. Your book. Her story.

"You need a haircut, Peas. You look . . . older."

"I *am* older."

"Don't get mad."

"I'm not."

"Yes, you are. But you won't show it. You're not being honest. Like that character in your last story. She's afraid to act. Afraid to be honest with her partner."

"She doesn't have a partner. The partner leaves."

"It's because the character isn't honest, even with herself. You ought to rewrite that story."

"Don't fucking tell me what to write."

Shouldn't have said that.

Shouldn't have. Shouldn't have done many things. Encouraging her to fly to Moscow for her high school reunion was one of them. Welcoming her old classmate into your house, hosting him under your roof, was another. Do not mull over the details. Do not inflict more pain. Need to switch topics. Cut your hair. Just cut it.

"I'm sorry, Peas. I am."

No, she is not.

Or maybe she is. But what difference does it make now? It won't change a damn thing. You know it won't. She's moving in with the guy. That sly, disgusting, worthless asshole, who's just using her to get a green card. But what can you do to stop her? Nothing. Absolutely nothing. The same feeling of total powerlessness as when your mother announced for the sixth time that she was pregnant. Your father's prideful grin wider than the table you all sat at. Your younger brother slipped from his high chair and pulled his pants down and started to wet the rug. Your mother, waving her thorn-pricked hands in the air, snapped at you to stop him, grab him, do something. Reaching for a dirty soup bowl on the table, your hand brought the bowl down to catch the urine. Your father threw his napkin on the floor. Your younger sisters slid under the table, tickled with laughter. But you didn't even smile. You thought it wasn't funny. You got tired of being a diaper disposal in that family. Tired of being in charge. Of being older. Always watching out for your siblings. Conceding to their selfish, baby ways.

"Peas, can you promise me something?"

"Anything."

"Don't say anything until you know what it is."

Look at her and then away.

Seek movement outside the table. Some sort of distraction that will ease the tension, relax your shoulders, relieve your gaze. It's getting late. The restaurant no longer buzzes with people. The waitress is sipping a glass of disturbing-red at the bar. You should go. Should pay for the dinner, get up, and leave. Kiss her good-bye. A friendly peck on the cheek. Do not ask for her new number. Just go. Leave.

"Will you stay in touch, Peas?"

"No."

Firm.

Shouldn't let her torture you anymore. Need to return home. Burrow in books. Unplug the phone. Write the best goddamn story you've ever written. Pray to get better and over, over her.

"Why, Peas? Why won't you stay in touch?"

"Why?"

"I asked first."

"It's no use. I see no point. No point whatsoever. It's all worthless and meaningless. A waste of time, energy, breath."

She's getting to you. She always does. She knows how. Knows the way. You've shown her. You let her in. And out. Have to shut that door. Shut it now. Change the lock. Seal the cracks. You can do it. You're an award-winning author. People listen to what you have to say. They praise your books, the books you wrote daily, nightly, hiding in the attic, while she waited for you in the kitchen, cooking and eating her meals in solitude, or in bed, dosing off with pages of your manuscript sprawled atop her blissful breasts.

"So you're just going to cut me out of your life for good?"

"For good."

"That's not fair, Peas."

"Fair?!"

The waitress turns to look at you. The bartender too.

Try not to raise your voice. Not to show your anger, your defeat. Curl your toes inside your shoes. Repeat, "Fair?"

"Yes. Fair. You aren't being fair."

She pisses you off. The very sight of her. This hair, swept casually to one side. These green, shady eyes. Her low, full-of-deceiving-tremor voice. Watch her hands slide under the table and pet that invisible belly of hers, the life that buds inside as the two of you speak. It could have been yours. She could have been yours. Selfish. You're being selfish. Selfish and scared. Scared that when she's gone from your life, you won't write a thing. Won't produce pages and pages of images she's taught you to envision, emotions she incites you to unleash. Your work will dwindle. You'll become the apparition your mother has become after your father left the family. The roses have grown wild, overtaking the garden, pushing against the fence.

Say, "Life isn't fair, is it?"

"No. Not always. But we choose what we want or don't want to be."

"I see. You chose some—"

Search for the right word.

Do not rush.

Try not to sound cruel.

He's the father of the baby she's been waiting for all her life. He is—"stranger." Yes. Stranger. You did well. No other description is necessary or preferable. Nothing suits better. "You chose some stranger over me."

"I didn't choose anybody over you. You'll always be—"

"What?"

She doesn't answer. Tightens her lips, pouts. The gesture that is all too familiar, all too adorable.

Press your finger to her lips then hide your hand in your pocket. Pray to disappear. Disintegrate. Turn into dust. Sift through the floorboards.

"You know I never meant to hurt you, Peas. But I always wanted a baby. I'm old-fashioned, I guess. I can't even tell my parents that I'm—"

"Gay?"

"They're Russian, Peas. They see women as mothers first and then as everything else. I know you think it's pathetic. But I've never lied to you."

"No. You haven't. Only about sleeping with men. Men, for Christ's sake."

"One. One man. Well, in my younger days, before we met. You said you tried sleeping with men too, but it didn't work out."

"No. It didn't. And I wasn't planning on going back either. And I certainly wasn't planning on cheating with a man. I wasn't planning on cheating. Period. I was happy with you. I thought you were happy too."

There.

You said it. All the right words in all the right order. All the spaces intact. Nothing to add. Nothing to take out. Ask for the check and get up. Do not look at her. Bite your tongue. Swallow your tears. Move.

"Of course I was happy. Even when I had to share you with your books. I knew you needed me, so I stayed as long as I could. But now my baby needs me. I need me."

Do not beg.

Do not say a word. Let her go. She has the right to be whom or what she wants. She has the courage not to drag you into this, not to force fetters of motherhood on your liberated, childless soul. If she stays, you'll become a diaper genie, Mom number two or number one. Doesn't matter. You'll stop writing. You'll cook, clean, nurse the baby you want as much as she does. You'll squander hours, like your mother, in baby sections of department stores, picking out cute outfits, toys, ridiculous tiny shoes. You'll be wasted. Spent. Miserable. You'll stop being you—this eccentric, five-foot-nine lesbian, worshipped for her prose, adored for her wit, defying the boredom of conventional marriage the world has imposed upon generations of sad, helpless women. You'll stop breathing.

Halt. Turn around. Crumple the restaurant check inside your pocket, eyeing her fair Russian face.

Say, "Be safe. Give me your new number. I'll stay in touch."

Gene Therapy

Some women on my mother's side of the family possessed magic powers—that is they could hear, see, and feel things other people couldn't. For example, in June of 1941, right before the war broke out, my great-grandmother, who'd just finished nursing her daughter, stretched in the grass and put her ear to the earth. She remained motionless for some time, but then jumped to her feet, scooped the baby in her arms, and ran through the field toward the village. As she reached her hut, she threw a blanket over the bed and started gathering her possessions, the few that she could carry. She piled shirts and underwear, cloth diapers and crib sheets, a small jar of lard and a hunk of soap. She was about to tie the ends of the blanket together when she spotted her wedding picture on the wall, her husband's genial face next to hers. My great-grandmother lifted the picture off the nail and added it to the hump of clothes on the bed. As she hoisted the bundle over her shoulder, she already knew that her husband, as well as the rest of the villagers, would be executed behind the old church, the village burned to the ground.

Years later, when I asked my grandmother Grusha why her mother hadn't warned the others, including her husband, who was at work on a collective farm that day, she said, "There was no time. The first German planes appeared in the sky just as she pushed the boat into the river. It was a crippled boat too; the bottom had rotted. Your great-grandmother had to bail the water out with her shoes. She'd also fitted a broken tree branch into one of the smaller holes, tying me inside an old pillowcase to the raised end, away from the water. The boat didn't have any oars and drifted downstream while my mother tried to steer it with her hands."

"How long did you drift like that?" I asked.

"Who knows," my grandmother said. "Days, weeks. Until one morning she woke up and found herself on a muddy bank of the Volkhov River, near the great city of Novgorod. Hundred kilometers away from her village. The boat was beaten to pieces, all but the place where the tree branch poked through the broken hull, with me still in the pillowcase."

While I was growing up Grusha had told me the story many times, never missing a detail. She also told me that soon after her mother had crawled ashore, she was discovered by a group of partisans living in the underground vaults of the Novgorod Kremlin. The Nazis had already occupied the city and were about to bomb St. Sofia Cathedral, built around 1050 by the son of Prince Yaroslav the Wise. The cathedral was the oldest structure in the city and probably in all Russia, with its white stone walls and five golden helmet-like domes. Even from afar, starved and emaciated, in a state that was closer to death than to life, my great-grandmother could see that the towers were missing the bells, the cathedral austere and silent behind the massive bronze gates. Later, as she joined the partisans, my great-grandmother learned that the bells had been hidden, along with other monuments and relics of ancient architecture, precious icons and frescoes, crucifixes, birch-bark letters, and the oldest Slavic books. Many citizens would be tortured to death by the Nazis, but no one would reveal what the partisans had done with the bells. Every day the Nazis would hang five people in the bell towers, waiting for others to confess. But they refused to talk, mute as the river.

My great-grandmother was captured late one night when she emerged from the vaults to procure milk for the baby. The next morning she was stripped naked and dragged across the city by her hair tied to a horse's tail. She had endured hours and hours of interrogations, lost teeth, fingers, skin. In the end they cut out her tongue and let her witness the bombing of the cathedral, where hundreds of terrified women and children had been herded like cattle. Within seconds after the explosion, the heavy oak doors crashed to the ground, revealing a heap of bodies in a pool of blood and smoke. Yet the indomitable walls survived, so did the towers, and that was when my great-grandmother knew that the Nazis would lose the war and they would never find the bells.

Grusha, of course, didn't remember her mother, who'd died soon after the bombing. My grandmother heard the story from another woman in Novgorod, who'd lived in the vaults with the partisans and raised Grusha after the war. The woman had no idea what had happened to the bells, and no one was left to ask. When I was still a child, I kept barraging my grandmother, as well as my mother, with the same questions: "How could the partisans hide those massive bells, the largest weighing twenty-seven tons? How could they have lifted them? Brought them down?" And the women would shrug and say, "It's a divine mystery, but it's all true."

* * *

WE'VE ALWAYS BEEN close—the three of us—and I could never imagine leaving Grusha and my mother or that someday they wouldn't be a part of my family. They were honest laboring women who'd endowed me with the kind of care and love that felt immortal. I reveled in that love and their ceaseless, heady nurturing. They talked about history and personal experiences, hunger and pain as though they continued living through them, as though nothing ever ended but coexisted in parallel worlds. They didn't joke much, and when they laughed on occasion, they opened their mouths wide, their laughter like a gurgle of water in the back of their throats. They bathed me, dressed me, and fed me, smearing sunflower oil on my skin and braiding my hair, sending me to school every morning. They stuffed coin rubles and knitted toys in my slippers on my birthdays and added chamomile flowers to my tea when I had trouble sleeping, their voices growing soft like yarns of wool. They sewed my first bra that made my breasts poke out of dresses in a sensual adult way, and when I had my period, they fried calves' livers to replenish my iron. Their cooking wasn't too elaborate, yet the meals they prepared agreed with the season and the weather.

We lived in a small log house on the outskirts of the city, facing the Volkhov River, where as a child I spent days swimming until my lips turned violet and my skin was prickly with goose bumps. Behind the house there was a patch of land, where the women planted anything that would grow, including pumpkins and sunflowers that stretched toward the sky and could be seen from the road, beckoning at strangers. The ardor, the zeal, with which Grusha and my mother worked on that land, grooming and combing it with their bare hands. From early spring until late fall they hovered among the rows, their robust arms outlined by crude cotton shirts, strands of hair like pieces of straw clinging to their sweaty faces. In winter Grusha fermented kraut in a squatty wooden barrel, and our pantry was stocked with jars of pickles, squash, and wild mushrooms like alien creatures preserved in vinegar. We owned chickens, pigs, rabbits, and one cow that produced enough milk to barter with the neighbors or sell at the market, along with eggs and pork. We had a small orchard too; the women pruned it every fall and spread manure under the apple trees that had been planted after the war and still yielded bountiful crops. The fruit, though small and crunchy, was nonetheless sweet; it kept well, heaping in baskets, so that even in the dead of winter our cellar smelled like summer.

Until I moved away I didn't pay much attention to the women's appearances, nor could I separate the two. They were coarse-skinned and rouged from being outdoors or cooking over open fire and had gray hair braided and pinned into heavy nests at the back of their heads. For women, they were tall, with splendid hips and bosoms that instilled comfort in babies and men. Both my grandfather and my father had died when I was still a baby, but the absence of a male figure in our household didn't affect my upbringing or self-esteem, the feeling of happiness and completeness that grew around me like garden vines around the picket fence.

* * *

IN 2003, when I was twenty-two and about to graduate from Novgorod State University, I attended an international science fair in Moscow, where I met my future husband. Fred was tall, handsome, with tan skin and dark roomy eyes, and a kind, pure expression of someone who belonged not only to a different country but to a different, bygone era of medieval gallantries and courtship. He held doors open for me, warmed my shoulders with his jackets, and listened to me mispronounce English words without a fleck of irritation. He was shy, studious, and trustworthy, if a bit sentimental. He radiated goodness and care, and his moods never depended on food or weather, the color of the sky. He was only two years older but had traveled extensively, ravenous for other cultures. We fell in love so quickly, irrevocably—a karmic gesture, you might say—that I didn't have the time to comprehend my future, what it would mean to marry a foreigner. A week after the fair, Fred returned to America, but we exchanged long, passionate letters until my fiancée visa came through, and I began tossing things into my suitcase: books, clothes, CDs and photo albums, household trinkets, years' worth of life to be carried overseas. Neither Grusha nor my mother objected to my marrying Fred, but they remained tight-lipped while watching me pack, handing me a birch-wood comb or a faded icon painted on a piece of cardboard.

The next morning, before a bus took me to the airport, Grusha and my mother scurried to the garden, scooped some dirt into an old hand-knitted sock, tied it, and stuffed it inside my coat pocket. "Keep it close," they said. "Always." They didn't cry even though I was about to, and they didn't promise to visit even though I kept begging them and refused to get on the bus until I saw them nod—a vague gesture that, perhaps, in my longing and eagerness to see Fred, I imagined.

Though I'd never before traveled outside of Russia, I'd adjusted to my new immigrant and married status with little difficulty. At the beginning everything appealed to me: food, people, TV shows, all swept into the afterglow of the honeymoon caresses. I didn't have a language barrier either, although at first I'd seemed immune to American jokes. And vice versa—they failed to laugh at mine. But I'd taken English classes both in high school and at the university, so I was able to communicate with Fred and his family without much effort, albeit with occasional confusion. For example, I wanted to buy potting soil but mixed up the words "soil" and "land." When I asked Fred where I could buy some land, he laughed and said, "How much land? And where at?" I looked miserably perplexed, and he brushed the hair away from my cheeks, smiling, tickling my jawline with his lips.

Months passed, and then years, but my mother and grandmother didn't express any desire to travel to America, claiming that they couldn't

leave the garden, the house, the land that demanded their labor and protection. I suggested visiting one summer with Fred, but they remained
silent, devoid of all curiosity, any urge to meet him. We still talked on
the phone, but their persistent reticence became cumbersome; less and
less I could relate to their lives, their self-imposed isolation from me and
the rest of the world. I complained to Fred, and he tried to assuage me
by driving to a Russian grocery store, for black bread and herring.

Five years into the marriage Fred and I had been admitted to
graduate school, both pursuing a degree in biochemistry, with a
special interest in molecular biology. Fascinated with genes and gene
expression, we studied the molecular underpinnings of the process
of replication, transcription, and translation of the genetic material,
the interactions between the various systems of a cell, including the
interactions between DNA, RNA, and protein synthesis. At Virginia
Polytechnic Institute in Blacksburg, we found part-time teaching
positions and spent countless hours at their research lab.

Our colleagues at other schools kept creating an assortment of
clones, with each one expressing a specific protein, in the quest for
a particular gene. The cells were cultured and then studied, and the
cells that produced the relevant gene were isolated for further study.
Gene therapy, however, appealed to us even more as a way of insert-
ing genes into a patient's cells and replacing the preexisting allele to
perform some therapeutic function. What had never occurred to us
at the time was the simple fact that cultural environment sometimes
behaves like a viral vector, much in the same way normal viruses
introduce their own genetic material into human cells.

What Fred and I also didn't know was that by altering one's genetic
environment, we altered the cells' inherited immunity, their resistance
to new strands of viruses. Sooner or later the patient's body weakened
in its attempt to reconcile the native cells with those being implanted.
It began to exile its own cells. Although we would never have any
scientific proof, nothing we could test in a lab and compile into a

dissertation, back in our graduate years we'd been convinced that science held answers to all the riddles of the universe, and we were eager to spend our lives proving it.

We rented a matchbox apartment downtown, biked to work, and ate most of our meals at The Cellar, where the chef wasn't afraid to experiment. The setting was simple and even crude, red walls, pale wooden tables and benches.

"Technically, lettuce is alive too," Fred said once at dinner.

"It has no eyes and no mouth and no ears. Its vegetative state is unlikely to evolve into a more sophisticated matter," I said.

"But it can still be genetically modified."

I smiled and raised a wad of salad to my lips. I tasted vinegar, perhaps too much from the dressing, and felt a bit light-headed; my fork fell on the table.

"What's wrong?" Fred's upper lip puffed out like a mushroom cap.

"Don't know. The salad tastes weird."

"Perhaps it does have ears and refuses to be eaten." Fred touched my hand, knitted the skin. His fingers warm, soothing.

The rest of the evening I spent on the couch, Fred a hovering presence by my side. He made me some chamomile tea, which, too, had an unpleasant, bitter sting. A few hours later, after cozying next to him, I managed to drift off while watching the History Channel, where they talked about natural disasters and how some animals would sense danger and stop eating or drinking.

"Pregnant," my mother and Grusha mouthed into the receiver the next morning. "A boy," they added, with a bit of puzzled reluctance as though I had a choice in the matter.

I felt nauseated and crawled to the bathroom, where I threw up.

* * *

THE FOLLOWING MONTHS became an eternity to me. What the doctors called morning sickness lasted days and nights. I arranged to go on medical leave without pay, but Fred often had to stay home too, because I couldn't get up from bed without falling back on it, my body as though pierced with hooks. I couldn't eat, except for a few slices of rye bread. Heat waves ran through my spine, a riot of flesh and muscles under my skin. My face thinned out and stretched, my complexion grew sallow. Grusha and my mother phoned regularly, and for those brief moments I would feel myself again, not pregnant or living thousands of kilometers away. The women sounded close by, their voices slipping through clouds and brick walls, lulling my weary flesh.

Twice I was about to lose the child and stayed at the hospital, where Fred kept a vigil by my bed, his cautious fingers sweeping the dome of my belly. Then the doctors told me that the placenta had begun to separate, I wouldn't carry the baby to term; after all those weeks of wait and struggle, they would operate, but they couldn't guarantee the baby would live at six months. Fred cried as he leaned to kiss a patch of veins like an imprint of a tiny foot above my navel. He held my hands and then my face, his lips raw, eyes dilated with tears.

Grusha and my mother called the night before the procedure. "Where's the sock with the dirt?" they asked.

"Sock? What sock?" I tried to concentrate. We had moved several times since I arrived in America, and the sock must have been left behind, thrown away by mistake.

"Come home," they said. "You're too far away. No one can help you there." Their words stung with urgency, and I felt compelled to obey.

In the next twenty-four hours I packed what little I could, and Fred drove me to DC, where I boarded a plane, despite my husband's protests and the doctor's warnings, the fear of a possible uterine rupture during a ten-hour flight. Fred wanted to escort me, but it would've taken weeks to obtain his visa, and the baby, of course, couldn't wait that long.

Contrary to the dreadful prognosis, I fell asleep almost as soon as the plane became airborne and didn't wake up until it was about to land, my body as though cocooned inside a soft invisible blanket. Once I stood up, however, I was sore, nauseated, and swollen. I wobbled through the airport terminal, hunched, the weight of my belly in my hands. Grusha and my mother met me at the doors, their heads covered with gray-wool shawls. From afar they didn't look any different than six years ago, the same tall, ample-hipped bodies, with tanned muscular arms and fierce bosoms. They pulled the duffle bag off my shoulder and my purse, draping a fuzzy shawl over my head, just like the ones they wore.

"It might get chilly," my mother said.

"The wind is stronger by the river," Grusha added.

As we exited the airport, my surprise escalated when I spotted an old-fashioned carriage—a horse and a buggy padded with hay and old quilts.

"Are you serious?" I asked, shaking my head.

They didn't answer but climbed into the buggy. Grusha grabbed the reins while my mother helped pull me in. The horse snorted and took a slow step; Grusha goaded it, tightening and wrapping the reins around her fists. Cars and trucks screeched by while our buggy crossed the two lanes of traffic and swerved on a deserted country road, rutted yet dry.

It was mid-July, clouds of heat and dust rising from the horse's weighty hooves. The sky was blue, combed with feathery clouds. In the distance the river shimmered, the sunlight trapped in its dark silky folds. Oddly enough I no longer was nauseated, my body anointed by a thick smell of hay and the horse's monotonous steps. My mother raised a basket on her knees and peeled away the layers of cheesecloth, revealing what was inside: hard-boiled eggs, herring, spikes of green onion, and a head of rye loaf. There was even a piece of gooseberry pie, tucked in a soft cotton napkin, and a bottle of water that somehow remained cool.

Insatiable, I drank and chewed, and my mother kept excavating more food from the basket.

"Eat," she said. "Eat all you can." Her voice came in gusts, tearing through the clatter of hooves and wheels. "And when the time comes, we'll boil you *hash*."

"*Hash*? What *hash*? When will I see a doctor, a gynecologist?" I asked.

"You are not. We'll take care of you and the baby. The land will provide."

My body shuddered and broke in heat waves, from all the food I'd ingested and also the wind that grew rebellious and unyielding as we approached Novgorod. The five golden domes of St. Sofia Cathedral burned in the late-afternoon sun. The bell towers were still empty, still silent, like mouths without tongues. All of a sudden I began thinking about molecular genetics and how if a gene could be expressed, it could also be suppressed, silenced. My fingers probed the hump of my belly, which had ripened in just a few hours, and I could see an islet of healthy pink skin where the T-shirt rolled up above my belly button.

* * *

IN THE COURSE of the next weeks other transformations began to take place inside and outside my body. Gone were the pains, the nausea, the feeling of tension and miserable displacement, the throbbing pressure in the lower abdomen. I could sleep through the night, my body in perfect alignment with my spirit. My breasts swelled even more, perched on top of my belly, which doubled its size. My hair was much thicker and shinier, lying braided across my shoulder, the old-peasant way. My cheeks grew plump and magenta-pink, as though rubbed with beets, which the women urged me to eat raw out of the garden. They made me work there too, waking up at dawn, before the heat began to scorch our backs. They allowed no gloves or shoes, only loose cotton garments and large straw hats. The three of us squatted between the rows, the soil cool and dewy underfoot. We pulled weeds, tied and retied tomato bushes disheveled by wind or birds. Plucking radishes, carrots, cucumbers, and green onions, we carried the vegetables inside our skirts, hems folded. When I got hot or tired, I dipped water from the well and splashed it on my face and neck, the icy drops stinging my flesh, turning into rivulets.

Sometimes when my back and feet ached from squatting or bending, I plopped in the grass and watched the women work in silence, the air thick, musty, sweet with pollen. Fields of wheat sprawled around, tall and bountiful; they rustled their silky stalks in the breeze, and nothing else could be heard for kilometers. The longer I sat, the more I could feel the earth sprouting its roots through me, binding me to the place of my birth.

"This soil," Grusha said, "feel how rich it is, how fertile." She patted some into my hand. "Your baby needs it. Just like you."

"But we must return to America. The baby needs his father. *I* need him." I'd been away for two months, calling Fred nearly every day. I missed him, his quiet assertive ways and soft lips, how he could add a romantic tremor to any rainy evening.

Suddenly I felt a pool of water spreading under me.

"It's time," Grusha said and beckoned at my mother, who carried an apron of wild mushrooms, shuffling through the grass. She paused, releasing the hem; the mushrooms spilled on the ground, but my mother didn't bother to collect them.

I was in labor for three excruciating days, during which the women cooled my sweating body with wet cloths and brought to my lips clay mugs of bitter herbs. I wasn't allowed to eat or drink anything else. Meanwhile, in a large cauldron the women boiled cow legs, from the knees to the hooves, cleaned from bristle and cut up. The *hash* had been cooking for the last twenty-four hours, and they kept skimming gray sediment, until the broth became clear and the skin and ligaments tender, easily detached. The smell drifted through the house, swirled up my nostrils; my body heaved and shook. The pain continued to move lower, pulling at my womb with its fibrous tentacles. I felt my bones sever from my flesh, my muscles contracting with the force of a choking animal. The women raised me up and let me sip the concoction, whispering about its healing properties, the power of marrow and tendons. The broth was translucent, pure, without salt or pepper or any spices, but as soon as I swallowed the first spoon, my body convulsed with pain. I pushed up and vomited all over my belly, minuscule red cells regurgitated amid the liquid mass.

When I opened my eyes again, the baby lay between my legs, purplish, shiny, squirming in a pool of blood and mucus. The women brought him to me—the umbilical cord dragging across the sheets—and pressed his scrunched, fist-like face to my lips. He was no bigger than a lizard, those gluey eyes and lucent body; he writhed and opened his tiny mouth, where I placed my pinkie. He suckled, then spat, then pouted, and finally cried. The women cut the cord with a knife and tied the baby's belly button like they would a balloon, then removed the afterbirth, from which they carved out an egg-shaped piece and ordered me to eat it. They pushed the bloody mass between my lips, their hot hands brushing my head and the baby's.

"He needs your strength," they said. "Now chew, chew."

* * *

SIX WEEKS AFTER the delivery, I flew back to America, to be with my husband—the desire to see him and to show him the baby had become unbearable. Fred called twice a day and threatened to leave his job and fly over if I didn't return. The women didn't contradict my decision but accepted it as they accepted thunderstorms and blizzards, the inescapable strikes of nature. They filled another old sock with garden dirt and made potato dumplings for the trip. They were quiet, carrying the baby to the checkpoint and entrusting him into my arms, crossing the air in front of his sweet plump face. Tears as heavy as river pebbles fell from my eyes, but I couldn't reach to wipe them and neither could Grusha or my mother. Slowly the women raised the collars of their weathered coats and trudged in the direction of the exit.

As soon as the plane took off, the baby woke up, ready to nurse. No one was sitting next to me, so I pulled up my gray sweater, which resembled a warrior's hauberk, that Grusha had finished knitting the night before. I brought the boy to my breast and, while he suckled, peered out the window. The city of Novgorod sprawled below: the churches, the old Kremlin, St. Sofia Cathedral, Lake Ilmen and Lake Ladoga on opposite ends of the Volkhov River. Boats furrowed the water; from the distance they appeared like tiny vectors binding to cell membranes.

The higher the plane climbed, the more the imprint of the city resembled a molecular structure of a living organism, the flow and exchange of genetic information within a biological system, the DNA spirals of bridges and groups of ancient buildings like cells collecting into the epithelium, the nervous, muscle, and connective tissues. For a moment, within that complex multicellular system of metabolic pathways, I thought I'd spotted a horse and a buggy on the rutted country road, plodding studiously along the river. The sun was red and low, half-sunken in the water, alloys of copper and tin in the dark bronze current. And just then I knew what the partisans had done with the church bells in 1941 and that the next time I would visit the place, years into the future, the women wouldn't be there. I'd be telling my son about his great-great-grandmother, the war, the missing bells, the story of his miraculous birth, and he'd be asking: "How could the partisans have drowned the bells and nobody saw them do it? How could Grusha and my grandmother have saved my life when no doctor could?" And I'd be shrugging and saying, "It's a divine mystery, but it's all true."

And What Rough Beast

I

Imagine a place far away, a farmhouse with rain-speckled windows and a woodstove, where a woman bakes breads, stews vegetables, and cooks all her family meals. She has long buckwheat hair that meanders down her back like a river. To her five-year-old daughter, she's an angel, a fairy creature, who gives life to everything she touches—flour, cloth, soil she tills with spellbinding ease and ardor. Seedlings thrive under her touch, dough swells and rises into mountains, chickens lay twice as many eggs. The woman has a sweet, lilting voice that splashes over her daughter like sunshine over the earth and causes golden tremors to run up the girl's body. She springs from her bed as her eyes behold the dear face, arms unfolding in sheer tenderness.

It's dawn, a scratch of a new day on the horizon, a lick of reddish light. The air is damp, bare. The sun yawns from a tangled patch of trees behind the barn and creeps up the sky, an egg on a skillet. The mother nudges the girl to get dressed and feed the pigs, one of whom will soon have babies. From the porch the ash-blond air lies above the hay bales like clouds, and the sky now is curdled milk. A flurry of crows in the trees. The pig's distended belly drags low as she waddles to the feeding trough filled with corn and bread mush, occasional grains left over from dinners. The pig's raw pink nipples are swollen, and just two can fill up the girl's slender fist. Last year when another pig had babies, it scooted on its side, next to the trough; her wrinkled brood latched on, huffed, and switched places. The fact that a pig has so many nipples and is capable of nursing five or six babies at once fascinates the girl but also disturbs her, urging her to peep inside her dress to discover two slightly asymmetrical buttons of pink flesh. She pats the front of her dress in place and aids her mother to pour water in a large tureen.

As always the day whirrs with chores and the shared closeness, the cohabitation of two females, their skin and labor, their thoughts, which pass between them like sun rays and strike smiles, a flow of energy. So many things need and deserve their attention, there's hardly time to stop and ponder over trifles. A tug and squeak of the well pump, the rusty mittens it leaves on their hands, or those crunchy beads of ice that float in the water; or how many logs it takes to stoke the woodstove and warm up the house where the windows fog from their breath. The kitchen window has no curtains but old cut-up sheets tucked in the frame; a candle melted in the bottom of a jar and a box of matches on the sill.

Sometimes after breakfast or in the early afternoons, as they sort grains together, separating black hardened granules from the rest of the kernels, the mother sings and the daughter listens or croons along. The mother's voice is soft and dreamy, the girl's is light and tingling, a river joined by a brook. All songs are crude folk songs, in which a woman is almost always addressing a man, either assuring him of her eternal love and devotion or soliciting his. The songs are fraught with longing that, the girl senses, could never be replenished or fully grasped. It spreads like dust about the cabin or lingers like that peculiar fleshy odor snarled in the folds of her mother's skin, her hair.

The girl is only five, but one song particularly strikes her because of its caressing tune and measured rhythm. It's simple but also unsettling, a tease of callous fingers on her ribs. She understands the words, their designated meaning, yet can't comprehend the speaker's urgency, her baffling desire to trail after her beloved. The girl usually sings the first couplets, impersonating a woman:

> *You are my dear, dear,*
> *take me with you there.*
> *In that far-far-away land,*
> *I'll be your faithful friend.*

And the mother answers for a man; her voice deepens, acquires coarseness:

> *You are my dear, dear,*
> *I would have taken you there.*
> *But in that far-far-away land,*
> *I already have such a friend.*

The song stretches into five or six more couplets and the speaker continues to offer herself to her beloved in every imaginable role: a wife, a lover, a neighbor, a sister, a housekeeper. Each time the man rejects her by saying that all those roles have been already filled by other women. The girl is confused by the song, by the implied humility of a man-woman union. It's the kind of feeling she gets— deep inside, in the bud of her body—from the dark, harrowed fields; or a cry of a soon-to-be-slaughtered animal; or the dumb panic of chickens, their pleading glare and already-sliced necks. Perhaps it is also in those moments that the first intimation of danger is conjured, the first apprehension of sex and the paralyzing inescapability of a woman's fate.

The girl lets the mother finish the song before venturing to ask, "That woman? Why can't she be alone? Why does she need that man?" At first the mother doesn't reply but keeps scooping the dry rice off the table into a tin bowl. The grains fall and swoosh like rain against tree leaves. The mother says, "A man shouldn't leave his woman. If he goes, you go. Or you make him stay. That's just how it is. It really is very simple. You're a tree—he's the roots. If the roots break, the tree dies. Understand?" The girl nods, although she doesn't, doesn't understand, not at the moment and not for many, many years, but she's never heard her mother talk so seriously about anything.

The water seethes on the woodstove, boiling over. The dishes are piled in a pan, rags draped over the sides, a sliver of soap in a cup. While the mother washes plates and skillets, yolk-crusted spoons and grease-gloved knives, the daughter dries them, standing on a rickety bench and stacking the dishes on a shelf.

The girl follows her mother step by step, from the kitchen to the pantry, from the pantry to the bedroom, where they shake blankets and amass a snowdrift of pillows against the metal railing of the bed. They brush each other's hair and rub oil on the tips before plaiting; the heavy braids swing at their waists.

After a while the roast simmers in the belly of the oven, and the girl and her mother are taking a bath in a large washtub filled with sudsy water and a handful of plums too sour to eat. They arrange the plums like purple gems around their wet necks. They laugh and hook toes and glance out of a steamed window, making fist-size clearings to glimpse their man, who should be coming home just about now. He's a barn of a man too, with a roughed frame and calloused hands. His hair is the color of rust and his skin is mushroom-brown from working in the fields all summer. His square figure looms large and larger with each advancing step. Both, the mother and the daughter, know the man's features to the last mole, the furrow between his raised brows, the finger-thick veins on his neck, or how he sometimes pulls to one side when he walks, limping as he ascends the hill. They can discern, even from afar, a wedge of tension in his prickly jaw, a hard, unpleasant certainty in the familiar drag of a stride as he places his feet a bit too close and sturdies himself then staggers along.

For just a moment the air holds a keenness, the silence close and deep. They hear the man stumble through the yard and enter the cabin, yelling out their names, capsizing a chair, and another, the fruit bucket.

The thunder of apples on the floor.

II

THE NARROW COUNTRY road is choked with bushes and trees, a sweep of junipers, a grip of shaggy pines, century-old oaks and maples, whose single red leaves dangle like tongues from thick, sprawled limbs. For miles around the fields are cluttered with boulders in waist-high weeds, the orchards abandoned to crows. They migrate from tree to tree, a pack of raucous resentful birds, flapping their black wings at a silver station wagon as it tears through the brush. When the couple pulls up to the farmhouse, they are surprised to discover, in a dapple of yellow light, a row of horseshoe pits and rusty stakes tufted with grass like old graves. The yard is large, strewn with random objects: an upturned child's basin, a faded plastic pitcher, a cracked-in-two flower pot, a lopsided sandbox made from a truck tire, a wheelbarrow overflowing with rainwater and bird droppings. Not far, a tractor squats in high weeds, the seat is missing. A short walkway from the house, where the sun slices off the tips of pines, there's a sunken barn and the remnants of a coop.

The station wagon halts, the engine revs and dies.

"Something happened," the woman says before sliding out of the driver's seat. She's been eating her favorite Angelino plums, and her lips are tinged with juice.

"Nice guess," her companion says. "Why are we here? This place gives me chills."

"You love the chills."

"If you say so."

"Let's snoop inside," she offers.

"What for?"

"Curiosity."

He shrugs, his foot rising over a busted stone.

The house is cold and vined with shadows; a few dusty rags are tucked around the window frames. On the kitchen table a stub of a candle inside a jar. A massive woodstove occupies a better part of the room, blackened with soot and grease. Next to it they discover a shelf with pots and cast-iron skillets wrapped in dust. A bit higher is another shelf with tools: shears, a three-pronged hand tiller, an ice pick, a rat trap, a box of nails. The tin sink is rust-eaten. Floorboards are warped and creaky.

The man saunters after the woman from the kitchen to the pantry, which is separated from the main area by a filthy curtain that could've been an old sheet or part of a nightshirt grazed with holes. Behind the curtain the couple finds canned tomatoes and beans with squares of jelled fat, a shelf of plum preserves, as indicated by the barely readable labels.

"Do people still can?" the man asks, his words echoing through the shadowiness of the empty house. "I mean not in the cities. I know they don't in the cities."

"Yeah. They also have gardens, grow things."

"Grow and kill."

The woman stops short, turns to face the man. A trace of discontent on her weary face. "What do you mean?"

"I mean cows and chickens. Pigs."

"Oh," she says. "Right."

The bathroom has an old oblong washtub like a dead body ossified in the middle of the floor. A chamber pot sits next to the commode, both are blotched gray. The sink, originally eggshell color but now also gray, is square and on a heavy pedestal that reminds the man of a colossal erect penis. He thinks of another woman, somewhere in the city, getting dressed for a dinner he won't be able to attend, not unless he leaves now.

"Why are we here?" he asks, impatiently.

"I told you."

"I forgot. Something about your new poem."

"A sestina. I can't decide on the last word. You have to select six end-words for the first stanza. Like *farmhouse, plums, babies, angel, song,* and one more. The words repeat in the remaining five stanzas only in a different order. And then, of course, the three-line envoy has to include all six words—three at the end, three midway. It's complicated."

"I'd say. I thought poetry was fun."

"To read, not to craft. The sestina originated as a love poem somewhere in France. Troubadours sang their verses and were quite competitive, each trying to top the next in wit and the complexity of style. Then the sestina migrated to Italy."

"Of course. All the world's greatest pleasures come from those countries—love, sex, wine, food. What's left for us?" He curls the woman's hair around his finger, taking a step closer, her slim body is fitted against his. She has small tight breasts that poke through her shirt; as always, she isn't wearing a bra but a camisole. His breathing changes, and so does hers.

There's a game they used to play when they first met and sex was as welcoming and mysterious as a night sky beaded with stars. They would crash parties, pay surprise visits to their friends and neighbors, invade summer cottages or vacation rentals locked for the season, finding a spare key or an unlatched window. They would sneak in people's bathrooms or closets, retire to empty balconies, live in strange homes, make love on nuptial beds. She'd always initiated it, of course, seduced him with a thin tremor of her voice and hops of phrases like dream potions brewed in the dark.

"I found this article awhile back," the woman says and pulls away from his kiss. "About a farmer's wife who killed her five children and arranged them in bed in the order they'd been born, from the youngest to the oldest. She then undressed and lay next to them, which was how her husband found her when he came back from work."

"Jesus." The man blinks, and again, trying to erase the image.

"When I did some more research, I found out that she was pregnant when that happened."

"The postpartum *and* another pregnancy?"

"Yes. But also something tragic occurred when she was five."

"Abuse? Sexual?"

"Maybe. Or domestic violence. I couldn't find out exactly."

"And the child?"

"They had to perform an emergency cesarean at seven months, afraid she would harm the fetus."

"It lived?"

"Yes. A girl. A female."

"How awful," the man says. "Bizarre."

"The farmer's wife, in her sixties, just died in a mental hospital, choked on an apple. The bizarre thing, as you put it, is that no one admits to giving her the apple. She never had any visitors either."

The man rubs his eyes, gnaws at the flesh inside his mouth.

"But there's more." Now the woman has slipped behind him, and her voice has gone soft, curled to a whisper. His neck tingles with her breath.

"More?" he asks.

"Yes. This place, this farmhouse—it's her childhood home."

The man turns around, observes the woman, flecks of crimson in her dark eyes, as when she's finished one of her poems and can't wait to share it with him. He senses the heat her body radiates under the tight clothes. She inches closer, and he leans against the sink as her upper lip sweeps across his lower one. Her hand caressing the hump of flesh inside his jeans. "Let's stay here," she says. "Pretend being them, a farmer and his wife. There's food in the car, and the pantry."

"No," he says. "Are you mad? I have to be at work." His fear rises, but also his desire. He wants the woman to stop, and he doesn't, her hot fingers slipping through his zipper, forming a ring around the base of his penis.

"What if I were to tell you there's no gas in the car and the closest station is miles away? It's getting dark," she murmurs. "So very dark."

"Look, I get it—the farmer's wife, she was crazy, depressed, pissed off at her husband for giving her all those babies. But what do I have to do with it? You aren't pregnant, are you?"

The woman's other hand is reaching inside his shirt, tugging at the little coils of hair on his tan muscular chest. She pinches one.

He trembles. "Don't do that."

"Suppose she wasn't crazy?" She pinches another hair. "Suppose she did it out of love? Suppose he was about to leave her and she wanted him to stay? She was hurting so badly, yet couldn't express herself. She had no words—nothing sufficient enough."

Suddenly the man has no desire to have sex, his erection is nothing but a habit, an involuntary response of dumb flesh at the moment of dirty provocation. He thinks about the other woman, who knows nothing about this one or her unfathomable poetry, her desire to bend and forge words, to herd them together and break them apart like wooden blocks.

"That's horrible," he says, fully engorged and breathless. A tremor runs up his thighs, his anus tightens.

"Isn't it?" the woman says and slides away from him, just in time, then shakes her long red-streaked hair. She walks toward a squalid window and rubs it with her fist, allowing the dim glow of the evening sun to creep over the floor.

She begins to whistle, then hums, then croons. It's a love song. Soft. Lullaby soft. The heart stills from such softness.

No Other Love

She arrived at our house in Richmond on an early spring afternoon in 1999, after being absent for over twenty years. Clouds forged a roof above the city, the sky darkened, and rain poured over the yard, the trees brought low, weeping. Dressed in a green parka and rubber boots but without an umbrella, Bonnie stood in the doorway, dripping water on the rug. Her thick eyebrows were still black, still distinct in their shape, resembling a set of open wings. A wet duffle bag hung from her shoulder, her hair long and silver-gray, like rain itself.

"May I come in?" she asked in a low, ragged voice, as though fighting a cold.

"Yes," I said, after a slight hesitation. "Of course. Let me take your coat and your bag."

She handed me both then took off her boots. She needed to use the restroom, and I pointed down the hallway.

Minutes later, when she joined me in the living room, her hair was brushed back and her hands smelled of lotion, a tinge of citrus. In her loose flannel shirt and baggy jeans she seemed to have gained weight. She stood large, her face a convocation of moles and wrinkles. Music reached our ears, a few massive chords and a purr of notes growing into a steady harmonious flow. The melody was strong and impulsive, heartfelt too. My daughter Bell played piano in the study. Her teacher, Valeriy, a forty-year-old Russian musician who'd emigrated from St. Petersburg when it was still called Leningrad, spoke with a growl of an accent. Behind the double wood-and-glass doors I could see his figure, like a shadow, garbed in all black, sauntering back and forth, gesticulating heavily. He was thin and somber, with a short graying beard and curly brown hair, perhaps too long for a man his age, but not for an artist.

"No. You play with sausage fingers. You must go deep into the keys when you play Rachmaninoff. Deep. Deep. We must feel his pain and pride. Again, try again. Look at these trees outside. They're angry and humble. That's how you must play. Remember—music is bigger than us." His voice was loud, his *r*'s snarling.

"Your daughter?" Bonnie asked, nodding toward the study.

"Yes." I reached into the china cabinet and retrieved two wineglasses.

"Why do you let him scream at her?"

"He doesn't scream. It's his personality. He's really quite charming."

"We were all charming once."

I raised my eyes. "What do you want, Bonnie? Why did you come?"

"I don't have a home, temporarily. I just need to stay a night or two, a week at most. Willis gave me your address."

"I don't have a guest room."

"I'm not a guest. I can sleep on the floor."

The study opened and Bell and Valeriy emerged, in silence. Bell was a little flushed, and Valeriy picked up his trench from the back of the couch and draped it over his shoulders. He looked stern and frugal, making one think of those interminable winters he must've endured as a child. He bowed and placed a soft kiss on my hand. My skin, my body, rippled with shivers. Having known him for a year, his foreign gallantries were still a surprise to me. I thought them to be outdated yet dashing, like the berets and trenches that he wore.

Gently he let go of my hand just as I asked, "Good lesson?"

"Yes," Bell answered.

"Fingers not good, lazy," he said. "Must play from here." His fist thudded against his chest. "Not here." He pointed at his head. "Soul versus mind. Yes?"

"Yes, yes. Makes perfect sense," Bonnie said, approaching. "Music is love, and love knows no reason."

Valeriy regarded Bonnie with his dark gimlet eyes. "Indeed," he said. "No reason."

"Bell, Valeriy," I said. "This is Bonnie—my mother."

* * *

I WAS TWO when Bonnie had left Willis, my father, fifteen when she first returned—humble yet poised, burnished by years and the sun. Her short auburn hair curled behind her ears, her face and arms as tan as her cowboy boots. I remember her standing in the doorway of our old house in Boones Mill, framed in the waning light, her eyes a deep, sad blue.

"Hello, Helen," she said, her voice startling in its softness. It reminded me of woolly worms I discovered inside empty flower pots every winter. "I'm—"

"I know who you are," I said. "Willis is at work. He won't be back until late."

"Well, maybe it's good. Maybe you and I can talk. Catch up."

I watched her face lighten for a moment before growing doubtful just as quickly.

"There's nothing to catch up on," I said as I backed into the house and climbed up the stairs.

She didn't leave, and she didn't dare to enter but sat on the porch swing, wrapped in muggy Virginia air, until my father's truck roared through the gravel driveway. From my bedroom window I watched him get out, slowly, adjusting his greasy baseball cap, and trudge up to the house, where Bonnie waited, rubbing her arms, then stretching them out halfway, then dropping them back to her sides. I raised my window, hoping to hear their conversation, but Willis didn't say anything, only nodded and picked up her duffel bag. I had a suspicion that perhaps he knew she was arriving that day, or perhaps he'd been expecting her every day since she'd left.

I reheated pizza for dinner and ate it in my room while they had a long talk in the kitchen. But try as I might, I couldn't decipher anything beyond a few strained words, tails of phrases. There'd been an affair—hers—and there'd been an agreement that my father had neglected. "You promised, you promised," Bonnie kept repeating. And my father said, "It's your fault. It's all your damn fault." He didn't lose his temper though, and neither did Bonnie, but at some point he got up, knocking the chair on the floor, and walked out. I heard the water run in the sink, Bonnie washing and putting the dishes away, and then all became quiet and the house surrendered to the darkness.

An hour or so later I climbed out of my bedroom window onto the roof, where my boyfriend Tyler already waited, smoking and gazing at stars, tiny grains of silver in the cobalt sky. We kissed and tongued and prowled under each other's clothes, his hands cupping the tender swells of my breasts, mine inspecting a hardened protrusion inside his pants. I felt new, achy, exposed to the universe, suspended between angst and desire.

"You're of a treacherous nature, Helen," Tyler said, breathing into my ear. "Just like Paris, I'm seduced by your beauty." He was two years older, obsessed with Homer and ancient history.

"Didn't Paris abduct Helen?" I asked.

"The sources are contradictory. But she must've complied. Just three days later she and Paris had sex. She'd already forgotten Menelaus and their daughter, Hermione. She betrayed them."

I shrugged and kissed him on the mouth, and then lower, where the buttons of his shirt pulled loose. He had such sweet, taut flesh, with curls of bronze hair on his chest and belly. I closed my eyes, feasting my way down. He made a sudden move, and I raised my face, acknowledging Bonnie's figure in my bedroom window.

He sat up, and I did too, my cheeks suffused with heat and embarrassment.

"Leave, please," Bonnie said to Tyler.

But I said, "No. Stay."

Tyler's eyes switched back and forth between Bonnie and me. He fumbled with his zipper, stuffing his shirttail down his jeans.

"You're only fifteen, Helen. Don't start your life the way I did," Bonnie said.

"I'm not you," I said. "I'll never be you."

She didn't reply but exhaled a weary sigh, her troubled face pulling into shadows.

It was the end of summer, and the grass showed dead patches, began to wither. So did our garden, where, except for pumpkins and a few sunflower plants, the vines looked sad, enervated by the long hot season. Willis didn't welcome my mother back, but he made room for her in the house just as I made room for her at the table. They continued to sleep in separate beds, but I did notice Bonnie changing into colorful button-up shirts before my father would return from work. She tried to clean and cook for us and even baked blackberry and peach cobblers with bubbly sugary edges, where the fruit had melted into the dough, but our table times remained awkward; we scraped plates in silence or resorted to news on a portable radio.

My father was a curt, irascible man of few sentiments. He could be easily provoked but not easily appeased, even though his anger rarely spread past the immediate argument. Like a house fire contained within one room, his rage, his pain, seemed to be contained within him. He seldom yelled at me or praised me, stingy with hugs or good-night kisses. He owned a gun, which sat next to his bed for years. He forbade me to touch it, although once, when I was twelve, he tried to teach me how to shoot, taking me to an empty field on the outskirts of the town, where crows gathered in long, muddy ruts. My shots missed, each one of them, and he seemed to be more relieved than disappointed, driving me to Sal's restaurant afterward, where we gorged on pasta and meatballs. His priorities for me were food, hygiene, religion, books—in that order. He believed that reading created more problems than it solved. And that people who wrote books did so to escape real labor; it was a shame when a man couldn't fix his own roof or build a fence, or when a woman couldn't cook a simple meal or raise her children. "God gave you a life," he'd say, "and it's up to you to make sense of it." My father worked as a plumber, and there wasn't a house in our town of Boones Mill where he hadn't repaired a leaking commode or replaced rotten pipes. People respected him and invited us to their homes during holidays; some pitied us, I suspected.

One Sunday, after Bonnie had been staying with us for a few weeks, my father went to church, and I ventured into the kitchen to hunt for food. I smelled bacon and eggs and dark-roasted coffee, its rich bitter aroma. Bonnie hunched over the counter, her finger trailing through a page of an old recipe book.

"Good morning," she said, without turning. "I'm making spoon corn bread. Your father's favorite. Wanna help?"

First I felt the urge to back out of the kitchen and pretend that I was never there, but the moment had slipped away, and before I could escape, I had a strip of bacon in one hand and a measuring cup in the other. Bonnie poured more coffee for herself and then for me in a tall white mug with a faded cardinal and a broken handle.

"Need to throw that mug away," she said.

"I love the mug. It's mine."

"No, it's mine. But it's bad luck to drink out of a broken dish, especially for a young girl." She cracked eggs one after another into a glass bowl, the yolks still intact, quivering on the bottom.

"I'm not superstitious," I said.

"I wasn't either at your age."

"When did it change?"

"When I broke the mug. I dropped it on the floor right before our wedding."

"You're making this up, right?"

She sighed. "Let's start, shall we?"

I measured the flour, and she sifted it in a separate bowl. While she added a cup of yellow cornmeal, I poured buttermilk and melted butter.

"The secret is—you whisk the eggs first but don't add them to the corn-and-flour mixture until the very end, right before baking. Then the spoon bread remains moist and fluffy."

I sipped my coffee; the jagged places on the mug were smooth from the years of handling. As Bonnie folded in the eggs, I dotted the dish with more butter, and she placed the bread in the oven. She pushed the door shut and straightened her shoulders, hands on hips, an arch to her back. A wispy strand of hair curled at her ear, her neckline so delicate, so graceful in the morning sun. I tried to imagine being inside her, being a part of her strong curvaceous body, shielded by her flesh and bones. But no matter how hard I tried, she remained insurmountable and distant—years away.

Much as I feared gossip and adjustment when school started, Bonnie didn't stay. In the fall, when we harvested pumpkins and piled them by the door so from a distance they resembled a jumble of severed heads, Bonnie migrated farther south. My father didn't insist, and I felt relieved and betrayed at the same time. She wasn't someone you could love instantly and effortlessly or admire out of respect; and yet she was a woman whose body spoke the same language as mine, and whose presence in the house had become noticeable. She wasn't a perfect housekeeper, but she was spontaneous and inventive, hanging new burgundy drapes in the living room and assembling wild lively bouquets from field flowers. There was a sadness to her and a tenderness a mother should have, and irrefutability, a harsh bluntness a mother shouldn't.

The evening before Bonnie left, she entered my room and sat down on my bed, her fussy hand repositioning a stuffed rabbit among the pillows.

"They gave it to me at the hospital after you were born. The night you'd picked. It was a blizzard like no other. The roads were a mess; our car wouldn't start. The snow kept falling and falling. Willis ran toward the interstate and brought back a guy with a snowplow. He drove us to the hospital. I was terrified, shaking from cold and pain. One of the nurses kept saying, 'You think this is hard. Wait till this baby is born and demands food and clothes and attention.' She brought me the rabbit." Bonnie poked the old toy in the belly.

"Take it. It means more to you than it does to me," I said.

"Don't be rude, Helen. Someday you might be able to understand."

"Understand what?" I stood by the window, fumbling with a pack of cigarettes.

"Youth is unforgiving. We all make mistakes."

I stared at her, that stranger who was supposed to be my first and closest relation in the world. Her eyes dim, a frown pinched between her brows.

"You're becoming a young woman, Helen. There're men out there, all sorts of men. Some will take advantage of you. Others will let you take advantage of them. Don't settle, don't feel like you have to. Find what makes you happy and hold on to it."

I lit a cigarette, a cloud of smoke filling the space between us.

* * *

AFTER BONNIE LEFT, life reverted to its parochial, small-town course, a doom of tedium and ceaseless household chores, mounds of schoolwork. I thought of her every now and then, but my father and I avoided talking about her except when I would accidentally add a third plate to the table. Then he would tell me what a different person my mother used to be—sweet and reasonable, eager to raise a family. "If it wasn't for that man, the climber," my father said, "things would've been different between us. He was a thief and a liar. Treated mountains better than people. And they aren't. They aren't nothing but rocks—dumb, sad rocks." I listened to him and thought that I understood his hurt and his loneliness. Like the mountains, it would always be there, solemn, indestructible, confronting him from afar.

Bonnie wasn't present at my high school graduation or my rushed wedding, with a pig roast, a bonfire, and bluegrass music that could be heard to the top of Mill Mountain. Neither was she present during the delivery of my only daughter. Sometimes, while nursing Bell, I felt painful contractions reverberating through my body and thought of my mother, but not Bonnie, not as I knew her to be—an aloof stranger who'd gone through thirty-six hours of labor to deliver a child only to abandon her a few years afterward—but some other woman, a light, vibrant, softer person who'd been nursing her daughter in the dark while crooning a lullaby, gazing at the night sky charted with constellations. Yet there was no longing in my missing Bonnie. I didn't really know her.

In the years after Bell was born, we'd moved first to Charlottesville, where Tyler attended the University of Virginia's law school, and then to Richmond, where he joined a small reputable practice. I had enrolled in a community college and then transferred to Virginia Common-wealth University, working toward my bachelor's degree. While Bell napped, I studied and read—all the classics I could find in a local library, including *The Iliad* and *The Odyssey*. The Greeks fascinated me, their lack of self-consciousness and their relationships with the gods, who had caused and directed all humans' actions and thus could be blamed for their mistakes. Tyler would laugh at my sudden discoveries of the Greeks' flaws, and if something slipped out of control in our daily schedules, he'd joke that the gods had abandoned us, forgotten to intervene. Those were the longest and the happiest years of our marriage. We loved and we struggled—not so much financially, but emotionally and physically, depleted of parental help and guidance; both my father and Tyler's mother remained too far away. But we managed, and we conformed. Surprisingly we had more sex when Bell was little and we were at the mercy of her moods and sleep habits than when she grew older and we encountered hours of free time.

During Bell's teenage years Tyler had been made partner, burrowing into work with envious zeal, and I finished my master's degree and found a job teaching English in high school, where Bell was already a student. Truth be told, I'd turned into the kind of mother that Bonnie wasn't to me—obsessive, overindulgent. I worried day and night about my daughter's future, her safety, the choice of a mate. I often panicked when she forgot to call me or refused to discuss a certain topic: boys, sex, the need to see a gynecologist. I began having dreams of Bell's disappearing, her being kidnapped and locked in someone's basement; or her running away to some godforsaken country, where she'd then be sold into prostitution by drug lords. As pathetic as my dreams sounded to Tyler, who'd once caught me spying on our daughter, slinking on the other side of the road, opposite from where she was walking to school, I couldn't shake my fears and my gloom. More and more my heart trembled at the thought that one day Bell and I wouldn't be a part of the same family, and that there might be secrets between us too ugly, too painful to share. Still, even among my deepest fears and mother-flaws, there had never been a doubt, doubt that Bell couldn't or wouldn't love me the way I loved her.

One evening, after we just finished watching *Terms of Endearment*, she nestled closer to me on the couch and asked, "Will you try and stop me from dating a guy you don't approve of?"

"What guy? Is there a guy?"

Bell smiled. She had such a warm, sensitive mouth; even as an infant, she suckled so gently. "Maybe. But I don't want you to freak out."

"Me? Freak out? No." I laughed and tapped her forehead with my finger. "I'm open to all your loves, no matter how unworthy or short-lived."

"Promise?"

"Promise. No stranger shall come between us."

Then Tyler ambled into the room and watched us cuddle for a minute. "I want food, and I want a vacation," he said. "How about Florida in the winter?"

"California," Bell and I answered in unison. "In the summer."

* * *

MUCH TO MY surprise both Tyler and Bell adjusted to Bonnie's unbidden presence in our home without a smidgen of inconvenience. They welcomed her as they would an old friend, comfortable if a bit odd. Tyler, whose genial nature overruled my impatience, called her Miss Bonnie while offering her a glass of wine at dinner, commenting on her blouse, her lovely smile, or her skill of carving up a whole chicken, not a spot of grease on the tablecloth. Bonnie received Tyler's attention with gratitude and, in turn, flirted with her son-in-law by complimenting his suits and ties, a new haircut, which had revealed his face, those trusting blue eyes. Bell, at first shy and unsure, drew toward Bonnie like a garden vine toward the sun, seduced by its vibrancy and omnipotence. After just a few days, she offered Bonnie her bed while she switched to a broken futon we'd been meaning to throw away. The two of them spent evenings in Bell's room, peering in photo albums and giggling at old pictures or reading and comparing horoscopes, their fates aligned on a magazine page. They whispered, they conspired, they huddled on the bed, blinking tears through old movies, *Casablanca, Kramer vs. Kramer, It's a Wonderful Life.* Bonnie had assumed the role of a grandmother with the same ease she'd appeared or disappeared from my life. It seemed as natural to her as the change of seasons, one submitting to the next in their sure, ineluctable succession.

As much as I'd hoped Bonnie would leave, I still couldn't bring myself to ask her to. She pretended she was expecting some important letter and insisted on bringing in the mail every morning, but we both knew it was a lie. Bonnie wouldn't receive a letter because nobody would bother to write one. I had an idea of writing it myself, of documenting all the uneasiness and irritation her persistent careless ways had caused me—the clothes she tossed on chairs and bathroom floors like shed skin, her ten coffee cups crowding the counter or her long gray hairs coiling in sinks and on the couch, all the shirts and sweaters she borrowed for one day and that somehow remained in her permanent possession. But I never did write that letter. Nor did I tell Bell that her and Bonnie's growing intimacy irked and distracted me, that I worried about her getting too attached, too dependent on Bonnie. I didn't want my daughter to live in a dream, where the most bizarre, chaotic things appeared plausible.

While Tyler and I were at work and Bell at school, Bonnie shopped for groceries and surprised us with homemade soups or meat loaf, a vegetable casserole. One day when I came home earlier than usual, I found her sitting on the couch, her hands on her lap. There was no book or magazine beside her, and the TV was off. She was wearing a robe but no slippers; her cheeks were flushed, her hair clipped into a bun as though she were about to take a bath but got distracted.

"Bonnie? Is everything all right?" I asked, for a second thinking that perhaps there was, in fact, a letter and she'd just received it.

She wrinkled her forehead, her expression brooding. "Why didn't you have another child, Helen? You still can. You're only thirty-six. I'll help you."

"What on earth, Bonnie? I don't want any more children. The way life is."

"Life is the same, people are different. Different but also the same. Do you know what I'm saying?"

"No. Not really. Why didn't *you* have more children? With that other guy, the climber?"

"Dan. His name was Dan. He had cancer. He died."

"Sorry," I said. "I had no idea."

"You couldn't have." She took a deep exonerating breath. "They say loss is easier when you have time to prepare."

I pondered her words. "Is it? Is it really?"

"No," she said. Her full lips trembled, unfolding. "I never wanted to leave you, Helen, but Willis made me. He wouldn't let me come back either."

"But you could've sent a letter, could've called or visited after Bell was born and we moved away."

"I tried. Many times. But I didn't want to ruin your relationship with your father."

"Then don't start now."

* * *

AT THE END of the third week, after Bell's piano lesson, Bonnie offered Valeriy a drink, and he eagerly accepted. As I poured the wine, Bonnie positioned herself on the couch, across from Valeriy, and pelted him with questions about his atrocious Communist upbringing.

"It wasn't Communist, but Socialist. And it wasn't that bad. We lost so much since then."

"Like what?" she asked.

"Courage," he said. "Honor. Love."

"How is it there now?" I asked, pushing the tray of snacks closer to him.

"Terrible. Corruption and pretense. It's everywhere, even in music." Valeriy swallowed a square of cheese. He seemed hungry, discontent.

"It's everywhere here too," Bonnie said. "All is corrupt. Capitalism is about who owns more."

"But music is freedom. It's about feelings. Passion. Desire. Impossible to own or hold permanently."

Bell was playing the piano again, a tender, melancholy piece that made us pause for a moment.

"Jo Stafford," Bonnie said. "'No Other Love.'" Her head swayed, gaze dissolving in the distance. "*No other love can warm my heart. . . .*" Bonnie's voice grew velvety-low, and her singing plucked at the heart.

"Chopin. Étude number three in E major," Valeriy said. "Nice voice. How you know the words?"

"I used to look like Stafford in my younger years," Bonnie said. "I know a lot of her songs." She picked up the wine bottle, but Valeriy intercepted and lifted it out of her hands then poured.

"What's really odd," he said, "is that Chopin, who was an incurable romantic, also composed 'Funeral March.' Love. Death. All so close for him."

The music stopped, and Bell walked out of the study, wearing tight jeans and a pink shirt. Her coppery-brown hair draped around her neck.

"You played well," Valeriy said.

"Yes," Bonnie and I echoed. "Very."

Bell's face glowed. She had such delicate skin; it revealed a prickle of emotion.

After Valeriy left and Bell retreated into her room, Bonnie helped carry the glasses to the sink. "He really likes you," she said. "I foresee trouble."

"Trouble? Who are you, Cassandra?"

"No. But I'm old, and I forget things, so I say them as soon as I think them." Her lips wrung into a smile.

That night I couldn't sleep, the sheets chaffed my skin, my senses like that of a nubile animal, sharpened by the moon's ominous glow. I finally got up, draped a jacket over my shoulders, and tiptoed into the yard.

The night was cool, the sky clear, pricked with stars.

"You're still smoking," Bonnie said, standing a step behind me, but very close.

"Occasionally," I said, without turning. "I like looking at the stars."

"God made stars so humans didn't feel so lonely. But come to think of it—they give you the loneliest feeling ever, don't they?"

I shrugged. "Maybe. Or maybe we only look at them when we're already lonely."

We kept silent for a moment, and then Bonnie said, "Thank you for letting me stay. Bell is a special girl. Like no other."

I continued to observe the sky. A plane blinked in the distance, a live star maneuvering between others.

"Just don't break her heart, Bonnie," I said. "Please."

* * *

THE FOLLOWING SATURDAY Bell and Bonnie went shopping for a prom dress. They returned with a horde of packages spilling out, escaping their arms like small children. Both seemed happy and out of breath, both collapsed on the couch—feet stretched out, eyes shut, faces upturned toward the ceiling, the expression of sheer satisfaction on their grinning lips.

"What's all that about?" I asked. "How much did you spend?"

"Bonnie paid for everything," Bell said, eyes still shut. "We had fun."

"Everything? What everything? And where did you get the money? You said you were broke."

"I never said that," Bonnie answered, her grin drooping into a frown.

"We're going to California this summer," Bell announced.

"We?" I asked.

"Bonnie and I."

"That's right," Bonnie confirmed.

"I don't think so," I said. "We're supposed to go together. All of us."

"We can all go," Bonnie said.

"It's a great idea." Tyler appeared in the room, sipping beer from a cold bottle. Beads of water gathered below his stout fingers. "Wonderful bonding time."

"No," I protested. "I want us to go as a family. Bell leaves for college soon after."

"Bonnie is family," Bell said. "She's my grandmother. I want to spend time with her."

"Thank you, Bell," Bonnie said. Her eyes blinked open at my disgruntled face. "Relax, Helen. I'm not trying to encroach on your family time. But I wish you were more considerate, more spontaneous. Feelings change, mature. Isn't that what Valeriy said?"

"We like Valeriy." Tyler nodded. "So direct, so R-r-russian."

I drew a fistful of air then blew it all out. "You barge into my house, you charm my family, and now you're telling me to be more considerate? Why, Bonnie? Why can't you leave us alone?"

My words didn't seem to upset her, or if they did, she wouldn't show it. She stood up, readjusted the couch pillows, and went to the kitchen to start dinner.

She departed that evening, despite Bell's fervent pleading. "We could do so many more things together," my daughter cried. "We can go hiking and swimming and camping. We can make fires and cook all our food, like you used to with Dan. We can travel after my graduation. We can see the Grand Canyon, Yosemite, Muir Woods."

But Bonnie was unwavering in her decision, her lips pinched together in a straight line that had almost disappeared from her face. She didn't take any of the borrowed clothes or the money that Tyler had stuffed in her coat pocket, and it appeared that she left lighter than when she'd first arrived, that she'd forgotten something. I kept searching the house for her accidental belongings, but all I found was a used Band-Aid in the trash basket.

* * *

WE PATCHED IT, and we didn't. I apologized to Bell, and she responded with a cold nod, a semblance of forgiveness. She remained aloof and somber most of the time. Only during Valeriy's visits, did she reincarnate into her old self—sweet and vivacious, smiling. I, too, became aware of his presence, his hot lingering lips on my hand as he bent to kiss it. Nothing in his face or posture betrayed his feelings, his austere ways. He was gallant, and he was dutiful, his accent, his foreignness a stir for others, but not for him. On occasion our eyes would meet in a kind of frank, disarming embrace. But the moment would be so brief, fleeting, impossible to own.

I caught myself thinking about him more and more, especially at night, when the house quieted into darkness and shadows crept along the walls, those silent daring ghosts. Images inundated me, passion scenes from movies and books. How the lovers groped and pressed and rocked, fused by sweat, Valery's face hovering above mine, his lips grazing my neck, shoulders, breasts. I touched myself too, in bed, first inadvertently and then harder, a tremble of fingers between my legs, while Tyler slept, oblivious to my encroaching betrayal, all that was about to happen. I blamed Bonnie, of course, not only for tearing into my life like a gust of wind, dragging in memories and the old umbrage, but for voicing her ominous observations after that piano lesson. I blamed Tyler too—for his nonchalance, his generous nonconfrontational nature, his reverence of his job and the demands of his increasingly wayward clients. But then I also blamed myself for being so vulnerable, so inexperienced, for wanting more from life and my body. Doubts possessed me. I questioned the neat convenience of my marriage, my and Tyler's steady yet unsurprising sex, our settled uncomplicated happiness, which I'd taken for granted, like leaves on trees. I began to feel that my life lacked mystery, some secret meaning I was supposed to discover as I aged and matured.

The week Bell departed on a field trip, I forgot to call Valeriy and cancel the lesson. Whether I did that on purpose I can't say, because even accidents can happen on purpose, though not clearly defined or acknowledged, like an early intimation of danger. I hadn't planned on seducing him or being seduced—all of that had already happened—but in those hours before his visit, I grew restless and remorseful, tangled between guilt and desire, agonizing over a spark of an affair that would burn through my life for months, if not years. I remember wearing a silky wine-dark tunic, the color of Homer's sea, and a pair of woven flats with tassels at the front. My shampooed and still-damp hair cloaked my naked shoulders—the first thing his lips touched that afternoon.

* * *

HE CALLED ME Elena the Beautiful, from a Russian fairy tale. We met every week in his tiny attic apartment, hot and dark, with a rickety fan buzzing in the window. I would park my car across the street, at a Dollar General, and walk to Valeriy's building, eyes on trees rampant with foliage. The neighborhood was remote, yet friendly, with newly built playgrounds, pizza and burger joints, and a large CVS where I imagined Valeriy buying condoms. Sex was tender and guilty and new. The world was old, of course, but I was new in it, rediscovering, reclaiming my body piece by piece, where Valeriy's mouth and fingers brushed and caressed. Contrary to Tyler, there was no routine goodness in Valeriy's lovemaking, but raw primitive instinct. He stroked my hair, my breasts, my hips, persistently and with confidence, like piano keys. He kissed my back, my thighs, my crooked big toe. I didn't really know my body or how responsive it could be to a man's touch, so urgent, explicit. Unlike Tyler, Valeriy wasn't concerned with the appropriate, with how to please a woman, but strived to leave his mark, to singe, scar with desire. He abandoned the foreign civilities and became spontaneous, voracious, and as different as the composers he revered, Bach, Mozart, Rachmaninoff.

Afterward we lay naked, unraveled, passing a cigarette, in a web of smoke and childhood memories. The stories of Valeriy's Soviet upbringing fascinated me, the City on the Neva, where he grew up; the palaces; the white nights; the drawbridges on the opposite sides of which he and his first lover once stood, caught unaware, the sides rising, separating them farther and farther. He would never see her again, even though he would be returning to the bridge every evening for many months. His Russian world spun a cocoon around me, and I was lulled inside its bright mysterious shell, its novelty and its intricacy and its tanginess. And when it ended, when the cocoon unspooled and ruptured, the ghost threads falling off, dissolving under the gaze of my daughter, who had come too early, or too late, waiting for her teacher on the steps of his apartment, perhaps venturing for the first time, perhaps not, to surrender her body to a man she thought was worthy—when all of that became revealed—I saw Bell's sorrowful eyes glazed with tears.

What followed was an incongruous, desperate exchange of phrases, my meager attempt to justify my behavior and Valeriy's struggle to find the appropriate words, not too harsh, not too kind, to describe our relationship, our being together, a mess of sheets and clothes on the bed, a broken door latch. He and I must have thought that we could and should defend ourselves, treating the affair as one mad lustful moment, to which we'd both succumbed, seduced by the treacherous gods. But no matter what we said, we floundered in guilt, our arguments thin with lies. We sounded unconvincing, selfish, helpless, and cruel; each word like a stone hurled at Bell, stripping off her armor, her flesh, ravaging her love for a man she deemed immortal, like the music he'd taught her to play.

When Bell finally gathered words in her mouth, she didn't sound hysterical or accusing. She seemed embarrassed more than angry. She said, "I'm sorry. I'm sorry I came. Intruded like that. How could I? I'm sorry. Please forgive me."

Her hands clutched a music folder, its corners frayed to pulp, excoriated. She kept patting it and hugging it as if it were an injured animal about to die.

* * *

SUMMER SMASHED AT our door with more rain and wind. At times I worried it would tear the roof off the house and all the water would pour in, flooding the rooms. I imagined the three of us, Bell, Tyler, and me—swept by the mad current, in a whirlpool of useless possessions— sheets, dishes, furniture, books, and the old piano with a Chopin score still opened on the rack. But the house endured, and so did we. Valeriy stopped giving piano lessons and soon deserted the city; I would never hear from him again. Bell enrolled at San Diego State, and I moved out of the house after finally admitting the affair to Tyler. Nobody was urging me, and Bell had kept the dreadful secret through all the family dinners and getaway weekends. She excused her sullen reticence with hormones and homework while I was desperate to touch her, to rock her in my arms, as if she were still a baby, but she remained outside of my reach.

Tyler didn't suspect a thing, even after Bell's departure for college, and yet his honesty, his trust, rivaled my lie. Time and again I stood facing him, wrapped in deceit. I thought he could see through it, could see how disheartening and embarrassed I appeared when we were alone, how clumsy and reluctant in bed. But he was blind to my guilt, as my father was once blind to Bonnie's.

"How long?" he asked after I'd confessed.

"A few months," I answered, as though months—as opposed to years—could excuse my infidelity.

"Why? Why, Helen?" Tears stood in his eyes, and I felt mine surging.

I reached for his shoulder, my arms around him for the last time. We wept as our life washed down our faces, slivers of old happiness, of rusted desire.

The following months, years, lumped together—unremarkable. I had a few brief relationships with men, who possessed neither Tyler's goodness nor Valeriy's rawness. I continued to teach English in high school, and while I reread parts of *The Iliad* to my students, I kept wondering how different the story would have been if told from Helen's perspective, or if Aphrodite hadn't rescued Paris and led him to bed with Helen before Menelaus had a chance to kill him in a duel. I could almost hear Tyler saying in his offhand jovial tone, "But Helen wouldn't have been born if it weren't for that same divine intervention. What begins in a fight ends in a fight."

Bell graduated, married, became a geologist, devoting herself to the studying of rocks. She didn't own a piano and stopped playing entirely.

At the wedding I remember Bell making one single joke when she'd introduced me to her husband's family as the beautiful Helen of Troy. Everyone laughed, and Bell bent over and gave me a peck on the cheek, like she would any old relative. Tyler sat at the table next to Bell, a mellow woman draped over his arm. He had gained weight, grown a beard, and appeared happy and confident. He smiled and waved at me, and I did the same, once again disarmed by his kind nature, the ability to knead the severed pieces into a new plausible whole. My father didn't come to the wedding, alluding to bad weather and his aching knees, but Bonnie was there, residing in the opposite corner of the room, stiff and gray-haired. We didn't speak, only nodded from a distance, two humble duelers contemplating the first shot.

∗ ∗ ∗

IN THE NEXT decade I tried to reconnect with Bell, to salvage and rebuild our relationship, but she wouldn't oblige, cold like a star—eons away. I only saw her a handful of times and always in the presence of a third party: her friends, her husband, the in-laws. We talked on the phone some, slipping in and out of the familiar, designated subjects.

"How's the weather in Virginia?"

"Cold and rainy."

"Hmm. It's warm and pleasant in California."

Once, after the birth of my first grandchild, as I was driving past the apartment building where Valeriy used to live, I slowed down, parked, and got out of the car. Not knowing why, I climbed the steps, all the way to the top and listened, my heart breaking into thunder. After a while I ventured to knock, but no one answered while I stood there, facing the same weathered red door, where one life had ended and another began. The day was hot. A fan whirred in the window; the sun shimmered over the steps and the tiny porch. I squinted, shielding my eyes, and then I remembered something, something I hadn't thought of before—there was no piano in that apartment, no old keyboard. I'd never heard Valeriy play, except in our home, a few measures, a musical sentence, but never a complete piece or a song, nothing but a cluster of notes that reverberated in the air long after he was gone.

Bonnie had several mini-strokes and then a massive heart attack. She died on a gray winter morning, Bell weeping silently at the foot of the bed. In Bell's home, in Bishop, California, I viewed old pictures of my daughter and my mother: on a deserted beach; in the Sierra Mountains; among the ancient bristlecone pines; at Yosemite, overlooking the valley, the immensity of rocks and sky around them. There were pictures of Bonnie holding Bell's children, right after they were born, red and squirmy, their scrunched faces no bigger than peanuts. There were pictures of Thanksgiving dinners and Christmas parties and, what I'd suspected—Mother's Day weekends. All those holidays my grown daughter had refused to spend with me.

At the cemetery Bell sobbed, patting her face with a Kleenex, one wet tissue after another. I stood next to her, flanked by my grandsons—seven and ten—their small hands warm inside mine. Snow surprised us; large shaggy flakes sifted through the sky and powdered our hair and faces. The mountains seemed to come alive, swelling and trembling, as though they, too, had succumbed to grief. We were urged to retreat to our cars, but Bell stayed for a long time, mantled in snow.

I ended up spending a week in Bishop. Bell had a modest home, untidy yet welcoming, with bushels of plants climbing out of their pots and various odd-shaped rocks peeping from shelves and tables. Bell's husband was an amicable man who never raised his voice, reminding me of Tyler. He owned several sporting-goods stores, and his business seemed to have picked up with the advance of winter. While he was at work, Bell and I busied ourselves in the kitchen, cooking meals and watching the children wallow in the snow. They bellied through the yard like slugs, tossed snowballs, built fortresses and funky unidentifiable creatures.

The evening before my departure, we made meat loaf and spoon corn bread, using Bonnie's old recipe. Bell poured red wine in tall goblets.

"Thank you," she said. "For coming all this way."

"How could I not? She was my mother."

Bell folded her lips and crossed them with her finger. In loose jeans and a man's shirt, she looked sturdy, dependable. Her long hair was drizzled with gray, her face mapped out with fine lines. She was much thicker in the hips and arms, and from a distance she appeared older, more of a mother than a daughter.

"I know you and Bonnie had some unresolved issues," Bell said. "But she did love you."

I swallowed the wine; it tinged my mouth with sharp, spiced fruit.

"Bonnie left me when I was two," I said. "She missed my birthdays, my graduation, and my wedding."

"Bonnie didn't just leave. She had to. Willis found out about the affair and broke into the guy's house with a gun. He was mad with jealousy. He threatened to kill them both and then himself."

I set my glass on the table; some of the wine sloshed out, speckled the wood.

"Bonnie agreed to go away and stay away if Willis would allow her to visit. But he couldn't forgive Bonnie. He wanted to sue for custody. Bonnie knew she'd lose, and that you'd be hurt even more." Bell brought the wineglass to her lips and took a thirsty sip, then another.

For a while no sounds reached us, as though inside a tomb, its stone walls sealed with moss and time. I didn't know whether to believe Bell or not, whether Bonnie had indeed told her the truth or Bell was simply defending her grandmother in hopes to end a lifelong feud. Willis had died a few years earlier, so there was no one left to prove or disprove Bell's statement. The silence was indefinite, our eyes drawn to the window, where the boys had finished rolling a snowman. They foisted long sticks for arms; each took off a mitten and pulled it over the stick so they resembled hands. Then one drew his scarf under the figure's gelid lopsided head, the other gave it a smile with small pebbles.

It was growing dark, and the sky broke out with stars; the shell of a moon over the mountains all blurred and crooked, whitewashed.

I could think of no words, none to accuse or justify Bonnie or Willis, or myself. I placed my hand on the small of my daughter's back and rubbed it gently while Bell remained still, allowing me to continue. I didn't know when I would see her or the boys again, where we would go from there, or how we could mend the past. All I knew at the moment was that Valeriy was wrong—once you voiced your desire, you owned it, from the first choked sigh to the full-throated moan; and that Bonnie was right, at least partially—the stars did give you the loneliest feeling, but not unbearable and only until dawn.

Pictures of the Snow

A week before her disappearance, Ann entered the La De Da clothing boutique on West Main. She asked to try on a soft-green silk blouse and a pair of matching trousers. The color complemented her winter skin and earth-brown eyes. She had lost weight in the past few years, her muscles diminished from the lack of exercise, but at her age—sixty-four—she was still attractive, with her full mouth and a heap of auburn hair on her slim shoulders.

Ann fidgeted with the pants, the hem dragging even if she stood up on her toes.

"Can you shorten them by Monday?" she asked.

The owner shook his head. "It's less than five days. By Wednesday, at best."

"Wednesday is too late," she said. "I'm going away on Monday. I'd like to wear them."

"I'll see what I can do."

Ann occasionally shopped at the boutique, even though it sold expensive designer clothes Richard couldn't justify paying for, not even if he were a doctor or a lawyer. And he was neither. He'd worked as a journalist for a local paper until they divorced a decade ago, then he retired from the job, moving to Mattituck, New York, while Ann stayed in their family home in Charlottesville, Virginia. Their children, Michael and Lena, were both married, living in Boston and New York City. They didn't argue against their parents' breakup, although both seemed disheartened. Lena was better about calling and checking up on Richard; Michael took the responsibility of managing Ann's investments because she could never secure a full-time job, the logic of finances escaped her. She was smart and had made good grades at school, but her teenage habits seemed to have lingered. Despite her Russian heritage, she was fragile and wispy, volatile. Richard once compared her to the fog falling over the mountains in great waves. No matter how beautiful or dense it seemed, one could never hold it in place or keep it from disappearing.

"All right then," Ann said to the owner. "I'll pay now and pick them up later."

"Shall I call you when they're ready?"

On the bottom of the receipt, she wrote down her home number then scribbled Richard's under it. Unlike the rest of the world, Ann didn't care for cell phones; she often forgot to charge hers, leaving it at home.

"If it's after Monday," she said, "call the other number."

* * *

RICHARD FINDS OUT about this exchange when the boutique owner, David Boucher, phones on Thursday. His name is French, he explains, and is pronounced *boo-shay*. Richard thinks that the man could have been Ann's lover. The name would have appealed to her, like French wine or dessert, Ann's favorite macarons. Richard has just sat down on the porch to drink a cup of coffee and read his morning paper. The call has startled him, and when Boucher tells him that Ann's outfit is ready for pick up, Richard says, "She isn't good at keeping track of time. It may be a week or a month before she remembers."

"Strange. It seemed urgent."

"It always is. Feel free to call me again if she doesn't show up by Christmas."

"But that's two months away," Boucher says.

"Exactly. Give her time."

Richard hangs up but remains seated, his gaze on a mob of birds crowding the sandbar. He remembers when he first brought Ann here, how mesmerized she became with the place, with that particular part of the landscape. She walked barefoot along the narrow strip of land wedged in the middle of the inlet. "Look," she said, toeing a swirl of foam and sand. "I'm walking on water." And then she laughed, the birds scurrying everywhere on their taut, string-like legs.

Eight years older than Ann, Richard is a tall wiry man with a full head of blond hair faded gray. From afar it almost looks white, like feathers only not as soft. Also from afar, he seems quite youthful; his back straight, his gait steady. But at a closer encounter, his age is evident: his skin has weathered to the texture of tree bark, grooves and dark blotches, shaded with beard. He remembers how Ann said it resembled dying moss, just as dry and sparse. When she felt bad, she could be cruel in her assessments. Richard doesn't give a damn now and can pretty much say anything back to her, but not to the children, who, having been brought up by a depressed mother and a workaholic father, still managed to graduate college, secure jobs, and avoid medication. They've inherited neither their mother's frailty nor their father's obsession with words and seem utterly in charge of their lives. Richard often marvels at their sense of reality, at how in touch they are with every little thing that aids and propels their existence. If they have dreams, he isn't aware.

Richard lives in his parents' beach house, where Ann and the children spent summers while he worked. After the divorce, Ann wished to stay in the mountains; Richard preferred the ocean. She said the mountains gave her courage, and he was buoyed by the water. Neither desired to remarry, agreeing to leave both properties to their children and let them decide who would end up with which house, even though Lena and Michael said they didn't want either one, didn't want their past to encroach on their future.

It was Ann's decision to split up, and Richard didn't object, especially because she'd told him about it in a letter sent from Canada. By that time Richard and Ann hadn't had sex for three years and slept in separate bedrooms. They were like two boats stranded in fog, never finding a harbor. At first Richard wasn't disheartened about the divorce, but somewhat relieved because he thought that he could give Ann what she craved most—freedom, both physical and spiritual, the kind of freedom that she lacked while being married. But later Richard thought that perhaps he'd surrendered too easily, abandoning Ann to her struggles and her medications: Zoloft, Prozac, Paxil, Celexa, Cymbalta, Remeron, Bupropion. Richard knew that all antidepressants increased suicidal behavior, but mostly in young people and only at the very beginning or when the dose was changed. And yet the feeling of personal failure and guilt persisted.

The beach house has been recently remodeled after the hurricane last October. Richard was in Boston, visiting his son, or he would have drowned, swept away like his furniture. He would have died. When he thinks of death, he isn't scared or upset, but he doesn't want it to be that kind of death, a stupid one. Ann would have scoffed at this—as though there could be a smart death. Even before they divorced, years before, her attention often strayed when he talked about such matters—life, death, global warming—her gaze drifting to the mountains, their prideful demeanor. Once she said, "You should write about them. The fog too. How free it is, unburdened, painless. How it can appear or slip away, unnoticed."

It isn't as though Richard has never written about the fog or the mountains—he has, many times—but he ended up making cuts at the last minute either because there wasn't enough space or because the writing seemed artificial. He was a reporter and dealt with people rather than nature, or how people abused and fought that nature. Neither in life nor in his writing did he welcome beauty for the sake of beauty. Beauty itself had no meaning unless serving some larger purpose. For Ann beauty has always been random and unattached. The beauty of life was in its momentum; the beauty of death in its constancy.

* * *

ANOTHER WEEK PASSES before Richard resolves to give the boutique owner a call. He isn't worried, he tells him, not yet, but perhaps he should check into it since he can't reach Ann by phone, at home or on her cell, and both answering machines are full. By now he also knows that Ann couldn't have slept with Boucher. Other than his name, there's no mystery to him, no great power to surrender to. Still Richard isn't concerned about his ex-wife's absence; puzzled is more like it. It won't be the first time that Ann left home and didn't tell anyone; sometimes she felt the need to go—the impulse, the urge, so alien to Richard's structured existence. She grew restless with people and places, the nagging predictability of everyday hustle. What's new is that Ann bothered to leave his number with Boucher, meaning that she was planning in advance and wanted Richard to know. The thought unsettles him.

In the kitchen Richard fusses over dinner: pasta primavera, a baked chicken breast, a glass of red wine—for the heart. He has a healthy heart, but at the moment it feels tight, uncomfortable, as though he needs to burp or drink more water. Which he does, a glassful, before calling Michael.

"I don't know when I talked to her last, Dad. Been awhile. Why?"

Richard stares at the old picture on the fridge, which has oddly survived the hurricane. It's warped and stained: the four of them on their backs floating in the shallow water. Legs apart, arms apart, holding hands. Giant starfishes in ridiculous oversize hats and sunglasses.

"She's sort of disappeared again," Richard says. "And she hasn't done it since the divorce." He lifts the picture off the fridge and peers at their faces, especially Ann's, who's smiling a tight smile as though afraid the water would leak inside her mouth and fill it with sand and shells, tiny crabs.

"I wouldn't worry yet." Michael is being his calm, lawyer-self. "She'll come back. She always does. Remember the fair?"

"That's different. She wasn't taking her medication. She got confused. She thought the man was her grandfather who'd vanished during the Blockade."

"But she's never met her grandfather. Don't you see? Mom is being Mom. She feels better among strangers. Give it until Christmas, then start looking for the body."

"Michael."

"Kidding."

Michael has always been Ann's favorite. As a child he was chubby, clumsy, and loved to sleep. Ann called him Mishka, "bear" in Russian, as she patted and nuzzled his hair, thick and brown like tufts of fur. She spoiled him with gifts and tales while Richard tried to make him useful, so he could aid society when he grew up. Michael loves Ann the way he's never loved Richard, even after she left him in a grocery store. He was ten and refused to go home with Richard, convinced that she'd come back. She did, only a week later, when Richard had already called the police and filed a missing person report. He almost hadn't slept while she was gone and lost ten pounds, a piece of his heart too.

Richard places the picture back on the fridge, securing a seagull magnet over it. He doesn't recognize anyone in that picture, only the sandbar, the waves, and the birds—so many, plucking invisible morsels of vegetation from the water.

* * *

ON HIS WAY to Charlottesville, Richard stops twice to refill the car; he also calls Boucher to confirm that Ann hasn't picked up the clothes. He feels a bit nervous but refuses to succumb to a futile emotion like panic. He understands that none of it is his fault: Ann's perpetual wandering, her depression, her restlessness, or his failed love, their broken home, from which all those years he tried to steal, like a thief, a nugget of warmth or comfort, a fragment of some eternal feeling that would cushion his old age. Not her estrangement either, the distance he fought to overcome in the past until it grew too heavy, too cumbersome, threatening to squash the last bits of goodness that still existed between them. He isn't to blame for any of that; still, he feels responsible and also scared, and not just for his children, what Ann's absence—should it become permanent—can do to them, a void it will create, a cold stark abyss he'll attempt to feel with words, but what it can do to him too. In some odd way his life depends on Ann's existence, her presence in the world. It gives him stamina and vigor—to know that she's there, in their family home, surrounded by the mountains and all that sentimental clutter, his parents' old dishes, Lena's and Michael's baby photos, their toys and schoolbooks, the first primitive typewriters that Richard hunted at flea markets. It is as though by staying alive and healthy he's determined to prove his worth to her, his righteousness, his ability to enjoy life even when it holds no excitement and no great mystery, nothing but this mundane, day-to-day puttering, the bleakness of a winter sky.

The drive ends up being pleasant, and as he gets closer, Richard contemplates the mountains in their autumnal glory. The colors are raw, jubilant, and he has succumbed to memories crowding his chest. Michael wallowing in a heap of leaves in the yard, only his head visible like a mushroom cap. Ann, pregnant with Lena, watching him by the back door, hands on hips. Her face as plump as her belly, rouged by hormones and whatever she was cooking that day. Smells haunt him too, smells of childhood and adolescence, of something left behind: his mother's meat loaf and spoon corn bread, the smoke from his father's pipe. He hits a bump, biting his lip, and now there's a tinge of blood in his mouth.

Richard decided to make the trip to Charlottesville after his daughter brought up the conversation she'd had with Ann last winter. It'd been snowing in the mountains, and Lena thought it was unsafe for Ann to drive to the airport. Most flights would have been canceled anyway. It was snowing in New York too. Ann said the snow was gorgeous, that it was almost as beautiful as Russian snow although she could hardly remember it; she was just a girl when they'd left the country. But she remembered scooping it in her fists in the yard while waiting for her parents to take her to school. She ate it too, and it tasted sweet like powdered sugar. Or at least she imagined it did. She put it in her pockets and her book bag because she thought she could keep it.

Later in the conversation Ann told Lena that she'd read an article about assisted suicide and how some countries, like Norway, allowed it, and how the relatives didn't even have to be informed. It was the person's choice, her privilege. Shouldn't it be like that everywhere?

"What are you saying? It's horrible, whatever the implications," Lena said.

"What's horrible is for someone to continue to live in pain," Ann said.

"Are you in pain? Do you feel depressed? Have you switched medications? Found a new doctor?"

"I have. In Canada."

"Canada? Why Canada? When did you go to Canada?" Lena asked.

"When I visited my parents on Thanksgiving. You were too busy to go with me."

"I had a presentation to make, prior commitments. We talked about it—I don't mind going, but I need to know in advance. I have a husband."

Ann's parents have been living in Canada ever since they immigrated. It has been their choice. They visited their daughter a few times but refused to move to the United States. While Russia was meddlesome yet obsolete, America seemed too impersonal, too frigid. It lacked culture and character. Richard tried to argue for the sake of his wife and children, but failed to sway them. Instead they said that he and Ann should move to Canada and buy a farm in western Ontario, close to the lake.

Lena has warned Richard about calling her grandparents until he's able to share some information. They're old and intolerant of pretty much everything: heat, cold, wind, rain, snow, elections. They still live in their old home but with a Russian housekeeper, who comes in every day and occasionally spends the night. He should talk to her first.

In Charlottesville Richard drives through newly populated neighborhoods, the echoing dullness of apartment buildings and shopping centers in place of once-lush forests and fields. The town is ripe with student life; the University of Virginia, Richard's alma mater, has long secured its prominence. He had too much hair back then and too much vigor—his ambition underscored by his desire to write. He strived to know the unknown, to understand his subjects and dig into their past, to reveal all that had been hidden, buried under a pile of dirt. Years didn't prove him wrong, but they didn't prove him right either, for the more he worked, the more the truth escaped him; or rather there were many truths that rivaled one another, and he was free to pick one and sell it to the public. He hadn't met Ann yet and regarded dating and girls as an unwelcoming yet necessary distraction. It was never about love or virtue but sex—the raw, the primitive, the wild. Time was infinite. It carried no meaning, no threat. It was a summer sky, blue and omnipresent, mapped with constellations, his future thousands of light-years away.

Richard has always believed that his life had a purpose, a destiny. But try as he might he can't describe what it is or even what it was, now that the children have grown and he and Ann divorced. He thinks of the hundreds of pieces that he wrote and how each time he finished one, he felt he'd lost something: faith, magic, the mystery of the unknown. He imagines not being able to talk to Ann or visit her ever again, and he's overwhelmed with pity—for himself, for her, for the life they struggled to build and failed, for the ghost of their love that still haunts him, years later.

On the road since 8 a.m., Richard is exhausted; his limbs groan like rusted springs. He's also famished. For dinner he stops on Campbell at a quaint French place, where Ann once found a tiny live snail in her salad. It's Thursday, and the restaurant is crowded, mostly students, but a few older joyless couples. He orders a glass of Avalon Cabernet, 2009, while flirting with the waitress.

"A good, dry year," he says. "Want to taste it?"

"No, thanks," she says. "I'm not allowed." She's hardly thirty, yellow hair, sweet unblemished face. Her full breasts are harmonious with the rest of her figure, her narrow waist and luscious hips.

"After work?"

"Not tonight." She smiles vaguely, the skin around her mouth is still soft, like new leaves. Richard feels that perhaps he can persuade her, at least once, to share his table and maybe his bed.

When Ann had an affair, just before they divorced, with the owner of an art gallery in town, Richard had one too. Yet he didn't feel vindicated because she did it first and also because he slept with a bartender, a middle-aged brusque woman who'd first gotten him drunk then fucked him in her car. She was married too. There were times in Richard's life when he felt pathetic, but then there were times when he felt helpless. After sleeping with the bartender, he felt both.

His dinner is uninspired: steak and french fries. Bloody, greasy, and oversalted. He ignores the pyramids of dessert offered by the tempting waitress, her voice low and velvety, like late-summer water at the lip of the sandbar. Richard leaves her an outrageous tip.

It's dark and bristly outside, and he wraps his jacket around him, raises the collar. The sky is fringed with clouds, the moon low, baring its cold puckered face. He hasn't smoked for ages, yet he lingers on the sidewalk, where a man is lighting a cigarette. He loves to inhale smoke, can almost taste a tinge of bitterness at the back of his throat.

* * *

RICHARD PARKS HIS car next to Ann's, the same dusty-blue Honda she's driven for the past decade. He glimpses a stack of magazines on the backseat, an umbrella, and a rain jacket, but no keys. He climbs the porch steps, misses one, and nearly falls, grabbing the shaky railing. The house lock hasn't been changed since his parents lived there. Richard has kept a spare key, in case of emergency. He still won't admit it is such a situation, but at least he has an excuse to enter without knocking.

"Ann?" he calls into the darkness. "It's Richard. Ann?"

The place is damp and smells of withered grass. He trips on a pile of books in the foyer, and they scatter all over the floor, the ancient Persian rug his parents had rescued at a yard sale. The colors have softened over time, the wool thinned in spots.

Originally the rug lay in the living room, and when Ann changed Michael's diapers on it, Richard held a box of wipes, ready to clean whatever mess awaited. It wasn't the money or the property he protected but the memories. A place where he, too, was a child. Ann nursed Michael for almost two years; she didn't nurse Lena at all. She was too sad to let her daughter suckle. How absurd was that? Richard learned to bottle-feed, to change diapers, to clip thin, almost translucent, nails. He gave Lena baths and occasionally felt like a pervert wiping her genitalia or rubbing anti-rash creams on those delicate folds of pink flesh. He blew air on her naked body because she loved it and because it tickled her. Her innocent laughter his near shame.

Except for the stack of books in the foyer, the rest of the rooms are in order, just as they'd been when they lived there as a family. Pictures hang everywhere, the evidence of their youth and happiness. Fragments of luckier times preserved under the glass. The four of them in Yosemite; at Cape Cod; feeding pigeons on Piazza San Marco. There are as many people on the piazza as there are birds, an importunate voracious horde.

It's been a few years since Richard visited, so he can't tell if anything is missing. Ann's clothes fill the closets, shoes on the low built-in shelves. Her jewelry box rests on the dresser, with a string of pearls drooping lazily on one side. Richards squats and peers under the bed. The suitcases are still there, two scuffed Hartman pieces from the time when the children were little and Ann traveled with them to Canada or occasionally followed Richard on yet another assignment.

In the living room a leather chair appears to be new, also a lamp, or maybe just the shade with its thick silky thrum. It reminds Richard of the waitress's hair. For a moment he imagines driving back to the restaurant and offering her a ride home or bringing her here and fucking her on the Persian rug or in Ann's high-poster bed. He cringes from the absurdity of his desire, augmented by age and this house, where his youth still resides.

"Past is the only constant," Ann once said.

"Past can be changed, to some degree, to aid the future."

"The future doesn't exist, Richard. It's like rewriting something that hasn't been written. Maybe that's why people are so screwed up, so desperate, trying to conform to some fictionalized version of themselves."

How Russian of her, he thought—the recalcitrance, the unwillingness to accept change, the overrated addiction to pain. Her generalizations, her truths, resembled those from Tolstoy's novels. Richard always felt that no matter how much he read them, he wasn't any closer to understanding them. Something always seemed inaccessible, just like his ex-wife.

Richard fiddles with Ann's laptop, which he can't get into without a password. He tries the children's names and birthdays, important dates and places, the city of Leningrad, where Ann was born. He can't tell what exhausts him more—the trying or the futility of the effort.

He finally dials Ann's parents, hoping to talk to their housekeeper, who picks up on the fifth ring. She speaks with a harsh accent and a mouth full of cookies. She apologizes for the crunching sounds, but Richard is unconcerned. Has Ann visited or called in the past week? When was the last time they saw her? Is there any way to find out the name of the doctor she was seeing?

"No need to worry her parents yet," he adds. "Confidentiality is the best thing."

"I understand," she says, her tone is stern, robbed of Western cheer. "Ann didn't see any doctors. She went to a reading."

"A reading? Where?"

"In Toronto. Someone famous."

"A woman?"

"I don't know. Can't remember. It's been a year. The last time Ann called was on Monday two weeks ago. We had dressed herring for dinner. Her favorite. She said she could smell it all the way in Virginia. She seemed happy."

Richard winces; his heart, an old startled bird, flopping about his chest.

For as long as he's known Ann, she's never been happy, but she can say cynical or tragic things in a facetious manner, and everyone believes her. Everyone but Richard, who understands that sometimes truths grow out of lies, pleasure out of pain.

From the china cabinet, Richard pulls out a bottle of whiskey, probably as old as his parents' dishes that Ann had fought to keep. They aren't exquisite or even pretty, large pink flowers on a cracked eggshell surface. Most of the dishes have chips; many have been broken, including an oblong serving platter for a family turkey.

The whiskey tastes rancid, and Richard discards the rest in the kitchen sink.

The cabinets and the fridge are nearly empty, except for a box of rice crackers, tea, oatmeal, honey, and coconut sugar. A piece of dry bread in the toaster. He remembers one Sunday morning, a year after his parents had died. Ann was sitting across from him, spreading butter on her rye toast. She always made perfect toast, a perfect sandwich, a perfect meal, as though trying to compensate for everything else in her life she failed to control. The sun dispelled the clouds, and everything in the room acquired a strange mellowed shape. Cabinets and dishes and Ann's face. There was tenderness in it and melancholy and purity and confusion. She seemed far away, as far as the mountains or the trees growing on top of them. Her eyes were half-closed, but she continued to chew, tearing one bite after another. He remembers making love to her, right here in the kitchen, passionately, desperately, trying to reach, to touch that untouched part of her. How thin she was, weightless, like a ghost forged out of fog and summer air, slipping through his arms.

* * *

ANN'S CELL PHONE is nowhere to be found, but the majority of messages on her answering machine at the house are Boucher's and Richard's; also—one from the pharmacy, several from Michael, and the most recent from Lena, who calls her mother by her name, as she would a friend. She has news, she adds, "Important."

Richard knows it's a strategy of Lena's—bait the opponent. The promise rarely delivered as stated. He dials his daughter, only to tell her that the house is empty and that he'll visit the neighbors in the morning.

"Don't be ridiculous. She never talks to the neighbors. They're Republicans."

"Even the preacher?" Richard asks.

"Especially the preacher," Lena answers. "Ann distrusts God."

"Church, not God."

"All of it. The conformity. She refused to baptize us, remember? She said they lied about everything. The place stunk. Then she bought us ice cream, all we could eat."

"How can you remember that? You were three."

"I was five and got sick. Michael too. Ann vanished for three days as soon as we got better."

Richard doesn't answer right away; he feels an unspecified emotion similar to pain yet not physical.

"Are you happy?" he asks.

"Are you?"

"You mentioned something important."

"I did? Oh, yes. I'm getting a divorce and moving to Africa." The insouciance in her voice is almost Ann's after yet another long, drawn-out disappearance.

"What's wrong with your husband and this country?" Richard asks.

"I don't love either."

From past experiences Richard knows that Lena's statements are only half-truths bathed in wine and sentiment. She resents her true feelings as much as she fears them. It's been years since he made her laugh.

"Michael is coming over for Thanksgiving," he says. "You?"

"No. I promised Ann I'd go to Canada."

"Christmas?"

"Maybe. If I haven't moved to Africa." She laughs a tight laugh then hangs up.

In the hall mirror Richard views his face, a tableau of nervous disappointment. His eyes are bloodshot, making him look even older and more restless.

There's this place between him and Ann and the children, a dry place, a swampland turned to desert. Twenty years ago, when Lena was sixteen, she had sex with a boy who was seventeen, at some pool party, drenched in music and booze. She said yes, and then she said no, but the boy was too drunk and the music too loud. He claimed he didn't hear her. Lena stayed home for a week afterward. Her eyes red and swollen. Michael could have been arrested for beating up the boy, breaking his nose and ribs, but his parents insisted they handle both matters privately; all to blame, none to be punished. Teenagers. Sex and violence fed by a riot of hormones. Ann pressed Richard to investigate and write an article, expose the assault. Perhaps there were other cases involving the same boy.

Richard refused. "She said 'yes' then changed her mind. She was drunk too."

"Sometimes a woman doesn't want to have sex, even if she allows it to happen. Sometimes a 'yes' is a 'no.'"

Richard felt Ann's words somehow directed at him, the hurt in them, the accusations. He slammed the bedroom door then hit it with his fist.

When he thinks about it now, Richard understands it was shame that prevented him from writing the article. Not the shame of disclosing the truth before the world, not even the shame attached to the nature of such incidents, especially back then, but the shame from his own powerlessness. He felt mortified because despite all his love and care for Lena, he failed to protect her. As a reporter he should have acted; but as a father he was convinced that documenting the assault, revealing all the chafing granules of truth, would have made it indisputable and unbearable—for him, as well as for Lena.

He regrets it, of course.

"She hasn't spoken ill of her husband once," Michael tells Richard when he phones him an hour later. Back in the foyer Richard has squatted on the rug, sorting through a pile of books. All story collections by Alice Munro.

"Lena can be secretive, like your mother," Richard says and picks up *Friend of My Youth*, his favorite.

"Still, she would've told me."

"Right," Richard says then switches topics. "Do you like Munro?"

"Who?"

"Alice Munro. She won the Nobel."

"I guess. I only read one book," Michael says. His voice catches in his throat, as though fighting a sudden cough. "I may not make it for Thanksgiving," he adds.

"Christmas?"

"Maybe."

"Work?"

"Sort of. Might be trading firms again. It's hard to adjust to people sometimes."

No shit, Richard thinks as he slips the phone into his pocket and walks out to the car for his duffel bag. The night is cool and misty, the prickly freshness of the mountain air. The moon nestles in the clouds dragging in lazy swollen heaps. Leaves crunch and scatter underfoot; Richard kicks them in all directions.

* * *

FORTY YEARS AGO Richard took on his first research project about a Canadian short-story writer, who was gaining an audience in the United States and who had just published her third collection,

Something I've Been Meaning to Tell You. Richard, who hadn't been a great fan of short fiction, read the collection and admired the prose. The craft was so subtle, so intricate, he wanted to meet the writer in hopes of learning her secret, of understanding the magic that held the seemingly disparate parts of the narrative together. Richard's piece ended up being too long and virtually unpublishable, but it was then and there that he'd met Ann.

The interview was scheduled for the previous afternoon, but because of the storm, it had to be postponed. The wind drove the snow over the lake, sweeping towns in sheets of white. Stores closed, schools and gas stations, even the post office. Richard spent all that time in a hotel, drinking whiskey and reading Munro. On the third day the storm had passed, and Richard ventured outside. Some people from the hotel were driving to the lake to take pictures, and Richard tagged along. Ann, who lived in Canada then, had come to town for a wedding, which also had to be postponed. She sat in the backseat, next to Richard, holding a camera against her chest, as though afraid to miss something very important. She rarely made any comments or laughed at jokes, but watched the road, the sadness in her eyes exquisite. Even though he detected no accent, Richard sensed her foreignness, some unconquerable distance that excited his imagination. There was thought and sensitivity in her demeanor but also delicacy. Like snow that melted under the touch.

The lake was deserted, and at first they didn't know they were standing on it. The sun shone through the trees. A charged brilliance to the air. Nothing could be seen for miles, nothing but hills and caves and the infinity of the blue sky. Trees broke here and there; some were bent to the ground. They resembled old people maimed by age or disease. Also, not too far in the distance, under a willow tree, they spotted an abandoned boat, or rather the oars sticking out of the ground like a pair of mighty hands. Ann told him that a man had drowned there last spring, the body disappeared. She began to take pictures, as did others, but Richard kept worrying about the ice cracking and giving way under their feet, a mouth of dark water growing all around them.

In less than six weeks Richard's parents would die in a car wreck, and Ann would nurse him through grief and loneliness and more snow.

* * *

RICHARD SPENDS THE night in the guest bedroom even though he could have slept in his former bed. The radiators creak and belch, and he's awoken by the noise, drifting in and out of darkness, a skein of memories that unravel somewhere deep inside.

It's early morning and Richard fidgets about the house, peeping inside a pantry or a closet, where as a child he hid from his parents. He's obsessive and relentless, yet has difficulty verbalizing his desire, his urge to ransack the house. He has no idea where to look or what to look for, nor can he stop. It is as though he's goaded into action by some indomitable force or the fog that spills over the mountains, weaving a cocoon of layers around the house. Or it could be the house. All those people who once lived there, his grandparents, his parents, Ann and he, the children. All that commingling energy stashed under the floorboards, tucked away inside the wardrobes and moldy chests. The house is crowded with echoes of all things past, the ghosts conjured into being by the simplest of objects: a cup, a coaster, a snow globe. Richard lifts it carefully. Behind the glass is a perfect house, a perfect family, a perfect Christmas tree. A red sled heaping with presents. On the bottom of the globe there used to be a key that turned four times before a melody played. Some sweet, affable tune he can't recall.

Shaking the globe, Richard watches the fake snow twirl and fall.

He puts the globe back in its place and walks through the kitchen to the garage. There, on one of the shelves, among paints and cleaning supplies, empty jars and spare bulbs, behind a scratched wooden case of an antient typewriter, Richard finds a caved-in, water-stained shoe box. He sits on the floor and places the box between his legs, takes the photos out one by one. They are Ann's black-and-white pictures of the lake, somewhat faded and distorted, like old memories. His heart hammers under his shirt as he arranges the photos in no particular order and studies them for a while, the immensity of snow and trees. The entire landscape has been frozen, changed into unfathomable shapes that resemble people, or beasts, or angels. Ann isn't in any of these pictures, only Richard, alone, dressed in his duffel coat and wool hat pulled low, right above his eyes. His expression suggests wonder but also helplessness lurking behind his stiffened smile.

The whiteness is astounding.

Champions of the World

Milka Putova and I had been friends since the first grade, which was pretty much for as long as I could remember. She was short and thin like a sprat, and every boy in our class called her exactly that—Sprat. She had small acorn-brown eyes, set too far apart and slanted—a result of 150 years of the Tatar-Mongol yoke, as she often joked. Her face was broad and pale, her pulpy lips raspberry-red, especially in winter, after we'd been sledding or building forts all afternoon, snow crusted on our knees and elbows, our bangs and eyelashes bleached with frost. We lived on the outskirts of Moscow and tramped to school together, across a vast, virgin field sprawled around us like white satin. She'd walk first through knee-deep snow, wearing wool tights and felt boots, threading her legs in and out; and I'd trudge after her, stepping in her steps, sinking my feet where hers had been just seconds prior. She'd halt and scribble her name with her gloved finger, and on the way back we'd rush to check whether the letters were still there or the snow had drifted over them.

Milka's school uniform had always been pristine—first a brown dress with a lace collar and a black or white apron with soft shoulder pleats that resembled a butterfly's wings; and later, starting from the eighth grade, a navy skirt and jacket, crude cotton shirts, collars starched and crisp. Her hair was dark gold, straight and silky, cut in a neat semicircle around her jaw. She shampooed her hair every day, and I loved to smell it when we sat next to each other during classes, the delicate scent of apple blossoms wafting around, arousing my senses, resurrecting our summer trips to my parents' dacha. How we'd sauntered through a corn maze, the stalks three times taller than we were, fingering green husks, separating soft, luscious silk to check on the size and ripeness of ears. Or how we roamed birch and aspen groves and gathered mushrooms for soup, their fragile trunks buried in grass, their red and orange caps burning under the trees like fake gems. Or how we swam in the river, racing to the other side and back and then climbing a muddy bank and drying off on towels, motionless like dead, sunbaked frogs—bellies up. Tiny pearls of water covered Milka's body, the hairs on her arms and legs scintillated, as though dipped in gold.

We had our first periods—two months apart—and grew breasts and pubic hair, started wearing bras and shaving armpits. I sprouted up and gained some weight and resembled my mother more and more—an ample, soft-bosomed woman who seemed stronger than my dad or all the men in the world. But Milka remained a sprat—short and puny, with long, awkward limbs and a caved-in stomach. When she stretched on her bed or bedroom rug after school, I could count her ribs, outlined by her T-shirt. Her hair was still the same length, still redolent of summers and tart Antonovka apples my parents grew at our dacha. Back then we paid no mind to scrapes or bruises or even pimples, which we often squeezed on each other's backs, and those summers seemed as endless as the lives ahead of us. We thought our parents to be old and hopelessly outdated, wasting hours in lines for sugar or toilet paper. Generation Buckwheat, we used to call them. And my mother would say, "Let's wait and see what they'll call you." By "they" she meant our future children, and we'd guffaw and chime in unison, "We won't have children. We'll elope to Paris and live happily ever after." Like most Russians we'd never been outside the Soviet Union, so Paris to us was just as far and impossible as the moon.

We turned sixteen when perestroika started and history lessons were canceled, and neither teachers nor parents could answer our questions: Are we free now? Can we go anyplace we wish? Can we listen to The Beatles and Queen openly? Can we buy Levi's jeans? And if Lenin and Stalin were despicable tyrants who'd cheated millions of people out of their beliefs and murdered the rest of the innocent but insubordinate Russians, who is left to lead this country into the future? What is the future? Can we tour the Gulag?

Milka was a dreamer, and when we weren't together she spent all her time reading, seduced by worlds remote and beautiful and unlike the one we'd grown up in.

"You know, back in the eighteenth century, rich women didn't even nurse their babies. They used serfs for that. I wish I'd been born then," she said, lolling back on her bed. I stretched next to her, folding my hands like a pillow under my head.

Milka lived closer to school than I did, so after classes we often went to her place and fried bologna and boiled potatoes, sliced pickles her mother had canned in summer and drank plum wine her stepdad fermented in a tall glass canister year-round. After pouring some of the wine, we'd dilute the contents of the canister with cold water and set the canister back in its place, behind the living-room curtains. Satiated and a bit tipsy, we'd lie on Milka's bed or the floor and listen to Freddie Mercury ululating "*we are the champions*" on a beat-up cassette player. We loved that song, even though we couldn't understand some of the words. Still, we bleated along as loud as we could, secretly wishing for someone to hear us and turn us into the champions.

I said, "What if you were born a serf? You own nothing. Not even your tits. And do you know what they did to misbehaving serfs back then? They buried them alive up to their necks and let starved dogs finish them off."

"Then I would've married a prince and moved into his castle."

"A prince would never marry a poor serf. Why pay for something you can have for free?"

"What about Praskovia Zhemchugova and Count Sheremetev? She was his lover for seventeen years. And when she was no longer a serf, he married her." Milka rolled on her back, her body limp and lazy, her eyes clouded with dreams. She smiled, parting her lips, her upper front teeth like two pearls inside a half-open shell.

"She was an actress in his theater," I said. "She was gorgeous and could sing like a fucking nightingale. You have no such talents. Besides, she died giving birth to his son at thirty-four or something."

"That's old, especially back then. They started fucking at twelve or sooner."

"Which puts us years behind."

"Speak for yourself," Milka said.

"So you already had sex and didn't tell me?"

"Why? Was I supposed to call you right after and describe my torn hymen?"

"Ugh, I don't want to hear about that."

"That's why I didn't call you. But there was blood everywhere."

"How much blood?"

"I don't know."

"A spoonful? A cupful?"

"I didn't measure. A ladleful."

"Liar."

"Am not."

"Who's the guy? Anyone I know?"

Her face tightened and turned red like her lips. She shook her head, "Na. A neighbor. Nothing remarkable. He had a birthday a few nights ago, and I didn't have any gift, so I presented him with my virgin flower." Her lips folded in a scowl.

"Did it hurt? On the scale of one to ten?" I asked.

"Twenty-four!"

"That bad?"

"Even worse."

"But a girl from my swimming team said it was nothing, like pricking your finger."

"Well maybe she has a rubber pussy and can't feel a damn thing. Or maybe she's been stretching it with candles for years, so it won't hurt later." Milka laughed, a short, abrupt chortle, then said, "Don't you fucking tell anyone."

"No," I said. "I'll post it on a school bulletin board."

She pinched my thigh and dragged a pillow over her face. "*We are the champions . . . of the world*," blared the tape, and just then I thought about the world as this enormous, wondrous place I might never get to see. I also imagined people everywhere listening to the same song and holding hands and making a continuous circle, like a variegated gird or belt, all the way around the earth. And then I asked Milka, "What do you think it really means—the champions of the world?"

* * *

I HAVE BEEN living in America for nearly two decades—an eternity. I came as an exchange student right after high school, got married and stayed. My husband, Mike, worked for a construction company then, doing mostly remodeling: patching and painting, restoring old floors or kitchen cabinets, replacing carpets, laying tile, installing new windows or countertops. He's what people call a handy man—that is, he can repair anything that has been broken. We don't have any children despite the fact that we've been married for eighteen years. At first we tried with all the fervency and zeal of newlyweds. We had been full of hope and joked about it each time we'd failed. We changed sex positions and made love at all hours of the day and night; I stayed in bed for forty minutes afterward, my buttocks raised, hips propped up on pillows. I took my temperature with a basal thermometer and drew charts of my menstrual cycles, highlighting the days of ovulation in red. We consulted several OB/GYNs in the area, who did a sperm count on Mike and blew dye into my fallopian tubes to check for scar tissue or any blockage. Back in Russia my mother had procured some ancient herbs she claimed would help with fertility. She sent them to us and urged me to put the bag under the mattress. Nothing ensued. Years stormed by and slowed down and eventually came to a halt. We let things go and become a memory. Not a bitter one, just vague and distant, like the mountain on a snowy day. We know it is there, although we cannot see it.

Since then I've gone back to school and completed a PhD in comparative literature, and my husband has moved from remodeling to building, mostly residential, but occasionally a restaurant or a factory. He's well respected in the area and earns a good, honest living. He has gained weight and lost some hair—the rest has turned silver, glistening like fish scales under the sun. He's tall and brawny and resembles an ogre, who can carry a house on his shoulders. He has big, kind hands he wraps around me every night before we go to sleep. He nuzzles my hair and jokes that it smells like books. We are comfortable. We rarely argue or disagree or have long passionate conversations, and sometimes I think of us as two pet fish in our aquarium navigating through tall, wavering weeds, or hibernating inside a plastic castle, or hiding under a rock, ostracized by the glass walls. We depend on each other and those walls.

It's hunting season in Virginia. My husband's high-powered rifle is resting atop his camouflage attire—a pair of heavy-duty overalls, a windproof jacket, a cap with a wide, curved bill. Under the chair are the scuffed leather boots he greases with silicon for protection against rain and mud. Mike used to hunt bear, but nowadays he only hunts deer. You're allowed one buck per season, and some years there's a doe day. We don't eat venison, so Mike gives his prey to our neighbor, Jack, who has four children, a wife, and three pound-rescued mongrels. Jack works at the Volvo plant, making parts for trucks. His dream is to become a manager, so he can afford a decent nursing home when he ages beyond salvation and his wife and children are tired of passing him around like a useless family antique. Out the window I see two skinned, gutted deer hanging from the swing in his yard. At the bottom of the plastic slide, the heads stare at the decapitated corpses with their doleful glassy eyes. The mulch and sand around the swing are dappled with blood, and there's a puddle directly under the deer carcasses, and one of the dogs is lapping from it.

Back at my desk I examine a stack of research materials as tall and mighty as the Eiffel Tower. I've been devising a new course—Literature of Resistance—and have plowed through hundreds of articles and memoirs in the past few months. I've discovered a book of testimonies by Russian women who'd been imprisoned and sent to labor camps, or exiled in Siberia. While in the Gulag, all were violated, dehumanized, turned into submissive, inert creatures by the Stalinist regime. Their bodies became a public urinal, devoid of shame or feeling. Most women talked about their bodies existing separately from their minds, as though their heads had been cut off, their limbs numb and distant. One woman was six months pregnant when she'd arrived at Kolyma, and all she could remember about the next three years of her imprisonment was not persistent hunger or rape or the death of other inmates, but the slow and blunt determination with which the guards had beaten the baby out of her. She had lost her voice screaming and could not talk again.

When Mike returns from work in the evening and I ask him to look out the kitchen window, at the butcher's shop in our neighbor's yard, he says there's nothing wrong with it—the course of life—a little bloody perhaps, but only for a city girl like me. I keep staring out the window. It's dusk; the sun has fizzled out, a splash of color on the crepuscular sky. The deer heads are gone, but the carcasses are still there, turning slightly in the wind.

* * *

IN THE LAST year of high school, our class staged *Hamlet*, translated into Russian by Boris Pasternak. I played Queen Gertrude because everyone decided I was mature enough and had a womanly figure. And Milka agreed to impersonate Prince Hamlet because no boy would—since it'd recently become known that Hamlet might have slept with the queen. All the boys in our class said they would not fuck their own mothers even if someone paid them a million dollars. Milka shrugged and picked up a long, sharp-ended pointer from the teacher's desk and lunged forward a few times, left hand raised in the air. She said she'd avenge her father and Queen Gertrude and kill Claudius and anyone who would stand in her way, "*To be or not to be.*"

We memorized our lines and rehearsed for hours after school. We even watched *Гамлет*, a 1964 film adaptation, directed by Grigori Kozintsev and with an original score by Dmitri Shostakovich. My mother had sewn Milka's and my costumes, and we were able to borrow a foil from a fencing club. With her jaw-length hair, dressed in a short red-velvet cape, matching pantaloons, and my father's old white shirt to which my mother had attached a pleated-lace jabot and cuffs, Milka indeed resembled a prince—pert and defiant. Her gait was full of the unhurried dignity bequeathed to royal heirs at birth.

On her feet she wore a pair of men's black leather slippers she had to stuff with wadded newspaper because they kept falling off as she moved about the stage. She still looked bony, except for her breasts concealed under the jabot.

Our final history exam had been canceled because the board of education hadn't had the time to rewrite history books and supplement all the missing or purposefully warped information. Lenin's portraits were torn from the walls, stomped and pissed on, his busts and monuments dragged off the pedestals and shattered; chunks of marble and granite filched overnight.

A week before the performance, we walked back from school to Milka's place. It was early spring, the air sharp and breezy, redolent of fresh growth. Everywhere trees swelled and budded, leaves began to unfurl. The sun was high in the sky, melting the last, ashen patches of snow crusted on the curbs. I seethed with energy and gabbed about us becoming a revived nation, a new people, who would bewilder the world—Generation Glasnost—and about my hope of getting into the Institute of Foreign Languages and maybe studying abroad, and Milka visiting me. Or maybe we could apply together. She didn't say much, but nodded every now and then, her mind as far away as the crowns of poplars bowing in the distance. As we reached Milka's building of flats, she said she had vodka and cigarettes and we should celebrate—us having all those choices, all that freedom.

We burrowed in her flat, like we had for years, frying potatoes and listening to the Queen tape. We poured vodka out of Milka's stepdad's bottle and added some water to it. Milka didn't say much, but shuffled about the kitchen like an old woman, her slippers scuffed at the back. It looked as though she'd filled up in places, and I even joked that she no longer resembled a sprat but a full-grown herring. She forged a tart smile, and I pinched her ass, hoping to make her laugh. I felt silly and tipsy; my heart pounded under my shirt. It was a feeling of some great wonder I couldn't identify, as though I was about to discover life on Mars or see an American movie for the first time in my life.

In Milka's room we opened the window and lit cigarettes, hanging halfway out, blowing a quivering tail of rings in the air. I stuck my finger out and put it through one of Milka's rings, so it resembled a wedding band, but then it dissipated right in front of our eyes.

"I need a favor," Milka said, her voice hoarse, raspy.

"What?"

"You're my best friend, right?"

"Wrong. I'm your only friend," I said, flipping away the cigarette, chuckling.

"I need you to hit me in the gut."

I turned to look at her, but she continued to smoke, her eyes on the lilac tree in front of the window.

"What the fuck?!" I said. "Are you drunk?"

"Pregnant."

"Fuck! No!"

"Yes. And you don't know the worst part," she said and stubbed the cigarette on the windowsill blotted with pigeon shit.

"What can be worse?"

"It's my stepdad's."

I blinked and cupped my mouth, dragged my hand all the way down my chin and neck. "You're kidding, right? You're humping your daddy?"

"Shut the fuck up. It's fucking complicated. You don't know shit."

"What do you mean I don't know shit? You're screwing your mama's man. What else is there to know? You don't do that. Are you fucking crazy?"

"My mother used to put me between them when I was little and then later, when I was a teenager. As soon as he'd get a hard-on, she'd throw me out the door, so he could hurry up and screw her."

"Are you shitting me? Ugh, this is fucked up. We need to tell somebody."

"Like who? Who gives a fuck if your own mother doesn't? Anyway it's too late for the abortion. I had my period the first three or four months. It was light, but I still had no idea I was pregnant. My boobs were sore, but I thought—growing pains, you know. When I told my mother, she started crying and pleaded with me not to do this to her, not to steal this fucking man of hers. He's all she's got; she can't be alone. I'll get married and leave, and who will she have? She said we could sell the baby to some rich folks, but I would have to go away for a while, until the baby is born, to live with my aunt in Norilsk. Do you know where that is? It's fucking Kolyma. I have to get rid of this baby. I don't want it, and I don't want to sell it to some sterile fucks who can abuse the shit out of it."

I was silent. I couldn't say a thing, my tongue in my throat. I stared at a small rectangular aquarium on her desk, the walls overgrown with silt. Through the greenish, murky water I noticed a few small fish not really swimming but stalling in place as though waiting out a storm.

"I've thought this through. Women used to do it a lot, hit themselves in the stomach with stones or irons. And then, boom—a miscarriage," she said.

"I'm not going to hit you. I won't be a part of it. Don't even fucking try."

"Then you aren't my friend."

"I *am* your friend. But this is fucking crazy. And what are you going to do with the baby?"

"We'll bury it someplace."

"And what if it's alive?"

"We'll take it to the hospital and tell them we found it in a trash can in the yard—happens all the time."

"No, it doesn't. What the fuck is wrong with you?"

"I'm pregnant, and I hate it. I hate everyone. You too."

"Why me? What did *I* do? I'm the one who should be mad. I thought we were best friends. I told you everything, and you told me shit. You're ruined. Fucking evil. You could've slept with *my* dad and thought nothing of it."

"Why not? I'm already wearing his shirt for the performance. *There's nothing good or bad, but thinking makes it so.*" She gave me a mocking smile, but her eyes were cold and distant, like those of the fish in her aquarium.

Gasping I took a step back and then jumped at her and began to pound on her face and chest and everything I could reach. She didn't defend herself but retreated deeper into the room and cowered next to her bed as I rammed my feet in her crotch and higher, between her ribs.

* * *

I HAVE A recurrent dream in which I'm trying to cross a long, deserted bridge, although there's no one waiting for me on the other end. My legs are stiff and stone-heavy. I can't move. Or if I do move, I don't go very far and turn around after taking just a few steps. There're no visible obstacles or obstructions ahead. The planks are even and smooth, attached to nothing. It seems as though the bridge has been suspended from the sky, but I can't see the ropes. I have no idea what's beneath the bridge, or what exactly it connects, or why I have to cross it, so I stand, confounded by the urge to get to the other side, swaying lightly, like a tree in the wind.

Mike says I should see a shrink, like the rest of the world. Perhaps there's a greater post-Freudian mystery to dreams. Perhaps it's just my longing to travel back home, but not wishing to undertake such a strenuous journey. Perhaps I miss all the snow—it hasn't snowed much since our wedding in February of 1992. Perhaps it's the fact that we don't have children and aren't planning any further steps, to undergo artificial insemination or in vitro. We haven't talked about a possibility of adoption but once, leaving the matter suspended, indefinitely.

The truth is—I haven't been home for ages. My parents are getting old, so they aren't eager to make the trip either. My mother tells me that everything has changed—music, clothes, food. Stores groan with goods, but prices are rocket-high, so people can't afford much. Some threw their dogs out on the streets because they weren't able to feed them. And now there are all those strays scouring the city. My parents still spend summers at our dacha, raising flowers and making apple preserves. Last time I talked to them, a few weeks ago, they said they had to cut down one apple tree and would replace it with another, a sweeter variety. But they didn't mention which tree or what kind exactly they would plant instead.

Once again I hoped they could meet us abroad, in Rome or Paris, where Mike and I had vacationed a few summers ago. We'd signed up for a tour and flew to Paris, where we stayed in Hôtel Bel Ami on rue Saint Benoit. Like Moscow, Paris was a sullen beauty, engorged with people and dust. We climbed the Arc de Triumph and rode up the Eiffel Tower and marveled at the city below as if it were made of papier-mâché, its miniature streets running in perfect symmetry. We cruised on the Seine, which smelled of kelp and herring; the water mossy-green and turbid, with leaves, cigarette butts, and candy wrappers floating around. We took a day trip to Versailles and roamed its half-empty rooms once filled with gaudy dresses and talcum powder, wine and harpsichords, political intrigue. In the Musée d'Orsay we devoured three levels of art, moving in silent awe from Degas to Delacroix to Monet to Matisse. And while conquering the Louvre, we huddled, among thousands of other tourists, in front of the *Mona Lisa*, trying to capture the Madonna's enigmatic smile on a cheap camera. In Montmartre we bought cortisone ointment in a small apothecary because Mike's arms kept itching, and then sat on the curb, eating ice cream, studying cracks in the walls of old buildings.

There was an open space between two buildings, and we could see mountainous clouds squatting over the city.

On our last night, at dinner in a restaurant with an odd name, Bouillon Racine, I was telling Mike about the article I'd recently read.

"Kubler-Ross's new book—*On Grief and Grieving*—just came out. It's a follow-up to *On Death and Dying*," I said, sipping sharp, fruity red wine. "Basically she claims that like the dying, the grieving undergo the same five stages: denial, anger, bargaining, depression, and acceptance. We see it in literature too. For example, we can assume Hamlet acted the way he acted because he was grieving over his father's death, undergoing the aforementioned stages."

"Makes sense. Although I don't remember exactly how he acted," Mike answered, placing a cube of meat in his mouth, chewing.

"Well some critics insist Hamlet had a strong sexual desire for his mother."

"Because he was angry or depressed?"

"Or both. But I think there's more to grief than just those stages. And some people never accept the loss because their whole identity is inextricable from the deceased."

"I remember when our mother died, my sister and I, we were very confused. And my sister, who'd just married, decided not to have any children because she didn't want them to see her die and feel all the grief. Now what bullshit stage is that?"

"I think grief makes us uncomfortable. We act irrationally."

"Yeah. In the months after the wedding, my sister, she talked to herself all the time. Her husband didn't know if she was hallucinating or what."

"In some cultures the dead aren't really gone, so you keep conversing. Russians believe that after a person dies, her soul is around for nine days. Then it travels back and forth between heaven and earth for forty more days before leaving for good. But if a person committed suicide or was murdered, then her soul never leaves, but hovers among the living. Brings up the metaphysical questions about existence, yes? You think there's life after death?"

"No. This is it. This is all you get, so you better not screw it up. And my mother drank herself to death. So did she kill herself? Or was she poisoned by people who produced the shit?" Mike asked, washing the meat down with the beer.

A pale, gaunt woman walked into the restaurant with four children, who were like a swarm of bees around their mother's bright pink skirt. The youngest one—a boy of about three—clutched her hand as she trailed after the waiter. Her skirt was loose, fluttering about her ankles, which made it impossible to gauge the size of her hips. She wore a halter shirt without a bra; her stomach tight, her breasts small and pointy, as though she'd never carried or nursed a child. The restaurant was half-vacant, candles wavering on linen-draped tables. The woman paid no attention to us as she ambled by and chose the farthest table in the corner. She began pulling the chairs out and watching her children take seats one by one, the baby too. They fussed and clamored and swung menus at each other. From afar they resembled a nest of chirping fledglings, waiting for their mother to drop food into their mouths. The woman took a clip out of her hair, letting her locks fall to her shoulders. Her hair was dark like pumpernickel bread, although it could have been colored.

"Stop staring," Mike said.

"I'm not."

"Yes you are. You always stare at women with children. You know what *I* think?"

"No."

The candle on our table sputtered and went out.

"I think we should adopt."

"No," I said and downed the rest of my wine.

"Why not? We have the money."

I shook my head.

"What? What is it then?"

"I don't want to abuse someone else's baby." I grimaced, attempting to smile, and waved at the waiter to bring the check.

* * *

MILKA CALLED ME the morning after the fight, after she'd allowed my fists and feet to touch her unprotected, humble body. It was early, the sky shy with dawn. I had been on the cusp of sleep all night, so when the phone rang, I reached down to the floor and grabbed it.

"I'm having it," she whispered. "Can you come? I'll tell my mother I'm sick, and they'll be gone for work in a few hours. I'll leave the door open."

I got up and made the bed and dressed in my school uniform and packed my bag, my knees weak, hands trembling. In my jacket and a new beret my mother had knitted, I waited until 7:00 a.m. to wake my parents and inform them I had play rehearsal before classes. They nodded, rubbing dreams out of their eyes. "Did you fix yourself a bologna sandwich for lunch?" my mother asked. And I said I'd be eating at school; they were serving beef Stroganoff.

Milka lived twenty minutes away, but I made it in ten, running, taking shortcuts through muddy yards and playgrounds, climbing up a kindergarten fence and exiting on the other side. When I arrived at her building of flats, I was panting like a dog, tongue out, eyes bulging.

Her flat was quiet, the air still, as if inside an igloo swept with snow. I saw two sets of slippers under the coatrack and a newspaper tossed on the chair. Milka's bedroom was closed, and no sounds reached me. Without taking my jacket off, I tiptoed down the hallway and listened by her door, the book bag dangling off my shoulder. I thought I heard someone whimper, so I stepped back and then forward, pushing the door open, just with the tips of my fingers.

Milka half sat, half lay on the bed, her face puffy and smeared with blood, dried rivulets on her cheeks. The blanket was drawn up to her neck, shielding her scrawny body, her knees bent, legs somewhat apart. There was also blood in her unkempt hair as though she'd been wiping her hands through it.

"It's over," she said, her gaze switching from my face to the window, to the lilac tree bursting with tiny purple flowers.

"Over?" I repeated.

"Yes."

"Where is it?"

"Here." She nodded at her knees then exhumed her one arm from under the blanket. She began to peel the covers away, slowly, as though afraid that whatever hid underneath might escape.

I couldn't bring myself to look at it, so I shut my eyes and, jerking the beret off my head, pressed the wool to my face.

"Can you bury it?" Milka asked. "I'm too tired, and I have to wash the damn sheets."

"Where should I take it?" I mumbled.

"I don't know. Just don't bury it under no fucking windows, where dogs can get to it."

She wrapped the baby in her old T-shirt with faded rose print and then in a white towel, and I placed the bundle in my school bag, taking a few books out and leaving them on her desk, next to the aquarium. I couldn't see any fish but a fake coral reef and a few scrawny weeds.

As I was stepping out the door, I asked, "You okay? Will you be okay? I'll come back afterward, if you want me to."

She shook her head and curled into a fetal position and pulled the blanket over.

On the wall above the bed hung the picture of her father, who'd died in a car wreck when she was just a baby. It was a black-and-white portrait, large and square; the wooden frame chipped at the corners. The man in the picture had a smooth, shaved face. He smiled— lips curving in a pulpy half-moon—but his eyes held deep sadness as though he'd already known what would happen to him and his daughter and the grandchild.

Outside I stood on the empty street, watching a stray dog nose a pile of trash near a freshly painted dumpster. I thought of sneaking the baby in there, but then I remembered my mother preaching to my father that the dead had to be buried, laid to rest—otherwise they'd come back to haunt you—that if the government had bothered to give Lenin a proper burial as opposed to preserving and displaying his wretched body, our country wouldn't have been in such a pitiful shape seventy years later.

I tramped to the bus stop and brooded over going to a park and burying the baby there, under a tree. But I had no tools, and the ground was too hard to paw with my fingers, and I was scared that someone might see me and call the militia. Finally I decided I had no choice but to ride to my parents' dacha. We had a tool shed, and I knew where my parents kept an extra set of keys—in the outer house, inside a red plastic pitcher on the wall.

There were mostly women on the bus and a few older men, who carried mesh totes with newspaper-wrapped packages and fruit saplings sticking out like brooms—naked branches tied together at the lower end. I had an odd feeling that everyone on that bus was watching me and that they somehow could guess what was stowed in my bloated bag. The bus shook and rumbled, and I held tighter to my cargo, pressing it against my belly.

It was a brisk fifteen-minute walk from the bus stop to the village, to the side of which a small community of houses, like cattle, herded up on the hill. Each house was fenced off, and each piece of land that came with it was utilized, mapped out perfectly, establishing a sense of order in people's lives. There were virtually no yards, but narrow paved or trodden paths meandering between withered flower beds and fruit trees and compost piles. Most everyone in the community cultivated a vegetable garden and grew strawberries, raspberries, gooseberries, currants, and apples. That was how city people survived during winters—eating what they had canned during the summer. My parents raised apples, and that was only because they didn't have to do much to them but spread manure under the trees twice a year. My mother also planted bushels of flowers—narcissi, gladioli, marigolds, daisies. She insisted the world could use more beauty, if only seasonal.

When I arrived at the dacha, I climbed the wooden fence like I used to with Milka, the bag swinging off my neck. I noticed that some of the boards had come loose over the years, the blue paint had bubbled up and shriveled, begun to peel. From the pitcher I extracted the keys, and from the tool shed, a spade. I debated whether to bury the baby in the cornfield, or in the birch grove, or on the bank of the river. But the more I thought about it, the less any of those places made sense to me. What if Milka wished to visit the grave sometime and I wouldn't be able to point out where it was? And what if one of the neighbors saw me walking around, carrying a spade? They would most certainly tell my parents. So as I stood there, next to my mother's flower beds swept with leaves and twigs and palm-size patches of charcoal snow, I raised the spade and began to dig under one of the apple trees, its limbs covered in tight, pearl-pink buds. I rammed the spade into the ground and hacked away at the hardened dirt, breaking it up and chipping a piece at a time, trying to carve out a wide enough space.

When I finished, I put the spade aside and retrieved the bundle from the bag. The blood had soaked through the towel. The stains resembled small flowers or berries crushed in the snow. I went back to the shed and looked for some kind of burial box and found nothing but a small jar of nails and a rusty basin filled with my father's old shirts torn for rags. There was not much I could do but place the bundle into the hollow of the still-frozen earth. Although before covering the baby with dirt, I brought it back up and slowly unfurled the towel and the rest, parting the layers of fabric like cabbage leaves.

In there, curled on its side was a miniature person—a boy. He was scarlet and tiny, with an elongated, egg-shaped head; knees bent, fists clamped against the button mouth as though in defense. He just lay there, amid a tangle of bloody rags, like a skinned animal—a squirrel or a rabbit—a hump of bare flesh on a strip of snow. His eyes were shut, body pleated with wrinkles like the trunk of an elephant. When I drew my finger along his shoulder, it felt cold and hard and slick. There was a tiny hose protruding from its belly, torn and ragged at the end, as though chewed off. I took the beret off my head and gently lulled the baby inside, as we had lulled dolls inside paper boats before setting them afloat in puddles of rain. I lowered him in the ground, folding the towel on top. Tears washed down my cheeks; my skin tingled and burned. I gathered an armful of clumpy dirt, shoved and padded it back in place, and then scooped some soggy leaves. I watched them fall through my mud-caked fingers and land under the apple tree.

* * *

I LISTEN TO very little music in the house or the car. A lot of times I find it distracting and irritating, even on long car trips, when Mike and I visit his sister and have to cross the mountain. We don't talk much either but stare out the windows, passing a comment or two about the weather or the serene beauty of the place we live in, a deer grazing a tuft of grass on a rocky hill.

Some days Mike and I don't see each other but for a few hours before bedtime. He feeds the fish in the aquarium, and I brew herbal tea, and we relax, shoulder to shoulder, on the couch in front of the TV. After thirty minutes or less we carry our cups to the sink, brush our teeth facing the mirror, and retire upstairs, books or magazines in hand. Mike reads detective stories or flips through builders' catalogs, and I indulge in Russian poetry—my favorite Akhmatova, Tsvetaeva, Berggolts, Pasternak. Poetry appeals to me because it's succinct yet doesn't have to be interpreted any certain way. A few days ago, in my Literature of Resistance class, one of my students asked why most Russian poets had either been murdered or committed suicide, why most Russian writers had been mentally or physically ill, or both: Gogol, Dostoevsky, Chekhov, Bulgakov. And why all Russian literature is fraught with pain and suffering—everyone important to the story dies or is about to die, and there's no retribution at the end. Does life mirror art? Or art, life? Is it really all that hopeless? There was a heated discussion, a debate, a crossfire of opinions, but at the end I said, "Read Shakespeare, *Hamlet*—it's all in there—death, murder, suicide, and endless misery. And we're all willing participants."

Mike is home earlier than usual because we have to visit the neighbors and meet their new Russian baby. Their four biological children had the flu all winter, passing it on to one another like a pair of hand-me-down boots. The after–New Year's gathering was canceled, and then the semester started, and Mike and I went back to work.

"Ready?" he asks, peeping in the bathroom.

"Almost. I just need to do something with my hair."

"Looks good the way it is. I like it wild and curly. They won't care."

"Don't forget the gifts. The bag is next to the bed."

"What did you end up getting? Clothes or toys?" he asks.

"Neither. I bought a picture frame and a complete edition of Shakespeare's works."

"How do you know they read Shakespeare?" Mike's eyebrows arch, his forehead puckers.

"I don't. But perhaps they will now. At least the children."

He shakes his head, his hand rubs against his jaw peppered with short, graying hairs. "They'll think you're showing off, that you're some snooty city girl coming to their house and telling them what to read."

"I'm not worried about that. You?"

He shrugs and leaves the bathroom, and sometime later, as I finish drying and pulling my hair straight, I see him out the window scraping the driveway. It has snowed all day again, and the cypress trees around the house are robed white. The bird feeder must be empty because a cardinal is pecking at chunks of stale bread I tore up and scattered just an hour ago.

When we arrive at the neighbors' house, there's a bit of a commotion in the narrow hallway. I see a long, endless line of shoes against the wall and a huddle of coats on the rack. It takes us some time to hang ours; mine keeps falling down, and Mike keeps reaching for it on the floor. The dogs bark somewhere in the basement. The two older children are in their room, playing video games, their mother informs us, but the two younger ones, twin boys of nine or ten, swirl past us, up and down the steps with water guns in their hands. They squirt each other and accidently their mother, who yells, "Hey, hey—no water in the house. How many times do I have to tell you?"

Widget is short and buxom, with wide hips and a kind, enveloping smile. Or at least I think one must be kind to deliver and raise four children and adopt a fifth one. She wears a pair of loose jeans and a sweatshirt, stained in the front. Under a brown smudge of someone's thumbprint, I read: *Hearts Aren't for Sale.*

"Cool, isn't it? Got it at the flea market in Hillsville. Have you ever been there? It's a madhouse. You can walk and walk, for hours."

"No. I haven't been," I say.

"Mike should take you. It's every Labor Day weekend. And you can get anything there. I mean anything. We buy cheap shirts for the kids—they go through clothes like crazy. We like to look at antiques too. People certainly took better care of their stuff back then."

"Or maybe it was made better," Mike says. "Most furniture was solid wood and not particle board, sanded and varnished and put together by hand."

"True," Widget confirms with a nod. "Jack went to get beer. At the last minute he decided we needed beer. We don't keep any alcohol. We don't want the children to see us drinking."

"In Russia," Mike says, "there'll be teenagers drinking vodka on a bus or subway right after school."

"How would you know? You haven't been to Russia," I say.

"You won't take me. Although I can hardly get away in summer. And it's too cold in winter."

"Actually it isn't," Widget says. "We thought so too, before we went to Pskov to pick up our son. But it wasn't much colder, and not that much snow either. Wasted all that money on new down coats. Well why are we standing in the hallway? Come see the baby."

The house is sweltering hot and smells of cooked meat and hot cocoa. The living room is spacious, with a large couch and chairs, and I imagine the entire family nesting there for a movie, passing a tub of popcorn back and forth. The floors are carpeted and have toys and clothes strewn across. There are no paintings or vases or any embellishments, except for deer heads on the wall above the mantel and a maze of children's photos on the end tables.

We follow Widget into the master bedroom, where inside a pale wooden crib we discover a sleeping baby. He's dressed in a blue jumper and his head is gilded with downy-soft coils of hair. One of his dimpled hands is under his cheek, another lies on an old toy—a teddy bear with matted fur and a knot of torn threads in place of the nose.

"He brought that toy with him. It's been almost five months, and he still won't go to sleep without it," Widget says.

"I was like that too." Mike leans over the crib. "My mother told me that when the bear had literarily fallen apart, they had to buy a new one, exactly the same."

The baby pouts, stretching in his sleep. His mouth opens and closes, foamy bubbles at the corners.

"We're waking him up." I step back, ready to exit the room.

"No, no. He can sleep through an earthquake. In that orphanage there were so many children, I don't know how they ever slept," Widget says, dropping her mouth into her fist. "He's ten months, but he doesn't even sit up yet. The pediatrician said there's something wrong with his leg muscles. He might never walk. We're waiting for the test results, and we're seeing a physical therapist next week." She places her hand over the baby's, tracing his petite fingers with hers.

"Hey, we have something for you," Mike says and looks at me.

"Yes, we do. But you know what," I touch Mike's hand, squeezing it lightly, "I think it's not going to fit him. He's bigger than I thought. I'll exchange it and bring it by in a few days. Maybe I'll find another bear, just like the one he has."

* * *

THE PLAY WAS canceled because Hamlet had died. Pupils and teachers gossiped and speculated in low, mournful voices. The school life paused, and we avoided looking at one another, as though each had been responsible for Milka's death. I sat alone at my desk; her seat vacant for the rest of the school year. They didn't pester me with any questions, but the teachers stroked my shoulders as they walked by. One day during recess the principal hugged me and encouraged me to stop by if I wanted to talk. She said time healed the deepest of wounds, bridged the widest of gaps—one day I would wake up and realize how wonderful life was, despite all the grief and sadness.

Milka's parents wouldn't divulge what had happened or share any details. They became gatekeepers of Milka's death. They wouldn't answer phone calls or talk to anyone. At school we were told that Milka had food poisoning, and by the time her mother ferried her to the hospital, it was too late—Milka's body had failed. At home my parents would stare and barrage me with questions: Do you know anything that we don't? Was she upset, angry, hurt? Did she have a boyfriend? Could she have gotten pregnant? Did she talk about killing herself? Did you see her that day? Did you miss school because you were together? Are you telling us the truth?

I didn't know. I didn't know what the truth was or is, although I've tried and tried to understand it. Is it true how it happened? Or how we remember it happened? Or how we imagine it happened? I've read somewhere that truth is a formula of belief, but then if you can't prove it, is it still true? And if at some point your belief changes, does truth become altered? Do we forgive ourselves? Or do we keep waiting for salvation?

After the funeral I couldn't eat or sleep for weeks. I lay in my bedroom most evenings and nights, gathering tears in my fists and watching the sheers puff up on my window and go limp like a piece of a shroud. I listened to the trees shivering with new leaves and dogs barking somewhere on the street and my parents discussing my pitiful state in the living room. I imagined Milka jumping out the window, crushed on the pavement, or slicing her wrists and bleeding to death, or swallowing a bottle of pills, chasing it with her stepdad's vodka. I imagined her dangling from the ceiling light or stabbing herself in the gut. But nothing would satisfy me. I became pale and rickety, a skeleton in a sack, a ghost hovering about the flat or lurking behind school doors. Sounds hurt me, silence did too. Sometimes it felt as though my ears crawled with spiders spinning labyrinths inside my head. I shook it and shook it and buried it under the pillows so as to muffle that incessant, tedious rustling like raindrops hitting trees.

My mother left her job because she feared the worst. It was the only time she'd ever smoked. We even did it together, huddling on the balcony, puffing the days away. Cowering on a stool next to me, she'd rub my shoulder or comb my hair behind my ears, a gesture I found all too unbearable, but otherwise she was afraid to touch me, to scoop me in her arms or kiss my head as she always did. Occasionally she and I would go to the movies and instead of watching the film, I would catch her staring at me. Her face contorted with fear. She'd grab my hand and wouldn't let go until the end of the movie, and I could feel her heart throbbing in my palm.

The teachers showed compassion and paid little mind to my not studying in those final months before graduation, and when I received my diploma, my grades were just as high as they'd been all year, prior to Milka's death. That summer, with the urgent support of my parents, I matriculated into the Institute of Foreign Languages and, a year later, was offered a chance to study in the States.

* * *

SOMETIMES WIDGET ASKS me to babysit Kolya, if she's running errands or has a doctor's appointment. I can never say no, even when my desk is swamped with students' work. Kolya is two and a half now, and he can stand on his own or walk slowly, holding on to the furniture or my hand, his finger wrapped around mine. From the therapist I've learned various exercises designed to strengthen his muscles and help him use his legs more and more. Mike has built the boy a special walker, which is narrow enough for Kolya to navigate through almost any passageway. We fight about what to get the boy for Christmas, his birthday, and Easter, so as not to outweigh the parents. We argue about food and clothes: Is butter good for a child? Should he eat buckwheat? Is he dressed warmly enough? Or is he trapped in too many layers? I talk to Kolya in Russian, and Widget doesn't mind because she wants him to keep his heritage, his Russian soul. But above all she wants him to be happy. She told me once she'd heard some American actress say that in order to be in a Chekhov play, she had to live in Russia for a year, and not just to learn the people's customs and habits or what they ate and wore—she could've researched that on the internet—but to understand Russian misery and how to endure it properly. Widget laughed, and I did too, eyeing her broad familiar face.

It's early December but we've already had eighteen inches of snow. Kolya is bundled up in his brother's baggy coat and Russian felt boots—*valenki*—which my mother mailed in the fall. The air is crisp, biting the skin. Snow cushions roofs and porches, hangs off tree limbs like white fur. Kolya and I are in the backyard, building a fort and burying toys in the snow, occasionally discovering hardened dog feces, which I scoop and dump in Widget's trash receptacle. After a while Kolya wants to sled in a blue disk he spots at the bottom of a hill, not far from the house. His cheeks are ruddy like apples, and he giggles when I pretend to bite them. I ask him to wait while I haul the disk up the hill and come back for him. He nods and nods, like a clown in his large woolly hat.

As I trudge through the snow, I hear him fuss and whimper, so I turn around and see that he's attempting to walk, holding to the metal pole of the swing, lifting his leg up and forcing it down.

"Hey," I tell him. "You okay?"

He grins, blinking—nose cringed, hat low—and then separates his gloved hand from the pole. I watch him sway for a moment, arms balancing like the wings of an airplane. He takes a wobbly step, and another, threading his legs in and out of the snow, placing them where I made the dents.

"I'm strong," he says and tumbles over, laughing.

And I say, "Yes, you are. Very strong."

It's begun to snow, hatfuls. Flurries swarm in the air and plaster our faces and cling to our eyelashes and lips. In the distance the mountain is chalk-white, integrated with the horizon. But if I stare, stare long enough—I can see its crooked ridges, a hollow in the curve of its back.

What Isn't Remembered

The afternoon of their arrival in Cremona they gather in Piazza del Comune for a drink. Mana is sipping a Campari of a lush berry color; her body mellows, the liquor pools inside her chest then spills down her limbs. Nearly all the people in the group are musicians from the former Soviet Republics, but who now live in America. All still speak Russian. The language of the oppressor, they laugh, loud, with a neurotic twitch, and Mana does too, although she thinks of languages, English or Russian, not as the tools of communist or capitalist dominance but as bridges. It is all that one has, other than music. Languages fascinate Mana; words, like sounds, accumulate someplace hidden and untouchable. If one could only weigh all the words that one knows, take them in one's arms and turn them into food, or medicine, or water.

Mana and Victor met some of the musicians last summer, at the same Stradivari festival, and most are much older. Or maybe it seems that way after days of peregrination, airplane food, and lack of sleep. Time traveling. Ever since Mana left Russia, fifteen years ago, she's always wondered how one could leap forward six or eight hours and then leap back. Somewhere in the space-time continuum the two selves should've crossed paths. When flying to Italy, Mana occupied a window seat. She would press her hand to the thick oval glass, behind which clouds hung cottony-white, as though on a painting, and imagine the other Mana doing the same: the identical shape of fingers with their slightly protruding knuckles, a scar on her right thumb, where she had surgery to remove a suspicious growth.

The musicians are loud, despite the exhaustion settled in the crevices of their pallid faces. They're never in the sun, never long enough to acquire a tan. They look ancient to her, just like the music they play, or this gorgeous church—Cattedrale di Santa Maria Assunta (the Duomo, as it's frequently called)—built in the twelfth century. Mana has missed it. The tall, elegant portico with a narthex surmounted by an expansive rose window, where light lingers in the evening, illuminating hundreds of symmetrical petals and the pinkish nude hues of the stone. The facade of the cathedral resembles an open-air museum of sculptures, among which are the *Madonna with Child* and the *Labors of the Months*, linked to the zodiac signs and seen as humankind's response to God's ordering of the universe. Mana shivers, although the air is stifling, the sun a raw wound in the sky. She attempts to sit up straight, defying gravity, the invisible fetters on her hands and feet. The weight of Earth itself.

"Have you climbed the Torrazzo yet?" a woman next to her asks in Russian. She's tall, stately, with streaks of auburn in her black hair.

"No. My husband is too lazy." Mana nods at Victor as he recounts a story of his nephew, also a cellist, who fell asleep in a conservatory closet and missed his auditions for the Cleveland Orchestra.

"It's one hundred twelve meters, five hundred steps. The third tallest brickwork bell tower in the world," the woman says.

"Really? I only know that the clock is the largest astronomical clock. The dial has no numbers. Nothing but the sky with zodiac constellations, and the sun and the moon move through them."

"Maybe back then time was irrelevant, you know? Or maybe, when they put the clock on something that was supposed to last centuries, time became eternity."

Mana has never met the woman—she's sure—and yet the motherly softness in her voice feels familiar. Unlike Mana's mother, however, who died twenty years ago (Mana still remembers her eyes, so dark, so hopeless, rimmed in purple, the bare tremor of her eyelashes when she cried), the woman has large blue eyes, perhaps too large for such slender brows and thin, flat lips. Her nose is petite too, with a brown mole tucked under the right nostril. Mana guesses her to be ten, fifteen years older, fifty-five or less. Her low-cut blouse shows a wave of freckled flesh supported by a black bra; the scalloped lacy edge is peeping from under the green silk, making Mana think of the ocean, its wet, murky, fascinating depths. The woman wears no makeup and no jewelry, except for an oval watch on a thread of a chain reaching as low as her navel. A hypnotic tool. Mana stares at the watch for a moment before averting her eyes.

"Tori," the woman says. "Short for Victoria."

"Mana. Short for Manya, short for—"

"Maria." Tori laughs and nods at the waiter. "Russian names sometimes make little sense. You want another drink?" she asks and touches Mana's shoulder, gently, gently, the brush of a feather. Mana's lips move without sound; she lingers somewhere between waking and sleep, in a time zone of her own, where she's one of the birds, a pigeon on the piazza, scouring for bread crumbs or circling the Duomo, a lazy flapping of wings against a peach glare of the sun.

* * *

TORI IS A Philadelphia-based pianist. A fist of passion and technique. In the darkness of the historic Teatro Filodrammatici, where some of the festival events take place, Mana watches Tori and Victor perform Rachmaninoff's Cello Sonata in G Minor. It's been a week since they arrived, and they didn't rehearse but twice. They invited Mana to sit in on their practices, but she refused. Instead she sauntered along the narrow cobblestoned streets, marveling at two- and three-story houses of warm variegated colors and red-tiled roofs, with bursts of flowers on wrought-iron balconies and serpent vines twisting up the walls. She visited churches, where she felt lost amid the grandeur of altars and tombs, shopped, read, and drank bitter foamy cappuccinos.

The book she brought with her was Virginia Woolf's *To the Lighthouse*. In the past Mana had started the novel four times, but became bogged down in the exuberance of the language and the characters' ruminations before she could ever reach part two. The novel made her feel helpless; at the same time, it empowered her with a certain intimate knowledge she craved. While reading it she felt life slipping through her fingers as she endeavored, desperately, to hold it in place, to isolate bits and pieces of personal experience, hoping for some larger truth to be revealed at the end. When she finally finished the novel, a few days ago, tears rolled down her face as she heard the Duomo bells ring their solemn, lugubrious chant.

And yet she couldn't say for sure why the sad tenderness that gathered in her chest and then rose to her eyes made her hug the book against her heart and remain motionless for what seemed like eons. At the very end of the novel there was a description of a canvas, its shapes and colors blurred, and there was Lily Briscoe drawing a sharp line in the center. Just like Lily, Mana felt extreme fatigue, although she couldn't explain it (her jet lag should have already passed). Later that evening Victor asked, "What's it about? The book? How come it took you so long to finish?" Mana shrugged. "It's lifelike," she said. "You can't live it all at once. It isn't about one thing but thousands of things, thousands of shades of things. Like the Rachmaninoff sonata, how many times did you try before you could actually play it?"

"I'm still not sure I can. Not the way it's supposed to be played."

"See? The same here."

And then they went to bed; they didn't kiss or touch, not even in their sleep, as if there were a guardrail dividing the mattress in two halves. The center line painted by a thick brush.

The sonata is as heartbreaking as it is superior in composition and technique. The inexhaustible depth of themes. Perhaps the hardest piece ever written, at least for piano. Harder than all of Liszt. Before they met and practiced, Victor was nervous about Tori's skill, whether she was capable of such a massive undertaking, such feverish intensity, the escalating leaps and arpeggios, the choking fury of chords, which she would have to break open because of her small female hands. "Women can't play Rachmaninoff," Victor said. "They're too tender or too jittery. Erratic." But after the first rehearsal he came back to the hotel and said he'd need to practice some more. It wasn't Tori's skill he doubted, but his. All passed, of course. Nerves, late entrances, missed notes, slipped fingers and smeared bow touches, memory lapses. Now there's only this magnanimous, soul-crushing sound that has swallowed the theater, where Mana sits in the company of other musicians and their students, who, it seems, have forgotten how to breathe.

Victor looks tense, emotional, but Tori appears focused yet relaxed. Mana can tell that she enjoys the piece much more than Victor. Tori is also more at ease with the piano than Victor has ever been with the cello. Mana isn't sure whether it's her age or skill, or her being a woman, that makes Tori's virtuosic playing more musical, more natural. Her heart is in it, and so is Victor's, only hers doesn't threaten to leap out of her chest and smash against the keys. She makes no unnecessary movements to flaunt her skill but remains poised, in complete control of the instrument and her feelings. Mana suddenly remembers how Tori said during lunch one day that her marriage had ended because it'd run its course, like a piece of long, difficult, exasperating music. You played it, and you played it, and then you put it away.

Mana watches Victor hug the cello so close, the instrument alive in his hands. This gorgeous piece of wood and strings he bought last year, also here in Cremona, where the traditions of Amati and Stradivari have been immortalized, the pulse of centuries soaked into the wood. She can almost feel it, escaping from under Victor's bow. The bare vibrato of his fingers against the ebony scroll. She knows everything about those fingers, the kind of sound they can produce, the kind of metronomic cadence no old marriage escapes. At the end there aren't any surprises, although she forgets to applaud, but a moment later rises to her feet and shouts, "Bravo! Bravo! Bravo!"

* * *

IF SOMEONE WOULD have told Mana back then that she would sleep with a woman or divorce Victor years afterward, she would have laughed so hard everyone around her would have turned in amazement, wondering what was so funny and how they, too, could be a part of her senseless cheer. Because it does make you feel good to see others happy or in love.

On Sunday, after Mass, Tori offers to climb the Torrazzo. But first she suggests visiting the main part of the Duomo and viewing the artwork, sculptures, frescoes, and paintings, *The Annunciation* by Boccaccio Boccaccino on the arc of the presbytery.

Mana feels overwhelmed by the domineering beauty of the interior: the columns of Verona marble, the heavily ornate ceilings, the canonical choir with double stalls and the inlay of musical instruments, a giant cross inside a glass sarcophagus—the work of Lombardian goldsmiths. The decoration of the central nave includes thirty figures of the prophets holding scrolls with Latin inscriptions relating to the episodes in the frescoes above them. The last six frescoes are by Pordenone, made between 1520 and 1522. Mana can't read the inscriptions (she hardly remembers any Latin from her conservatory days, and her Italian is a pocketbook of tourist clichés), but Tori is capable of translating most of them because she studied Italian opera for many years. Although it isn't what she says but how she says it that makes Mana want to hear more, Tori's voice is a warm tide engulfing Mana. The woman's shoulders are bare, smooth, gleaming with lotion, and Mana has an urge to touch them, to draw a path with her finger along Tori's arms, so lean yet muscular and utterly hairless. Her desire is so bizarre, she laughs, the echo tracing the vaults, the pillars, the colorful mosaic windows.

When both women stand in front of the great wooden Ancona with the Assunta di Gatti, Tori says, "They don't really know whether Mary died a mortal death."

"Of course, she did," Mana says. "If she lived, she died. We visited her grave when Victor performed in Jerusalem awhile back."

"But didn't they tell you the grave was empty?"

"On the third day after the burial. She went to heaven, body and soul."

Tori twiddles the watch on the chain, still around her neck. "Maybe she didn't live at all. Maybe we don't live either. Maybe we're just imagining our own existence and projecting it onto others. Our suffering, our desires, our loneliness."

Mana's eyes are glued to Tori's watch. It makes little sense to her that she would wear a watch, if time is imagined, like the rest.

"It's a gift from my son," Tori says. "He lives in LA. It has a built-in calendar." She flips the watch open on one side, and then the other.

"Do you see him often?" Mana asks, although she already knows the answer.

"Once a year. He and his partner are very busy performing. Violinists. Both."

Mana assumes that Tori's son is gay, although she hesitates to ask. She feels uncomfortable for some reason. She has gay friends in New York, but she doesn't know their mothers.

"Do you have children?" Tori asks.

"No," Mana says. "We tried though. But it didn't happen. And we couldn't afford in vitro."

"Yes. I hear it's exorbitant."

"Especially for a musician and a teacher. And no insurance. Back then, I mean, we had no insurance."

"What do you teach? Piano?" Tori asks.

"No. ESL. In a community college. In Brooklyn."

Tori looks surprised, her brows arch, a trail of wrinkles on her forehead. "I've kind of assumed that you're also a musician."

"I was." Mana stops before the altar, where a bouquet of red roses lies withered on the marble steps. "I used to play piano, mostly chamber, until I got this thing on my thumb, and then it was over. My thumb lost all feeling. Mobility too."

"But you still play?"

"Only in my dreams. We sold my old grand and bought Victor's cello. He needed a new instrument, as much as he performs. We'd been saving for years."

"He's a strong musician," Tori says.

"Not as strong as you."

It pains Mana to admit that, and her honesty is a surprise to both of them. Tori touches two fingers to Mana's lips, sealing in other secrets or revelations that might follow. But who can do that? Hold back all that is about to happen? Tori's fingers are short, clean, with square, perfectly filed nails, without polish, the tips toughened by a lifetime of practice. Her gesture is sure and intimate, just like her playing, and Mana is swept with curiosity and gratitude, excitement and longing.

She can't quite verbalize her desire. Words shrivel and garble, a score of platitudes. She's reminded of her conservatory days, when she was about to learn a new, difficult sonata, and the anticipation made her tremble, the challenge worthy of her effort, those long, late, thirsty hours of stroking and striking the keys.

* * *

YEARS LATER, on her therapist's couch, when Mana would try to reconstruct and analyze her experience, she would always stop with the gesture of Tori's fingers pressed against her lips. It's the touching, the willingness, the intimation of sex, the warmth that washes over her, again and again, like the sun over the rose window of the Duomo. She wants to own the moment, so she can bask in its forestalling intimacy, the promise of pleasure before it turns into a heartache or disappointment, hundreds of shades of disappointment. Before the day transitions into night and into another day, a different kind of day— where they've never touched or kissed or ignored the hours, and where her body remains a stranger next to her husband's for years to come.

When asked to describe the hotel room, Mana wouldn't be able to do that either. She couldn't remember. She would close her eyes and imagine the walls, honey yellow, like the afternoon sun. There must've been a bed, and there must've been a window, but no drapes, just shutters, green wooden shutters that Tori had to pull halfway, so the light could still escape through the narrow slats. Mana watched it travel up the wall, where a painting of the bluest sea and fishing boats hung unframed. One boat appeared smaller than the other, stranded far from shore, a red eye of a lighthouse in the distance. Or maybe she imagined it, her body, wrapped in another woman's skin, drenched in heat and sweat, guilty, guilty, seeking an escape—a boat, a sea, a lighthouse. The rainbow of colors arching over her life like a bridge.

The festival ended two days later, but Mana never met with Tori again, missing her last solo performance, alluding to an abominable headache and the need to pack. At the airport, on the way back to New York, she heard one of the musicians say that Chopin's second scherzo was astonishing—highly strung, tempestuous, volcanic, relentlessly driven, with thundering octaves—a house fire, from which the pianist attempted to salvage a few personal belongings. A favorite painting, a photo album, some rare original scores, perhaps. Mana could see the rest burning to the ground, at her feet a glow of ambers.

* * *

ONCE, YEARS INTO the future, Mana heard the scherzo performed by an older woman in a church in Brooklyn, where she and Victor stumbled in by mistake. He listened without interest because he'd heard the piece too many times, and because he thought that only a few chosen people of Slavic heritage could perform Chopin without either being too stiff or too maudlin, swaying and weeping over the piano. But the old church and the Gothic setting—the gray stone walls, the vaulted ceiling, the mosaic windows brought out from the darkness by a gentle pulse of the evening light, the shiver of flames in red glass candleholders as though a flicker of hot tongues—all that made Mana focus on the music, how it raged from loneliness to despair to heartache, and then died down, turned into a murmur, a soft cooing of bodies. After the performer finished playing, the sound hung in the air, a few lingering notes, like an echo of one's youth or past desire. It was then that Mana remembered what Tori had said about the piece, about the middle section, marked *sotto voce*. She'd described it as a confession. A dialogue. Between a priest and a woman divulging her secrets. Her love affair, perhaps. He's trying to calm her down, and she's trying to express her feelings, to tell her story, relive the passion.

Mana shared Tori's interpretation with Victor as they walked out of the church and sauntered along the street, unexpectedly deserted. "Do you agree?" she asked.

"Maybe. Or maybe she was talking about herself. Someone said she'd been through a nasty divorce that involved an affair. Her affair with another woman. It drove her husband nuts, and he smashed his car through the woman's house, killing her and her mother."

Mana stopped in front of a large puddle, where pigeons, dirty and clumsy, plucked bits of food. "That's awful," she said. "Why haven't you told me before?"

"I don't know. Why?" Victor stopped too and offered her a hand, so she could cross the water, but she walked around it.

"I hope the husband went to prison for murder," she said.

"Probably did. Although it's her fault. She should be in prison too."

Mana stared. "You don't know what the marriage was like."

"Still—she's the one who slept around."

"If you imprisoned people for infidelity, there'd be no one left to play music. Or write books. Or make movies. Or sweep streets."

"What are you saying?"

"Nothing."

"I haven't cheated on you."

"I didn't ask."

"But you implied."

"No. I didn't."

"Have you? Cheated?"

It would've been so easy to say no; it would've been easy to say yes too. And then to say that she was joking, that she wanted to test him, to gauge his reaction. But she chose silence because she never really considered that one time with Tori an infidelity, but rather an experience, a fleeting glimpse of ecstasy, a burst of light on a crepuscular sky that fizzled out, turning to shimmers and then to nothingness, right after it'd happened. Or maybe it hadn't. Hadn't happened, but she imagined it, just as she imagined playing the scherzo in the church, knowing all too well that she had neither skill nor stamina. Still, she imagined throwing herself at the piano, as though it were a bed in a tiny hotel room, hot, damp, musky. There, ensconced by the honey-yellow walls, existed another Mana, her other self, who entered that room and did those things, again and again, those shameless beautiful things for which she had no names, only colors. There was yellow, and blue, and green, and crimson red, the color of the waning sun when it touched the lip of the sea, somewhere far, far in the distance.

* * *

FROM VICTOR, months after the divorce (when both of them cried as though two old, shaky relatives who couldn't stop reminiscing, caught unaware by age and illness, life's turbulent, dark-hued cadenza), she would learn that Tori remarried a gifted cellist five years her junior, with whom she performed and who accepted her lesbian past, the tragedy of losing her lover to her ex-husband's violent prank. Victor called the new man an idiot blinded by Tori's musical powers, but Mana considered him brave, brave and defiant, a provocateur, who welcomed chance and challenge. We were like that once, she thought. Brave, defiant, blind. No struggle was insurmountable, no piece of music outrageous or impossible. But when Victor had said that, she felt that she lacked gravity but also wholeness; she could remember musical bits, scraps and fragments of every piece she'd ever played or heard, but no one solid opus, no ballade or scherzo, sonata or sonatina, prelude or fugue. Not even an étude. She said she was sorry it didn't work out between them, life didn't work out, which was also like music—some perished, sank into oblivion; some crossed into eternity.

* * *

WHAT ELSE HAPPENS to Mana in the years that follow:

She sleeps with another woman but finds it distasteful and even crude.

She continues to listen to Rachmaninoff and Chopin and has enough savings for a used grand that movers carry up the stairs of her rented apartment on Ocean Avenue, charging her per flight, per step. She disposes of her sofa, and the old TV, and her dinner table. And then her bed. She sleeps on a mattress on the floor, next to the piano, which towers in the middle of her living room—its solitude and silence aligned with hers.

One weekend, she rereads *To the Lighthouse*, from start to finish, clutching the book hard, as though testing the novel's strength against the years. Just like before, she feels fatigued, exhausted to the last measure, from the book's virtuosic suite of characters, with their extreme contrasts of style, mood, texture, and the spacious musical structures of Woolf's language, its insistent beauty, a soiree of lilting themes and luminous, almost atonal, harmonies, a riptide of chords: major, minor, augmented, or diminished. The artist's farewell symphony, her ode to life. Mana finally understands why it takes Lily Briscoe years to finish her painting, and why she could never do it when all the people were still there, gathered around, crowding her days. And why, with a jolt of sudden intensity, she feels compelled to draw a line in the center of the canvas, dividing it in half—her life before and after.

There's another detail, another little episode that Mana has forgotten until now.

How when it was over, that afternoon in the hotel room, how she reached to brush a wet strand of hair from Tori's forehead, and how Tori caught Mana's hand, her sticky, trembling fingers that still smelled of flesh. "Time to practice," she said and pressed Mana's fingers into the pillow, getting up. When Mana raised her hand, it left an imprint in the creased white cotton of the bedding, which she rushed to smooth and straighten, apologetically, the pillowcases, the sheets, the covers. And then the colors smoldered into view, replacing words with images, images with sounds (the way she'd been taught to imagine as a child, touching a piano for the first time, gently, one key after another, applying little pressure). Yellow—like the sun;

blue—like a sea; green—like grass; red—like an apple, like a heart, like a fire, like a burn.

Tori's words echo in Mana's ears, a throb of disparate notes muffled by time and distance, as she recalls the two images of infants inside the Duomo. The first image was painted by Boccaccio Boccaccino in the scene of the *Marriage of the Virgin*; the other by Pordenone in the episode in which Christ falls under the cross. The images represent the synthesis and the evolution of painting in sixteenth-century northern Italy, which Tori also compared to the synthesis and the evolution of love and marriage. The first image is classical but static and idealized; the second, realistic and shows movement.

ACKNOWLEDGMENTS

It takes a village to raise a child, but it takes the world to raise a writer. I would like to thank everyone who made me laugh or cry (or both) in the past twenty years:

Jackie Ko, Kwame Dawes, Sheryl Johnston, Sacha Idell, the late Jeanne M. Leiby, the late Eric Trethewey, Richard Dillard, Amanda Cockrell, Jeanne Larsen, Liz Poliner, Donald Secreast, Tim Poland, Moira Baker, Kay Edge, Maria Bowling, Kelley Shinn, Francine Ringold, Cristina Garcia, the late Randall Kenan, Steve Yarbrough, Sherman Alexie, Amy Hanson, Matthew Lansburgh, Raul Palma, Liz Zemska, Sujata Shekar, Julia Lichtblau, Andrea Jurjević, Pang-Mei Natasha Chang, Renée Zuckerbrot, the Matushes, the Taylors, the Phillipses, the Newberrys, the Dodsons, the Cutters, the Erhlichs, the Rayevskys, the Morozovs, the Kromins, the Plekhanovs, the Goldshteyns, the Solovievs, Tanya Nadtochiy, Masha Baukina, Galya Suradze, Lena Ivanova, Stipe Ostović, Mila Makrova, Elena Efimova, Tatiana Early, Gevorg Sukiasyan, Leonid Mukhaev, Galina Vorotynova, Lesya Paisley, Lena Boeva, Trevor Moffitt, Kay Moon, Irina Akimova, Lena Hourihane, Svetlana Miller, Vera Tolpina, Terri Russell, Andrea Waide, Carrie Bruce, Kristiana Roemer, Mike Smith, Jim Weston, John Salmon, Barbara Mackin, Dan Tepfer, Hayk Arsenyan, Irina Morozova, and the late Peter Serkin; my nonpareil family—Randy Newberry, Albert Newberry, and Albina Ivanova—who inspire and invigorate me, and without whom I wouldn't have had any stories to tell; and the Literary Goddesses—Virginia Woolf, Toni Morrison, and Alice Munro. All of you are here, imbedded in my heart and these pages. . . .

Grateful acknowledgment is made to Moscow State Linguistic University, Radford University, Hollins University, and the University of Nebraska Press, as well as the following publications, in which these stories originally appeared, in slightly different form:

"Boys on the Moskva River," *Nimrod* 57, no. 1 (Fall/Winter 2013): 7–22.

"All of Me" reproduced from *Prairie Schooner* 91, no. 2 (Summer 2017): 140–51, by permission of the University of Nebraska Press. Copyright 2017 by the University of Nebraska Press.

"The Heart of Things," *Nimrod* 59, no. 1 (Fall/Winter 2015): 150–62.

"A Lullaby for My Father," *Flyway* (March 2019).

"Simple Song #9," *TriQuarterly*, no. 155 (Winter/Spring 2019).

"Nepenthe," *Southwest Review* 99, no. 2 (2014): 210–55.

"Beloveds," *Indiana Review* 42, no. 2 (Winter 2020).

"The Suicide Note," *Southern Review* 56, no. 1 (Winter 2020): 34–45.

"Second Person" reprinted with permission from *Phoebe: A Journal of Gender and Cultural Critiques* now *Praxis: A Journal of Gender and Cultural Critique* 19, no. 2 (2007): 65–69. Copyright 2007 held by *Praxis* for *Phoebe*.

"Gene Therapy," *Folio* 35 (Spring 2020): 59–69.

"And What Rough Beast," *Bellingham Review* 41, no. 76 (Spring 2018): 54–59.

"Champions of the World," *Southern Review* 47, no. 3 (Summer 2011): 487–507.

"What Isn't Remembered," *Southern Review* 56, no. 3 (Summer 2020): 345–54.

Grateful acknowledgement is also made to Peter Balakian for permission to reprint his translation of Grigoris Balakian's poem, "Lullaby on the Way to Zor," originally published in *Armenian Golgotha*. Translation copyright © 2009 by Peter Balakian.

Infinite thanks to Courtney Ochsner, an associate acquisitions editor at the University of Nebraska Press, Haley Mendlik, my project editor, and Debbie Anderson, my copyeditor—for their time and effort and astute skills.

To order or obtain more information on these or other University of Nebraska Press titles, visit nebraskapress.unl.edu.